The Secret Chronicles of Sherlock Holmes

JUNE THOMSON

Allison & Busby Limited
12 Fitzroy Mews
London W1T 6DW
www.allisonandbusby.com

First published in Great Britain in 1992.
This paperback edition published by Allison & Busby in 2014.

A CIP catalogue record for this book is available from
the British Library.

10 9 8 7 6 5 4 3 2 1

ISBN 978-0-7490-1667-8

Typeset in 11/16 pt Sabon by Allison & Busby Ltd.

The paper used for this Allison & Busby publication
has been produced from trees that have been legally sourced from well-
managed and credibly certified forests.

Printed and bound by
CPI Group (UK) Ltd, Croydon, CR0 4YY

THOMSON, a former teacher, has published over
ty novels, twenty of which feature her series
ective Inspector Jack Finch and his sergeant, Tom
ce. She has also written seven pastiche collections
Sherlock Holmes short stories. Her books have been
nslated into many languages. June Thomson lives in
gby, Warwickshire.

By June Thomson

THE SHERLOCK HOLMES COLLECTION

The Secret Files of Sherlock Holmes
The Secret Chronicles of Sherlock Holmes
The Secret Journals of Sherlock Holmes
Holmes and Watson
The Secret Documents of Sherlock Holmes
The Secret Notebooks of Sherlock Holmes
The Secret Archives of Sherlock Holmes

THE JACK FINCH MYSTERIES

Going Home

To H.R.F. Keating for giving so generously of
his time and expert advice

My thanks also to John Kennedy Melling and John
Berriman for their help and expertise on Victorian
Music-Halls and Victorian Pocket-Watches.

I should again like to express my thanks to June Thomson for her help in preparing this second collection of short stories for publication.

Aubrey B. Watson LDS, FDS, D. Orth

Contents

FOREWORD

by Aubrey B. Watson LDS, FDS, D. Orth

In the Foreword to *The Secret Files of Sherlock Holmes*,[1] I described how a certain battered tin dispatch box, with the words 'John H. Watson, M.D., Late Indian Army' painted on the lid, together with its contents, came into the possession of my late uncle, also a Dr John Watson. In his case, however, the middle initial was F., not H., and he was a Doctor of Philosophy rather than medicine.

It was sold to him in July 1939 by a Miss Adelina McWhirter, who claimed it was the same box which Dr John H. Watson, Sherlock Holmes' companion and chronicler, had deposited at his bank Cox and Co. of Charing Cross[2] and which contained records in Dr

---

[1] This first collection of hitherto unpublished adventures, supposedly undertaken by Mr Sherlock Holmes and Dr John H. Watson, was first published by Constable and Co. in September 1990. Aubrey B. Watson.

[2] Dr John H. Watson refers to this dispatch box in the opening sentence of 'The Problem of Thor Bridge'. Aubrey B. Watson.

John H. Watson's handwriting of sundry adventures undertaken by the great consulting detective which, for various reasons, had never been published. As a relative of Holmes' Dr Watson on her mother's side of the family, Miss McWhirter alleged that she had inherited the dispatch box and its papers which, finding herself in straitened circumstances, she was forced reluctantly to sell.

My late uncle, struck by the similarity of his own name to that of the other illustrious Dr John Watson, had studied widely in the Holmes canon and had made himself an acknowledged expert. On examining the dispatch box and its contents, he was convinced of their authenticity and was planning to publish the papers when international events overtook him with the outbreak of the Second World War.

Anxious about their safety, he made copies of the Watson documents, depositing the originals in their dispatch box in the strongroom of his own bank in Lombard Street, London EC3. Unfortunately, it suffered a direct hit during the bombing of 1942 which reduced the contents of the box to charred fragments and so blistered the paint on its lid that the inscription was indecipherable.

Left with nothing more than his own copies of the papers to prove the existence of the originals and unable to trace Miss McWhirter, my late uncle, fearful of his reputation as a scholar, decided very regretfully not to publish them in his lifetime and, on his death, the whole collection, together with the footnotes he had added, was bequeathed to me under the terms of his will.

As I pointed out in the Foreword to *The Secret Files of Sherlock Holmes*, I am by profession an orthodontist and, having no academic reputation to protect and no one to whom I can in turn bequeath the papers, I have decided, after much careful consideration, to offer these documents for publication although I make no claim for their authenticity.

The first account I have chosen for this second collection is the adventure of the Paradol Chamber, referred to in 'The Five Orange Pips' and assigned by Dr John H. Watson to 1887. It was one of a long series of cases which engaged Sherlock Holmes' attention during that year, not all of which were published although Dr John H. Watson states that he 'kept the records'. The account of the Paradol Chamber case was among those alleged to have been deposited in the dispatch box at Cox and Co.

With regard to the question of dating this particular adventure, readers might be interested in a short monograph which my late uncle wrote on this matter and which is printed in full in the Appendix.

The Case of the Paradol Chamber

I

It was not often that Sherlock Holmes called on me at my consulting rooms in Paddington,[1] preferring to remain in the seclusion of his lodgings at 221B Baker Street which he left only rarely.

I was therefore considerably surprised when one morning in November '87, not long after my marriage,[2] and my purchase of the practice from Mr Farquhar, the front door bell rang and my old friend was ushered into the room.

[1] Mr Sherlock Holmes visited Dr John H. Watson at his consulting rooms at the beginning of the adventures concerning the Stockbroker's Clerk and the Crooked Man, in the latter case staying the night. He also called on the evening of 24th April 1891 before he and Dr Watson departed for Switzerland where Mr Sherlock Holmes apparently met his death at the hands of his arch-enemy, Professor Moriarty. Dr John F. Watson.

[2] I refer readers to the Appendix where they will find, printed in full, the monograph of my late uncle, Dr John F. Watson, concerning the dating of certain events within the published canon, with particular reference to the precise year of Dr John H. Watson's marriage. Aubrey B. Watson.

'Ah, Watson!' said he, striding forward to shake me vigorously by the hand. 'I trust you and Mrs Watson are well?' On receiving my assurance that we were both in excellent health, he continued, 'I see that your practice is quiet at present and you are not over-burdened with patients. That being so, could you spare me an hour of your company? It is a case which I think may interest you. I may assume, may I not, that domestic pleasures have not quite blunted the edge of your former interest in our little deductive adventures?'

'No; indeed not, Holmes,' I replied warmly. 'I am delighted to be asked. But how can you be so sure that business is slack enough to allow me to take up the invitation?'

'Two reasons, my dear fellow. Firstly, the condition of the boot-scraper by your front door. Although it is miry underfoot after last night's rain, so little mud has been deposited on it that I deduced only one or two patients could have made use of it since it was cleaned earlier this morning. Secondly, I noticed the extreme tidiness of your desk. Only a man with time on his hands would have arranged his papers in such immaculate order.'

'You are quite right, Holmes!' I exclaimed, laughing not only at the simplicity of his explanation but with pleasure at his renewed company.

'Then are you prepared to accompany me to Baker Street? I have a cab waiting.'

'Certainly. I shall be but a few moments informing my wife and writing a note to my neighbour, also a medical man, who will take over the practice while I am away.[3] It is a reciprocal agreement. What is the case?'

'I shall explain once we are in the hansom,' Holmes replied.

Having made these necessary arrangements to cover my absence, I hurriedly put on my topcoat and, seizing my hat and stick, joined him outside in the cab. As soon as it had started off and was rattling on its way to our former lodgings, Holmes produced a letter from his pocket which he handed to me.

'It arrived only this morning by the first post,' he explained, 'hence the necessity of collecting you in person rather than summoning you by telegram as the client requests an interview at eleven o'clock. Read it, my dear fellow, and tell me what you make of the contents.'

With that he folded his arms and leant back against the seat, allowing me to peruse the letter in silence.

It bore the previous day's date and an engraved address: Windicot Villa, Little Bramfield, Surrey, and read:

Dear Mr Holmes,
May I request an interview with you tomorrow morning at eleven o'clock in order to discuss a matter of extreme delicacy? It concerns a close

---

[3] It would appear that Dr John H. Watson had at least two medical acquaintances who were willing to take over his practice in his absence. In 'The Adventure of the Crooked Man', one is referred to as Jackson, while in 'The Boscombe Valley Mystery', Mrs Watson suggests that Anstruther might oblige. Dr John F. Watson.

acquaintance of mine who appears to have returned from the dead. I prefer to give no further details at this stage.

I apologise for the short notice I have given you but the case is of great urgency.

Because of its unusual nature, I shall be accompanied by my solicitor, Mr Frederick Lawson of Bold, Brownjohn and Lawson of Guildford, Surrey.

Yours sincerely etc.

Edith Russell (Miss).

'A curious case, is it not, Watson?' Holmes asked when I had folded up the letter and handed it back to him.

'A return from the dead!' I cried. 'Miss Russell must have imagined it.'

'That may indeed be so. However, I prefer to wait until I have heard Miss Russell's account before indulging in any speculation, either scientific or metaphysical. It was for this reason that I wanted your presence at the interview. As a medical man, you will no doubt be able to confirm whether or not Miss Russell is of an hysterical or over-imaginative disposition.'

'Of course, Holmes,' I assured him, gratified to be asked for my professional opinion.

We arrived at Baker Street only a quarter of an hour before Miss Russell and her solicitor. Even so, I was hard put to it to contain my curiosity and, when they were shown upstairs, I rose to my feet as they entered the sitting room, eager to study their demeanour, especially that of the young lady.

Miss Russell was tall and graceful, with an air of breeding and quiet intelligence about her features; in no way inclined, I thought, to be of a nervous disposition.

Her solicitor, Mr Frederick Lawson, was also young, distinguished-looking and possessed of a similar sensible, no-nonsense attitude, apparent in his firm handshake and his direct gaze.

They made a handsome couple and, from Lawson's solicitous manner towards Miss Russell, I suspected at once that his feelings for her were more than those of a legal adviser towards his client.

Once the introductions were over and Holmes had received Miss Russell's agreement that, as his long-term and trusted colleague, I should be allowed to remain, Mr Russell opened the interview with a short, introductory preamble.

'Miss Russell has already written to you, Mr Holmes, explaining to you very briefly the background to the situation but not, in her preliminary letter, referring to anyone by name. As the persons involved are distinguished members of the highest society, I know that we may rely entirely on your discretion, as well as that of your colleague, Dr Watson, not to allow any of the facts ever to be made public. That being said, I shall leave my client, Miss Russell, to make her statement to you in her own words, as she has already given it to me.'

Lawson then fell silent and Miss Russell began her

account in a clear voice and an unhurried manner which showed few signs of nervousness apart from an occasional clasping and unclasping of her gloved hands as they lay in her lap.

'First of all, Mr Holmes, I must explain a little of the background to the events which have brought me here to ask for your assistance.

'My father is a retired City banker, a widower, suffering from a heart complaint. On the advice of his doctor, we moved from London to Surrey where my father bought Windicot Villa, a house situated on the edge of the village of Little Bramfield which is a few miles from Guildford. The nearest residence to ours, a mere half-mile away, is Hartesdene Manor, the home of the young Marquis of Deerswood and his uncle, Lord Hindsdale, the younger brother of the Marquis's late father who died in a hunting accident. Because Lord Deerswood was left an orphan, his mother having died many years ago in a Swiss clinic – of consumption, I believe – Lord Hindsdale was made the young man's guardian and continued to live at the Manor after the Marquis came of age and inherited the title.

'About seven months ago, I made the acquaintance of Lord Deerswood under rather unusual circumstances. Like his mother, the young man suffered from poor health and, for that reason, rarely went into society, nor were visitors encouraged to call. He was, I understand, educated at home and has – or rather had, up to the time of his death – led a life of almost total seclusion. However, although he was seldom seen in public, he was permitted a little light exercise and he would walk his dog, a spaniel called Handel, in the nearby fields and lanes, always accompanied by a groom.

'It was during one of these excursions last spring that I first met him. I myself was returning from a walk when I saw him and the groom crossing a meadow close to the house. They had reached the stile and the groom, who had safely climbed over it, was holding out a hand as if to steady his master, when Gilbert, as I came to call him, appeared to lose his balance and fell, striking his head against the post.

'I ran up to give assistance and, as the house was nearby, I suggested that we took the young man there. He seemed dazed, as if suffering from a mild concussion, but was able to walk and, between us, the groom and I supported him back to Windicot Villa where I gave him what medical attention I could. Meanwhile, the groom ran on to Hartsdene Manor to raise the alarm. Shortly afterwards, the uncle, Lord Hindsdale, arrived in the carriage and the young man was taken away.

'About a week later, the Marquis, in the company of his uncle, called at the villa to thank me formally for my help and when, in the course of conversation, I happened to mention my love of flowers, Lord Deerswood invited my father and myself to the Manor to inspect the hothouses there.

'It was the first of several visits I was to pay over the subsequent months in which my acquaintanceship with Gilbert deepened into a true friendship. I found him a lonely young man, very much to be pitied; eager for the company and conversation of people of his own age. We shared many interests and the time I spent with him passed most pleasantly. Indeed, I felt as warmly towards him as I might towards a brother.

'The only drawback to our friendship was the attitude of Lord Hindsdale. He seemed very fond of his nephew – too fond, perhaps, for he was, in my opinion, overprotective towards the young man, although this was understandable considering Gilbert's poor state of health. Indeed, there were several occasions when my visits to the Manor were cancelled on Lord Hindsdale's directions because he considered Gilbert too unwell to receive callers. He is a proud, rigid man, Mr Holmes, and I felt he disapproved of my growing friendship with his nephew.

'I come now to the events of last summer. Gilbert and his uncle had left Hartsdene Manor in order to spend August in another family residence, Drumpitloch Castle, on the Scottish coast. About a week after their departure, I received a letter from Lord Hindsdale – such a terse communication, Mr Holmes! – informing me that his nephew had been drowned in a boating accident. He gave no further details and I had to discover the facts of Gilbert's death from the reports in the daily newspapers. Perhaps you, too, read them, Mr Holmes?'

Holmes, who had been listening to Miss Russell's account with keen attention, replied, 'Indeed I did. Pray continue, Miss Russell. Although the body was never found and it was assumed it had been swept out to sea, there was a memorial service, was there not?'

'Yes, there was, Mr Holmes. It was a private ceremony, held at St Saviour's church in Little Bramfield, which only immediate members of the family and the servants attended.'

For the first time, Miss Russell's calm manner failed her and her voice faltered as if remembering that occasion to which, despite her friendship with the young Marquis, she had not been invited.

I saw Frederick Lawson lean forward anxiously in his chair but, after a few moments' silence, Miss Russell had sufficiently recovered her composure to continue.

'I heard nothing from the new Marquis of Deerswood, as Lord Hindsdale became on his nephew's death, and my connection with Hartsdene Manor appeared to have been severed. However, three nights ago, at about half-past ten, my father and I were driving back from Guildford where we had dined with Mr Lawson who, over the years acted as my father's solicitor, and has become a close family friend. The road passes Hartsdene Manor and, as we drew opposite the gates, I glanced across at the house, thinking I confess, of Gilbert's tragic death. I was seated on the right-hand side of the carriage and, the blind being up, I had a clear view of the garden which fronts the Manor. There was a full moon so there is no question that I was mistaken in what I saw.'

'And what was that, pray?' Holmes inquired. He seemed impressed, as I was, too, by the concise nature of her account although a tremor in her voice spoke of deeper feelings.

'I saw Gilbert walking across the lawn. He was facing towards me and his features were quite distinct although thinner and more haggard than I remembered them.'

'Was he alone?'

'No; he was accompanied by two men, one of whom I recognised as Macey, the butler. The other I had never seen before. He was a tall man, exceptionally broad across the shoulders. There is one other fact which I must acquaint you with, Mr Holmes,' and again her voice trembled with emotion. 'Macey and the other man were grasping Gilbert by the arms as if trying to force him back inside the house. And his poor face! It held an expression of such terror that I shudder even now to recall it!'

'What did you do?' Holmes asked gently.

'I called on the coachman to stop but, by the time the carriage had halted and I had jumped out and run back to the gates of Hartsdene Manor, the garden was empty and there was no sign of Gilbert or the other two men. It was, of course, too late to make inquiries. Besides, I was greatly distressed by what I had seen and needed time to consider calmly what action I should take. After discussing the matter with my father, I consulted Mr Lawson the following day and, on his advice, I drew up a letter to Lord Deerswood, asking for an urgent interview, but without giving any details, merely stating that it was a personal and delicate matter which could involve legal complications. For this reason, I requested that Mr

Lawson, as the family solicitor, should be present.'

'A most wise decision,' Holmes murmured. 'I understand that, on his nephew's apparent death, his uncle inherited not only the title but also the estates, which are considerable.'

'Yes, indeed, Mr Holmes. After Gilbert, his uncle was the next direct heir. Because of this legal aspect to the affair, I felt I could not undertake the interview alone and my father's heart condition does not permit him any undue anxiety or emotion. The interview with the new Lord Deerswood took place yesterday morning.'

Miss Russell turned to address Frederick Lawson.

'As it was held under your direction, I think you should describe exactly what took place. I still find it most painful to recall.'

As she sat back in her chair, evidently relieved that her part of the statement was now over, Frederick Lawson took over the account, his handsome features grave.

'It was indeed a most uncomfortable occasion, Mr Holmes. As Miss Russell has already explained, Lord Deerswood is a very proud, rigid man, exceedingly cold in his manner. He listened in silence as I repeated Miss Russell's account of what she had seen and then he categorically refuted any suggestion that his nephew was still alive. Miss Russell was mistaken, he insisted, although he did not deny that an incident had taken place in the garden two nights earlier. However, the man she had seen was not Gilbert but the groom, Harris, who had been taken suddenly ill and whom Macey and another servant had walked about the lawn in order that the fresh air might revive him. As Harris bore a resemblance to his nephew, this was how the mistake must have arisen.'

'Is that possible, Miss Russell?' Holmes asked.

'Certainly not!' she exclaimed, a flush of indignation colouring her cheeks. 'I know Harris very well by sight and, although he bears a superficial likeness to Gilbert, both being dark-haired and slight of build, there is no question that I could have confused one with the other.'

'And what of the third man, the one whom Miss Russell did not recognise? Did Lord Deerswood give any explanation for his presence?'

Lawson looked a little abashed.

'I fear, Mr Holmes, that, in the embarrassment of the occasion, I failed to press Lord Deerswood for an account of the man. When Miss Russell declined to accept Lord Deerswood's explanation, he became quite angry, in a cold, controlled manner, and challenged us to bring anyone we cared to nominate to Hartsdene Manor in order to search the house and to prove to our satisfaction that his nephew was nowhere on the premises. With that, he brought the interview abruptly to a close and we were shown out. Later that morning, after consulting Miss Russell, it was decided that we must, on principle, take up the challenge. Miss Russell felt that she could not let the situation rest there. Having heard of your reputation as a consulting detective, Mr Holmes, as well as your discretion in handling such confidential matters, I advised Miss Russell to write to you.'

'I shall be delighted to inquire into the affair,' Holmes replied with alacrity. 'The case has many singular features. However, there are two provisos which I must make.'

'What are those?'

'That my colleague, Dr Watson, should accompany me. You would wish to do so, would you not, my dear fellow?'

'Indeed I would, Holmes,' I agreed.

'I am sure that can be arranged,' Lawson said. 'Lord Deerswood made no stipulation as to the number of persons who would be allowed to examine Hartsdene Manor. And your second proviso?'

'That we undertake the investigation with the minimum delay before there is a change in the conditions regarding the weather and the fullness of the moon.' Turning to Miss Russell, Holmes continued, 'I wish to examine the scene of the curious incident you described under circumstances as similar as possible to those in which you yourself witnessed it. You understand, Miss Russell, that I am not for a moment doubting the veracity of your evidence? But I should prefer, in such a case, to make my own observations.'

'Of course, Mr Holmes,' Miss Russell readily agreed. 'Would tomorrow evening be convenient for you? You may stay at Windicot Villa overnight and the carriage will be placed at your disposal to drive past Hartsdene Manor at exactly the same hour at which I saw the events I have described.'

'Excellent!' Holmes exclaimed.

'Then if you care to catch the 4.17 train from Waterloo,

I shall see that the carriage meets it at Guildford.'

'The arrangements will suit you, Watson?' Holmes inquired when, having taken leave of Miss Russell and Mr Lawson and escorted them to the door, he returned to his seat by the fire. 'Mrs Watson will not object to your spending a night away from home?'

'I am sure not, Holmes.'

'A most estimable woman! And your neighbour will, no doubt, take care of your practice in your absence? So, that being settled, what did you think of Miss Russell, my dear fellow?'

'I thought her a most sensible young lady.'

'Not the type with an over-warm imagination, given to hallucinations or to seeing ghosts?'

'Not in my opinion.'

'My estimation exactly.'

'Who, or what, do you suppose she saw, then? She was altogether convinced that she had not mistaken the former Marquis of Deerswood, apparently dead these four months, for the groom.'

'Never speculate until you are in possession of all the facts, Watson. It is quite the wrong way in which to begin any investigation. Facts first; theory last. Now, my old friend, if you care to make a long arm and reach down from the shelves beside you my book of newspaper cuttings together with volume 'D' in my encyclopaedia of reference, we shall begin some preliminary research into those facts, you into the circumstances of Lord Deerswood's death, while I shall refresh my memory of the young nobleman's family background. May I recommend *The Times* cutting for the account of the accident? The date, by the way, is 5th August.'

We read in silence for several minutes, Holmes engrossed in his encyclopaedia, while I, having found the relevant page in his cuttings-book, perused the following account.

It had the headline TRAGIC DEATH OF YOUNG MARQUIS, and read:

Last Thursday afternoon, the Marquis of Deerswood was tragically drowned in a boating accident off the north-west coast of Scotland.

The young nobleman, who was staying with his uncle, Lord Hindsdale, at Drumpitloch Castle, a family residence, had taken a boat out alone in order to examine the caves at the foot of a nearby cliff when it is believed a sudden squall over-turned the craft. The weather at the time was unsettled.

When the Marquis failed to return, his uncle raised the alarm and a search was carried out. However, no body was found and, as the tide was on the turn, it is assumed that the deceased was swept out to sea.

A Fatal Accident Inquiry is to be held by the Procurator Fiscal at Glasgow.

When I had finished reading, I looked up to see Holmes regarding me quizzically.

'Well, Watson, have you any comment to make so far?'

'Only that the Deerswood family seems remarkably ill-starred.'

'A fate which appears to have pursued them throughout the course of their history,' Holmes remarked, tapping a long finger on the cover of the encyclopaedia. 'The second Lord Deerswood was beheaded by Richard III; another was arrested for his part in the Babington Plot of 1586 and died in the Tower of London of gaol fever before he could be similarly executed; a third was killed in a duel; and that is not to take into account the death of the apparently late young Marquis's father on the hunting field. under the circumstances, their family motto, "*Fortunae Progenies*",[4] has an ironic ring to it. So you made nothing of Gilbert Deerswood's demise?'

'No, Holmes, I must confess that it seemed straightforward enough.'

'You surprise me. Do you not recall Miss Russell's account of her first meeting with Gilbert Deerswood? She said that he was out walking his dog, the only physical exercise he indulged in, and was accompanied by the groom – mark that, Watson! – when he stumbled and fell while climbing over a stile. And yet we are supposed to believe that he was allowed to take a boat out alone on the sea, in adverse weather conditions.'

'Yes, of course, Holmes. I see your point. What, then,

---

[4] *Fortunae Progenies* may be literally translated as 'The Lineage of Fortune' or, more loosely, as 'Of Fortunate Descent'. Dr John F. Watson.

are you suggesting? That it was not an accident? In that case, could it have been murder?'

Holmes leant back in his chair, his expression indulgent.

'Go on, my dear Watson. Pray expound your theory.'

'Well,' said I, warming to the idea, 'the present Lord Deerswood may have murdered his nephew in order to inherit the title and estates. He then threw the body into the sea, overturning the boat to make it appear that the young man had been drowned.'

'No doubt also weighing the body down with stones so that it was never found?'

'That is certainly a possibility.'

To my discomfiture, Holmes gave a chuckle.

'An interesting theory, my dear fellow, but one that does not take into account Miss Russell's evidence. Despite my earlier warning, in your eagerness to speculate about the case, you have forgotten that she saw, or thought she saw, the young Lord Deerswood alive only three nights ago in the grounds of Hartsdene Manor. If that is so, it was a remarkably corporeal ghost which had returned from the dead and which needed two grown men to restrain it!'

'Then could he have survived the murder attempt and swum ashore, reappearing later at Hartsdene Manor to confront his uncle? Under those circumstances, the new Marquis of Deerswood could very well find the need to keep him under restraint.'

'With the collusion of the servants, no doubt? If your theory is correct, then why did his uncle not make a second attempt on his nephew's life and bury the body in the grounds if his purpose was to eliminate the heir and inherit the title? In addition, why should the present Marquis challenge Miss Russell and Mr Lawson to invite anyone they wished to search the Manor? Do you not consider that a curious response under the circumstances?'

'I do not quite follow you.'

'Then place yourself in the present Lord Deerswood's shoes. You have been accused in so many words, although no doubt Miss Russell and Mr Lawson expressed themselves more delicately, of falsely inheriting the title and the Deerswood estates, the true heir still being alive, a charge you most strongly deny. What would your response have been under the circumstances?'

'Why, to put my lawyer in touch with them, of course, and threaten legal action should they persist with their slander. So would any reasonable man.'

'Exactly! And yet Lord Deerswood failed to do so. Bear that in mind, Watson, when we undertake the investigation. May I suggest that you also consider two other facts which could be relevant?'

'What are those, Holmes?'

'Firstly that Hartsdene Manor was, according to my encyclopaedia of reference, built in the reign of Elizabeth I and, although it was considerably altered in the eighteenth century, a wing of that original Tudor building still stands. Secondly, that the seventh Lord Deerswood was accused of taking part in the Babington Plot.'

'The Babington Plot? You refer to the conspiracy to

29

assassinate Queen Elizabeth and replace her on the throne with Mary Queen of Scots? But what possible connection can that have with the present case?'

But Holmes refused to be drawn.

All he would say in answer was, 'Think about it, my dear fellow. It will make a useful study between now and tomorrow afternoon when I shall expect to see you here again in good time to catch the 4.17 to Guildford.'

I did as Holmes recommended and turned the matter over in my mind but I was no nearer solving the mystery when, the following afternoon, Holmes and I set off for Waterloo.

II

We were met at Guildford station by Frederick Lawson who explained that he was staying, like us, at Windicot Villa in case his professional services should be needed during our inquiries.

It was a five-mile drive to Little Bramfield near where Miss Russell and her father resided, and the route took us across a track of open heathland. In the fading light, it looked sombre indeed, its only vegetation rough heather and low clumps of furze with a few stunted trees which stood out against the darkening sky like crippled sentinels, standing guard over the desolate landscape.

The journey was almost complete, apart from the last half-mile, when Frederick Lawson drew our attention to the right-hand side of the road where we had our first sight of Hartsdene Manor.

It stood a little back from the verge, a square, severe-looking house, its grey-stone facade in the Palladian style unrelieved by any softening benefit of shrubbery or climbing plants. A formal rose-garden and a stretch of lawn fronted the house while a gravelled drive led from a pair of wrought-iron gates up to a plain pillared portico.

In a few seconds we had passed it, but Holmes appeared content with that first fleeting glimpse for he settled back against the upholstered cushions with every sign of satisfaction.

Shortly afterwards, we arrived at Windicot Villa, a commodious, red-brick residence. Here we alighted and were welcomed by Miss Russell who conducted us into a comfortable, well-furnished drawing-room where a cheerful log-fire was burning on the hearth.

Seated by the fire was an elderly, white-haired gentleman whom Miss Russell introduced as her father; a courtly personage of the old school whose frailty of appearance confirmed his poor state of health.

For his sake, the conversation was general although, after dinner, when Mr Russell had retired to his room, we turned to discussing the subject uppermost in all our minds, Holmes confirming the arrangements with Miss Russell for that evening's excursion. The carriage would take us along the same road we had already travelled, turning at the crossroads before driving back past the gates of Hartsdene Manor at half-past ten, the same hour at which, four nights before, Miss Russell had witnessed the incident in the garden.

The weather had remained clear and the moon was still relatively full. The conditions should therefore be similar to those which she herself had encountered.

'And after that,' Holmes concluded, 'I suggest that the

carriage return here. As Dr Watson and I shall have further inquiries to make in the immediate vicinity of Hartsdene Manor, we shall make our own way back on foot. It is a mere half-mile walk and there is no need for the coachman to be kept from his bed. May I also request that two carriage rugs be placed for our use inside the brougham?'

'What inquiries, Holmes?' I asked when, the time for our departure having approached, we retired to our bedroom to put on our topcoats in readiness for the drive.

But Holmes declined to be drawn.

'Wait and see, my dear fellow,' he said, adding teasingly as we descended the stairs, 'Remember the Babington Plot!'

I could still make nothing of the connection and continued to puzzle over it as the carriage set off along the Guildford road, turning as agreed at the crossroads to begin the return journey.

It was a cold night with a touch of frost in the air and the trees, their branches denuded of foliage, stood very still and stark against a pale sky in which a great, white moon hung, so very bright and close that I could make out quite clearly the mysterious dark continents which marked its lunar surface.

Although Holmes had taken the right-hand seat, the one which Miss Russell had occupied during that earlier journey, I myself was able, by leaning well forward, to obtain a good view through the carriage window as we approached Hartsdene Manor.

On this occasion, it was not the house which engaged my attention but the garden. Through the open tracery of the wrought-iron gates, I could see the lawn quite clearly, the grass blanched by the moonlight and by the covering of thick dew which was rapidly turning into a crisp, white frost. There were no trees nearby to cast any shadows and those which lined the drive presented in their leafless state no barrier to observation.

The lawn, and anyone walking on it, would have been instantly visible to an observer travelling along the road in a carriage, a point which Holmes made when, having drawn level with the gates, we passed beyond them.

'I am convinced, Watson, that Miss Russell was not mistaken.'

A few minutes later, he rapped on the panel, a signal to the coachman to halt. We climbed down and the empty brougham proceeded on its return journey, leaving us standing by the roadside, the carriage rugs over our arms.

I had expected Holmes to walk back to the entrance to Hartsdene Manor. Instead, he followed the road a little distance in the opposite direction until, finding a gap in the thick hedge, he scrambled through.

Beyond lay a wood which must have formed part of the boundary to that side of the estate for, as we crossed it, I could see ahead of us through the trees the massive bulk of the Manor; or, rather, of a wing which, judging by its steep gables and irregular roof, formed the old Tudor part of the building of which Holmes had already spoken.

At the edge of the wood, from which point we had a clear view of this part of the house, Holmes halted and seated himself upon a fallen tree-trunk.

'And now, my dear fellow, we must wait upon events,' he announced in a low voice.

His manner dissuaded me from asking to which events he was referring and I sat down beside him in silence.

It was a long and bitterly cold vigil even though the carriage rugs kept out some of the night chill.

Eleven o'clock passed and then half-past, signalled by the tolling of a bell from the stable-block.

It was nearly midnight before any sign of life appeared in the darkened wing of Hartsdene Manor.

And then, just as I had begun to think that our watch had been wasted, a yellow glow appeared in one of the mullioned windows, wavering at first and then steadying as if someone had carried a lamp into the room and had set it down. Shortly afterwards a similar glow shone out through the panes of the adjoining window and a figure appeared against the glass, even at that distance distinctive in its broad-shouldered silhouette.

The next instant, both windows were darkened in turn as if heavy curtains or shutters were closed across them, and the façade was once more left in darkness.

'Come, Watson,' Holmes said softly. 'I have seen enough.'

The long wait, it appeared, was over.

We walked the half-mile to Windicot Villa at a brisk rate to get the blood moving again in our frozen limbs, Holmes striding out one pace in front of me, his long black shadow projected ahead of him in the moonlight.

He was silent and, knowing him in this abstracted

mood, I made no attempt to interrupt his train of thought.

It was only when we reached the gates of Windicot Villa that he ventured any remark.

With his hand on the latch, he turned to me, his face sombre.

'This case will end tragically, I fear, Watson. I must warn Miss Russell and Mr Lawson. But not tonight. I should not wish to give them an uneasy rest, the young lady in particular.'

Miss Russell and Mr Lawson, together with the housekeeper, a Mrs Henty, were waiting up for us in the drawing-room where a bright fire was still burning on the hearth and where hot soup and game pie were soon served.

Holmes said little about our night's investigations, merely remarking that they had been satisfactory, before asking Miss Russell a question of which, at the time, I could not see the purpose.

'Tell me,' said he, 'had the young Marquis of Deerswood ever travelled abroad to your knowledge?'

Her answer was quite positive.

'No, Mr Holmes, he had not. He told me once that he had never been outside the country. Why do you ask?'

'I am merely curious,' Holmes replied with a dismissive air and said no more on the subject.

True to his resolve, he made no reference to his fears about the tragic outcome to the case until the following morning at breakfast when he finally raised the matter. Only the four of us were present, old Mr Russell preferring to breakfast in bed.

His expression grave, Holmes addressed Miss Russell

and Mr Lawson across the table, expressing in the same words the anxiety he had already voiced to me the previous night.

'I can give you no more detailed explanation,' he concluded. 'However, in view of my apprehension regarding the inquiry I can proceed no further with the case without your permission. Even then, unless the present Marquis of Deerswood agrees, I fear that the full facts may still never be revealed.'

Miss Russell listened with bowed head and then, raising her eyes, looked him directly in the face.

'I should prefer to know the truth, Mr Holmes, however terrible it might be,' she said quietly. 'As far, that is, as Lord Deerswood permits it.'

'A most remarkable young lady,' Holmes commented when we set off once more for Hartsdene Manor, my old friend carrying in his pocket a letter of introduction from Miss Russell, countersigned by Frederick Lawson.

Coming from Holmes, it was a rare accolade indeed. There were no women he cared for and only one whom he had ever truly admired.[5]

The rest of the journey was completed in silence, I preoccupied with turning over in my mind what tragedy Holmes had referred to and how he had reached his conclusion, while Holmes was sunk deep in his own thoughts.

---

[5] Dr John H. Watson is no doubt referring to Irene Adler who, in Mr Sherlock Holmes' estimation, was always 'the woman'. *Vide* 'A Scandal in Bohemia'. Dr John F. Watson.

On our arrival at Hartsdene Manor, he seemed to recover some of his spirits, jumping down from the carriage and running up the steps to ring energetically at the bell.

The door was opened by a butler – Macey, I assumed – a solemn, portly individual who, on our presenting our cards and Miss Russell's letter, showed us into the hall where he requested we should wait.

While we did so, I looked curiously about me.

The hall was large and sumptuously furnished but neither the portraits hanging on the walls nor the rich oriental rugs spread across the marble floor could quite dispel the air of chilly gloom which permeated the place. It seemed joyless, as if the sound of human laughter had been banished long ago.

In front of us, a broad, heavily carved staircase led to an upper gallery and, as we waited below, a white and liver-coloured spaniel came suddenly bounding down the steps to sniff eagerly at our legs.

'Gilbert Deerswood's dog looking for its master, I dare say,' Holmes remarked.

His surmise seemed correct, for, having examined us and found us wanting, the dog slunk away disappointed to a far corner where it curled up on one of the rugs and went to sleep.

At this point, the butler returned to announce that Lord Deerswood would see us and we were conducted down a corridor to a pair of double doors.

They led into a library, also splendidly furnished

although it was not the book-lined walls nor the gilt and leather chairs which caught my attention but the tall figure of Lord Deerswood who had risen from behind a desk at the far side of the room.

He was a thin, dark pillar of a man, very erect and rigid, dressed entirely in black with the exception of a high, white, starched collar above which his high-nosed, aristocratic face regarded us disdainfully as a well-bred racehorse might inspect creatures of a lower pedigree from across a five-barred gate.

'I see,' said he, tapping with one finger on Miss Russell's letter which lay open on the desk in front of him, 'that Miss Russell and her solicitor continue with their ridiculous assertion that my nephew is still alive. Very well, Mr Holmes. The truth of the matter shall be put to the test. You and your companion,' and here he made a slight bow in my direction, for the first time acknowledging my presence, 'are at liberty to search the house from attic to cellar although I can assure you that you will be wasting your time. You will find no one in residence apart from myself and the servants.'

With that, he turned his back on us and jerked on a bell-rope beside the fireplace.

We waited in silence for the butler to reappear, a deeply embarrassing few moments in which I sympathised with Miss Russell's and Mr Lawson's ordeal when they had faced this man at their initial interview.

It was Holmes, not at all put out, it seemed, by Lord

Deerswood's haughty manner, who finally broke the silence.

'I understand,' said he, 'that Miss Russell saw two men in the company of the person she took to be your nephew. One was your butler. The other she did not recognise. May I inquire who he might be?'

Hardly had he finished speaking when there was a tap at the door and the butler entered.

Without so much as glancing in Holmes' direction, Lord Deerswood addressed the manservant.

'Bring Mr Barker here, Macey,' he ordered, adding, as the butler left the room, 'The man to whom you refer, Mr Holmes, is my secretary, Barker, who joined my staff only a few months ago which is no doubt why Miss Russell failed to recognise him. You shall meet him. I should not wish to give Miss Russell cause to believe that any circumstances concerning my household have been kept from her.'

He lapsed once more into silence which continued until the butler returned, accompanied by a tall, dark-featured man, immensely broad across the shoulders.

'My secretary, Barker,' Lord Deerswood said by way of an introduction at which the man bowed in our direction. 'And now,' his lordship continued, 'if you care to accompany my butler, he will show you any rooms you care to examine.'

He regarded us with the same cold disdain with which he had first greeted us as Holmes thanked him and we turned to follow the butler from the room. For my part, although I cannot speak for Holmes, I felt the man's eyes boring into my back as I made the long retreat from the desk to the double doors at the far end of the library, preceded by the figure of Macey, who maintained a silence as intimidating as his master's.

He broke it only when Holmes addressed him directly as we were mounting the stairs.

'It is merely the bedrooms that we wish to examine.'

'Very good, sir.'

We reached the upper gallery, a long passageway extending in both directions and with doors leading from it to at least twenty bedrooms, all of which we examined and all, with the exception of Lord Deerswood's own bed-chamber, apparently unused, the furniture covered in dust-sheets.

The former Marquis of Deerswood's room was similarly sheeted, the bed stripped down to the mattress and the curtains which surrounded the four-poster swathed in white cotton so that they resembled so many hanging shrouds.

As we entered the room, Holmes glanced down at the surround of polished boards which extended beyond the edge of the carpet, before raising a quizzical eyebrow in my direction. The implication was quite clear. The thin layer of dust on the floor, which had gathered since the room was last cleaned, bore no other signs of footmarks than our own. It was evident that the room had not been recently occupied.

As the butler closed the door on the last room at the end of the passage, he announced, 'you have now seen all the bedchambers, gentlemen. Do you wish to return downstairs?'

'What of the other wing?' Holmes inquired.

For the first time, I thought I detected a sign of unease on the butler's part.

'Only the servants and Mr Barker occupy that part of the house, sir.'

'Nevertheless, I should like to see it.'

'Very good, sir.'

We followed him down some steps and into another passageway. From its lower ceiling with its heavy beams, it was clear that we had entered the older part of the house, all that remained of the original Tudor manor house in front of which Holmes and I had kept our vigil the previous night.

The passage ran haphazardly, turning several corners and ascending or descending by means of sets of shallow steps so that it was difficult to grasp the plan of the rooms and their relationship to one another.

The chambers themselves were smaller and darker than those in the main part of the house and several of them also appeared to be unoccupied. However, we examined briefly Macey's own bedroom and those of the cook, the housemaids and Lord Deerswood's valet.

It was the room belonging to Barker, his lordship's secretary, in which Holmes lingered the longest although, at the time, I could not understand why this particular chamber should have aroused his interest.

There was nothing remarkable about it. Like the

others, it was low-ceilinged with old, linen-fold panelling on the walls and with a single mullioned window, fitted with wooden shutters, which looked out towards the wood, on the edge of which Holmes and I had sat upon the fallen log.

The furniture was of the plainest, a single bedstead with a night-table beside it on which an oil lamp was standing and, opposite it, an old-fashioned press of time-blackened oak which occupied almost the entire wall. An armchair and a square of drugget on the floor completed the furnishings.

Nevertheless, Holmes remained for several long moments in the room, opening the door of the press to look inside it and examining the shutters before turning back towards the door.

There were other rooms to see – a windowless linen closet which adjoined Barker's with the housekeeper's bedchamber next to it but Holmes merely put his head in a perfunctory manner inside them.

The tour completed, we returned to the head of the main staircase and went down it to the entrance hall which we crossed, it being clearly Macey's intention to conduct us out of the house.

Indeed, he was halfway towards the front doors when Holmes suddenly announced, 'There is one room I wish to re-examine. I am sure Lord Deerswood would not object, having already given us permission to inspect the house.'

The butler seemed nonplussed and, as he stood

hesitating, Holmes started back up the stairs, adding airily over his shoulder, 'There is no need for you to accompany us, Macey. Dr Watson and I know the way.'

As we reached the upper landing, Holmes glanced down over the gallery rail.

The entrance hall was now empty, the butler having disappeared from sight.

'Gone, no doubt, to inform Lord Deerswood of our intentions,' Holmes remarked. 'Come, Watson, the hunt is nearly over but we may not have much time to draw the last covert.'

'What covert, Holmes?'

'Why, the one where our fox has gone to earth, of course.'

'You seem very sure.'

'Indeed I am, my dear fellow.'

'How is that?'

'From our observations last night, coupled with what we have seen this morning.'

'But we have been shown nothing except a large number of empty rooms.'

'Oh, we have seen a great deal more than that, including the fingers on the right hand of his lordship's secretary. Did you not notice that they were stained, not with ink, as one would suppose, but with . . . ?'

He broke off as the spaniel we had encountered earlier rose from the rug where it had been sleeping and came to the foot of the stairs, wagging its tail with the same eager air.

'A canine assistant!'[6] Holmes declared and, snapping his fingers at it over the banisters, called it up to join us.

It obeyed with alacrity, bounding up the steps and following at our heels as Holmes led the way down the passage and into the Tudor wing of the house which, only shortly before, we had, to the best of my belief, thoroughly examined.

We halted outside the door to Barker's room, Holmes tapping on the panel as if expecting that, in our absence, its owner would have returned.

In this assumption he was correct for, having received permission to enter, we opened the door to see Barker in the act of laying aside a book and rising to his feet from a chair by the window, his expression full of consternation at our unexpected appearance, the spaniel at our heels.

It was apparent that the creature had never before been inside the room for it halted just within the door, uneasy at finding itself in such unfamiliar surroundings.

Barker had stepped towards us as if about to object to our presence when Holmes sent the dog forward with the words: 'Go, Handel! Seek your master!'

At this command, the spaniel ran towards the great

[6] There are several references to dogs within the published canon and two instances when Mr Sherlock Holmes made use of such an animal to assist him in his investigations. *Vide* 'The Sign of Four' and 'The Adventure of the Missing Three-Quarter'. In 'The Adventure of the Creeping Man', Mr Sherlock Holmes speaks of writing a monograph on the use of dogs in detective work in relation to the manner in which they reflect the characters and moods of their owners. Dr John F. Watson.

oaken press to sniff eagerly at its closed doors, its tail thumping against the carpet.

It was at this moment that Lord Deerswood appeared silently in the open doorway behind us, our first intimation of his presence being Barker's stammered apology.

'I'm sorry, my lord. I had no idea Mr Holmes or Dr Watson would return. . .'

Lord Deerswood advanced into the room and, ignoring Barker's attempt at explanation, addressed Holmes directly, his expression no longer supercilious but full of a brooding melancholy.

'I can see, Mr Holmes, that it is impossible to deceive you, a fact I should have recognised, knowing your reputation.'

Making a slight bow in acknowledgement, Holmes replied, 'My inquiries have led me this far, Lord Deerswood, but, without your permission, I shall proceed no further than the doors to this press. Although I am retained by Miss Russell, whose concern in this affair is, I should add, solely on behalf of your nephew, I have her agreement that she will desist from all further inquiries should you so desire it. If you wish Dr Watson and myself to withdraw, we shall do so immediately.'

For several moments, Lord Deerswood considered this proposition without speaking. And then he seemed suddenly to come to a decision for, turning to Barker, he inquired, 'Is all well?' On receiving the man's assurance that it was, his lordship continued, 'Then show them the Paradol Chamber.'

At this, Barker crossed to the cupboard and opened its double doors.

As I have already described, the press was large and its commodious interior was divided up into two sections, in one of which clothes were hanging on hooks. The other was entirely taken up by a set of shelves on which some shirts and underlinen were lying.

Stretching one arm inside the cupboard, Barker released some hidden catch at which the whole set of shelves swung inwards like a door.

With a silent gesture of one hand, Lord Deerswood invited us to enter, which we did, followed by his lordship.

Beyond lay a room of a similar size to the one which we had just vacated but so different in its furnishings and appearance that it was like entering another world. In place of the plain drugget, a thick carpet lay upon the floor while hangings of a similar richness disguised the shutters at the window in front of which stood a small reading table and an armchair. Other luxuries in the form of paintings and bookcases occupied the walls and the chimney alcoves where, on the hearth, a bright coal fire was burning.

The only incongruous fittings in this otherwise comfortably appointed chamber were the high iron guard which stood before the fire, the fine mesh screen over the window which would have been invisible from outside, and, most disturbing of all, a pair of leather straps fastened to the frame of a bed which was placed against the wall to the immediate right of the doorway.

On the bed, under the linen sheets and the thick

embroidered quilt, lay a young man, so heavily asleep that I suspected he had been drugged. He neither stirred nor opened his eyes as we entered but lay immobile, his head resting on the monogrammed pillows.

It was a tragic face despite its youthfulness for the man was only in his mid-twenties, but so ravaged that the features appeared those of someone much older who had endured many dark and bitter experiences.

'My nephew, the Marquis of Deerswood,' his lordship announced.

He was standing at the foot of the bed, gazing down at the motionless figure, his face as drawn and as haggard as the young man's with an expression of agonised compassion.

'If you have seen enough, gentlemen,' he continued as Holmes and I remained silent, 'I suggest we retire to the library where I shall give you a full account of how my nephew came to be reduced to this pitiable state. I know I may trust your discretion. Your reputation in that respect has also followed you.'

Again Holmes inclined his head and, preceded by Lord Hindsdale, to accord him his proper title, we vacated the chamber and returned downstairs to the library where, on his lordship's invitation, we seated ourselves before the fire.

III

However, it was Holmes who opened the interview, pressed to do so by Lord Hindsdale.

'Before I begin my own account,' he said, 'I should prefer to hear yours, Mr Holmes. It might save my having to repeat certain facts with which you may already be acquainted. Besides, I am curious to know by what methods you have so far proceeded in discovering the truth.'

'I know only what I have deduced from my own observations and a little research I undertook after Miss Russell and her solicitor first requested me to inquire into the case,' Holmes replied. 'There is no need for me to repeat her account of what she saw in the grounds of Hartsdene Manor; she has already given it to you herself. However, I should like to explain that her concern arose not out of idle curiosity or from a desire to spread scandal. She was – is – genuinely fond of your nephew and it was for his sake that she consulted me.

'Her statement prompted me to look up in my own records the newspaper reports of your nephew's apparent death in a boating accident last summer in Scotland. However, as I have already explained to my colleague, Dr Watson, certain features about the tragedy intrigued me. My curiosity was further aroused by Miss Russell's account of her first meeting with the young Marquis which occurred when he fell and hit his head while climbing over a stile.

'And then there was your family history, Lord Hindsdale, which went part of the way to solving your nephew's apparent return from the dead. It involved the arrest of one of your ancestors for his part in the Babington Plot in 1586.'

Turning to me, he added with a smile, 'I am afraid, Watson, that I caused you some bewilderment by referring to it. The explanation is, however, quite simple. The Babington Plot was a conspiracy to replace the Protestant Elizabeth Tudor by the Catholic Mary Queen of Scots.

'This suggested,' Holmes continued, resuming his narrative, 'that at the time the Deerswoods were Catholic sympathisers. Now, it was often the custom for recusant families during the reign of Elizabeth I to have constructed in their houses a secret chamber where the resident priest could be hidden should the house be searched. Although there was no reference in any books that I consulted to such a hiding-place in Hartsdene Manor, I nevertheless decided to put my supposition to the test. If there was a secret priest's room, it would be in the original part of the house.

'Consequently, Dr Watson and I kept watch last night on the Tudor wing where we saw a man, whom I later recognised as Barker, closing the shutters on a pair of lighted windows on the upper floor. However, when I examined Barker's room this morning, I observed that his bedchamber had only one window.

'Now, as the room next to Barker's on the right was a windowless linen closet, it could not have been there that the light appeared. It had to be some other chamber, situated between Barker's bedchamber and the linen closet, its presence concealed from the casual observer by the irregularity of the passage. I further deduced that its entrance must be through Barker's room. Your nephew's dog confirmed its position by going immediately to the large press against the wall when I ordered it to seek out its master.

'I was already curious about Barker's presence in your household. As Miss Russell did not recognise him when she saw him in the garden, he must have joined since her last visit here in the summer, a supposition you confirmed by stating that he had been recently appointed as your secretary. But I noticed that his fingers were stained with iodoform.[7] Only a doctor or a nurse would normally handle such a medicament.

'Given all these facts, I came to the conclusion that your nephew was alive but was kept concealed in a secret chamber, attended by a doctor or a male nurse, and was allowed out only at night. Only two explanations

[7] Iodoform is a compound of iodine, used as an antiseptic.

presented themselves. The first was some disfiguring illness such as leprosy[8] which I dismissed as a possibility as your nephew had never, according to Miss Russell, travelled outside this country.

'I was therefore left with my second hypothesis – which has proved only too tragically correct – that he was suffering from some mental aberration which made his appearance in public impossible. The fact that his mother had died in a Swiss clinic, ostensibly of consumption, tended to confirm my supposition.

'I should like to assure you again, Lord Hindsdale, that I expect no explanation from you but, if you should honour Dr Watson and myself with your confidence, no word of what we have heard or seen here today will ever be repeated outside these walls.'

Lord Hindsdale, who had listened to Holmes' statement without interruption, his chin sunk on his breast, now raised his head to look across at my companion, his austere face drawn down into deep lines of suffering.

'You are correct in every particular, Mr Holmes,' he said. 'For this reason and because I know you and Dr Watson are men of your word, I have no hesitation in confiding in you. Indeed, it is a relief, having borne the truth so long in silence, to speak openly about it for it has

---

[8] In 'The Adventure of the Blanched Soldier', Godfrey Emsworth was kept segregated in an outhouse by his father who feared that his son was suffering from leprosy. However, Mr Sherlock Holmes called in the eminent dermatologist, Sir James Saunders, who diagnosed pseudo-leprosy or ichthyosis, a non-infectious disease. Dr John F. Watson.

weighed very heavily on both my mind and my heart for many years.

'While still in his early twenties, my eldest brother, Gilbert's father, fell in love with and married a young lady, Blanche Seaford, a dazzling and enchanting creature. Her family was rich but obscure, having farmed in South Africa for several generations, and was therefore unknown in English society. On the death of her husband, Mrs Seaford sold up the family estates and brought Blanche, who was then seventeen, to London in order to complete her education. It was there that my brother James met and fell in love with her, marrying her on her eighteenth birthday. For the first two years, they were blissfully happy but, after the birth of Gilbert, my sister-in-law began to show certain symptoms which, over the next eighteen months, degenerated rapidly into lunacy. Later inquiries showed that it was an inherited madness. A grandfather had committed suicide; an aunt had died in an asylum.

'Although everything was done in an attempt to save her reason, she was beyond medical aid and, when her behaviour grew so violent and unpredictable that it was considered unsafe to keep her under the same roof as the child, my brother, with great reluctance, arranged for her to be admitted to a private clinic for the insane in Switzerland.

'We are an old, proud family, Mr Holmes, but tragically ill-fated. My brother, fearful of the effect it would have on his son if the truth were generally known, had it put out that his wife had died of consumption. In fact, she lingered on for another fifteen years, a helpless lunatic.

'My brother was most anxious about his son, his greatest fear being that Gilbert might have inherited from his mother that tendency towards mental instability. For that reason, he was kept at home where he was tutored privately in the hope that if he followed a quiet regimen with no excitement or emotional strain to tax the brain, he might escape the same fate as his mother.

'You are probably aware of the rest of the story, Mr Holmes. My brother was killed in a hunting accident when Gilbert was fourteen. As his guardian, I came to live here at Hartsdene Manor in order to supervise his education and upbringing. My brother and I had often discussed what should be done if Gilbert became insane. James was only too painfully aware that, should he die, a terrible burden of responsibility would be placed on my shoulders. It was no burden, Mr Holmes. I love my nephew as I would my own son!'

The stern features were convulsed momentarily with a spasm of emotion and he turned his face away, murmuring, 'Forgive me, gentlemen, it is a most painful subject.'

It was several seconds before he had sufficiently recovered his composure to continue his account.

'And then, last spring, Gilbert met Miss Russell and, as his father had done with Blanche Seaford, he fell in love with her at first sight. It was a hopeless situation. Marriage was out of the question as, by that time, he was already showing signs of incipient madness. Indeed, it was during a minor fit that he fell and struck his head whilst out walking and first became acquainted with Miss Russell.

'I was most reluctant to permit the acquaintanceship to continue but Gilbert pleaded so hard to be allowed to see her again that, very much against my better judgement, I finally gave way. It was an unwise decision. Further meetings only deepened Gilbert's feeling for Miss Russell although I believe the young lady felt no more for him than friendship and a strong pity; at least, I hope that is the case for her sake.

'By last summer, it was quite clear to both Gilbert and myself that his madness was not a passing aberration. The fits of insanity became more frequent and prolonged. In one of his lucid periods, we discussed his future quite rationally. It was Gilbert himself who suggested that we go to Scotland, where the family owns a castle on the coast, and that there his apparent death should be contrived in a boating accident. It seemed to him the best and cleanest escape from his tragic situation. That way, the truth need never be revealed. I should inherit the title and the estates without any legal complications and Miss Russell would be released from an impossible relationship.

'He further suggested that he be brought back here to be cared for.[9] He loves this place; it is his childhood home;

---

[9] As Mr Sherlock Holmes points out in 'The Adventure of the Blanched Soldier', it was not illegal to keep a lunatic on private premises, provided a qualified person was in attendance and the authorities had been notified. However, as this latter obligation had clearly not been fulfilled, Lord Hindsdale was breaking the law. Dr John F. Watson.

the servants are all old family retainers and therefore could be trusted. There was, moreover, the Paradol Chamber, the priest's hiding place, so named after the Italian craftsman, a Signor Paradolini, who devised it, and the existence of which you correctly deduced, Mr Holmes. There he could be kept safe from the eyes of casual visitors or curious neighbours.

'He also insisted I gave him my word that, should his madness grow worse, he would be sent abroad to the same clinic where his mother had been admitted.

'I agreed to his terms; there was no alternative. Consequently the boating accident was arranged in which Gilbert apparently died, his body being swept out to sea. A few days later, I brought him back here, disguised as a servant. Barker was appointed as his nurse and the Paradol Chamber was prepared for him. He occupies it for most of the time, kept docile by drugs and sleeping draughts during his most violent attacks, although there are intervals, usually at night, when his insanity is less pronounced and he is taken downstairs to walk about the gardens.

'It was on one of these occasions that Miss Russell caught sight of him. He had been walking with Barker in the grounds to the rear of the house, out of sight of the road, when a sudden fit overcame him and, breaking free, he ran towards the gates. Barker shouted for Macey to assist him and it was while the two men were attempting to restrain Gilbert and conduct him back inside the house that Miss Russell's carriage drove past.

'That is the full and tragic story, Mr Holmes. I know I can rely on you, and on your colleague, Dr Watson, never to repeat it.'

'You have our word,' Holmes assured him. 'However, may I be allowed to give you some advice, Lord Hindsdale?'

'What is that?'

'That you take Miss Russell into your confidence. She is a young lady of great good sense and strength of character. I am certain she would never betray your trust. But it would be cruel indeed, knowing the affection she has for your nephew, if you leave her in ignorance of the truth. Her solicitor, Frederick Lawson, may also be trusted.'

'Yes; you are right,' Lord Hindsdale conceded after a long moment's consideration. 'In fact, I shall ask Miss Russell for an interview in the presence of her solicitor this very afternoon.'

I do not know what was said between them but I assume Lord Hindsdale repeated in their hearing the account which he had already given to Holmes and myself, for during the course of the following months we received two communications from Miss Russell, one tragic in which she informed us that 'a mutual friend' had been forced to retire to a Swiss clinic through failing health.

The second, which arrived several weeks after the first, contained happier news. In it, Miss Russell announced her forthcoming marriage to Frederick Lawson, inviting

Holmes and myself to the ceremony which, unfortunately, we were unable to attend, Holmes being fully occupied by the Tillington scandal, for which he required my services.

As for the case of the Paradol Chamber, I have given my word that the facts will never be made public and therefore I have had to content myself with making only a passing reference to it within the published records[10] and with writing this secret account which will be deposited with other confidential material in my dispatch box at my bank, Cox and Co. of Charing Cross, knowing that no one except Holmes and myself will ever set eyes upon it.

---

[10] In 'The Five Orange Pips', Dr John H. Watson refers briefly to the adventure of the Paradol Chamber among a list of other cases which occurred in 1887 and of which he has retained the records. Dr John F. Watson.

The Case of the Hammersmith Wonder

'What an exceedingly depressing day!' Holmes complained. He was standing at the window of our[1] sitting-room in Baker Street, drumming his fingers on the pane down which the rain was pouring like a cataract. 'No investigation to stimulate the mind! No book worth reading! Nothing to look at except wet umbrellas and steaming cab-horses! We really must do something, Watson. I cannot tolerate another hour spent shut up between these four walls. I shall suffocate with boredom!'

He had been in a restless state of mind all afternoon, alternately pacing about the room or flinging himself

[1] Although the account is undated, the use of the word 'our' in this context suggests that Dr John H. Watson was living permanently at 221B Baker Street and was not there merely on a visit. The case must therefore be assigned either to the period before his marriage to Miss Mary Morstan in the late 1880s or to the time following Mrs Watson's death in the mid-1890s, after which he again took up residence in Baker Street. From the internal evidence, I am inclined to favour the earlier dating. Dr John F. Watson.

down on the sofa to stare moodily at the ceiling.

'What do you suggest, Holmes?' I inquired.

I was seated by the fire, reading the evening newspaper, with no real desire to venture out in such wild, wet weather.

'Let us see what the *Star* has to offer,' said he, striding across the room. Taking the paper from me, he rustled through the pages until he came to the section advertising the various places of entertainment.

'Which would you prefer? A concert at St James's Hall? A theatre? Or a return visit to Goldini's?'[2]

'Quite frankly, I should prefer none of them. It is a beastly night, Holmes.'

'What a dull fellow you are! A little wetting hurt no one. Aha! I see something here which will tempt you away from the fire. The French Nightingale is top of the bill at the Cambridge.[3] I thought that would rouse you!' said Holmes, quite recovering his good spirits at the alacrity with which I sat upright in my chair. 'She is a particular favourite of yours, is she not?'

---

[2] Goldini's was an Italian restaurant in Gloucester Road, Kensington. It was here that Mr Sherlock Holmes arranged to meet Dr John H. Watson for coffee and a curaçao, requesting him to bring with him certain house-breaking tools and a revolver. *Vide* 'The Adventure of the Bruce-Partington Plans'. Dr John F. Watson.

[3] I have been unable to trace the Cambridge music-hall, other than a smaller establishment in the East End of London, and suggest it is a pseudonym for the Oxford, where many famous performers appeared, which was situated in Oxford Street. It was demolished after the First World War. Dr John F. Watson.

'She has a very fine voice,' I replied, a little stiffly.

'And a quite superb ankle. Well, what do you say, my dear fellow? Shall we brave the rain and go to see her?'

'If you wish. It is entirely your decision.'

Holmes was still chuckling with amusement when, a little later and well muffled up against the weather, we hailed a cab in Baker Street and set off for the Cambridge, supping first at Marcini's[4] on the way.

Because of the rain, we had no difficulty in obtaining seats in the third row of the stalls, from which vantage point we had an excellent view of the stage and the chairman who introduced the acts.

I cannot say that the earlier part of the programme particularly engaged my interest. There was an indifferent low comedian, a group of slightly above-average high-wire performers, a contortionist in a leopard-skin leotard who contrived to twist his limbs into quite extraordinary positions, and a pair of performing seals which Holmes, for reasons best known to himself, applauded enthusiastically.

For my part, I reserved my admiration for Marguerite Rossignol who appeared at the end of the first half of the bill.

Those who have never seen the French Nightingale

---

[4] Mr Sherlock Holmes and Dr John H. Watson stopped at Marcini's restaurant after the successful conclusion to the Hound of the Baskervilles case for 'a little dinner' before going on to hear the De Reszkes, the famous Polish brothers, sing in Meyerbeer's Les Huguenots, for which performance Mr Sherlock Holmes had reserved a box. Dr John F. Watson.

perform have missed one of the greatest artistes ever to grace a music-hall stage.

She possessed not only a beautiful soprano voice, angelic in its effortless ability to reach a pure, high C, but also a full and yet graceful figure.

That night, as I recall, she was wearing a gown of lavender-coloured silk, a shade which showed off to the best advantage her abundant corn-coloured hair, elegantly adorned with a single aigrette plume, and a pair of shoulders which appeared to have been carved from white alabaster.

The setting also served to enhance her charms. She stood under an arched bower, covered with pink roses, and against a back-drop depicting a garden, full of flowers and blossoming trees.

I can picture her even now, that lovely throat extended as, after singing several ballads, she ended her performance with a thrilling rendition of Godard's 'Berceuse',[5] before the red velvet curtains closed before her to tumultuous applause.

My palms were still warm with clapping, when Holmes tugged at my sleeve with the prosaic suggestion that we made our way to the bar.

---

[5] Benjamin Godard, the French composer, was born in Paris on 18th August 1849 and died in Cannes on 10th January 1895. His best-known opera was *Jocelyn* (1881) which included the well-known 'Berceuse' or Cradle Song. Operatic arias became a popular music-hall feature after Charles Morton presented extracts from Gounod's *Faust* at his Canterbury music-hall on the night before its premiere. Dr John F. Watson.

'A whisky and soda, Watson? If we hurry, we shall be among the first to engage the barmaid's attention.'

It was Holmes who bought the refreshments, carrying the glasses over to a padded bench in a corner among the potted palms where I was sitting, my mind still captivated by the enchantment of the French Nightingale's performance.

'Well,' said he, regarding me with a smile, 'are you not grateful, my dear fellow, that I managed to persuade you away from the fire?'

Before I had time to reply, a commotion drew our attention to the far side of the room. A plump, pale man in evening clothes and, by his expression, in a state of considerable agitation, was trying to push his way through the crowd which now filled the bar.

Above the noise of laughter and conversation, I could hear his voice calling out in great urgency, 'Please, ladies and gentlemen, if I may have your attention! Is there a doctor in the house?'

It was such an unexpected request that at first I failed to respond and it was Holmes who pulled me to my feet, at the same time signalling with his arm.

'My friend, Dr Watson, is a medical practitioner,' he announced as the man approached us. 'Pray what is the matter?'

'I should prefer not to discuss it here,' the stranger replied, glancing uneasily about him at the curious faces which pressed in on us at all sides.

Once we had accompanied him outside to the privacy

of a corner in the foyer, he continued, mopping his moist face with a large white handkerchief, 'My name is Merriwick and I am the manager. A most appalling tragedy has occurred, Dr Watson. One of our artistes has been found dead backstage.'

'In what circumstances?' I inquired.

'Murder!' Merriwick whispered, his eyes almost starting out of his head with horror at the word.

'Have the police been informed?' my old friend asked. 'My name, by the way, is Sherlock Holmes.'

'Mr Holmes? The great consulting detective?' It was highly gratifying to hear the tone of astonished relief in the manager's voice. 'I have heard of you, sir. It is fortunate indeed that you were among the audience tonight. May I retain your services on behalf of the management? Any adverse publicity could be disastrous for the Cambridge.' Merriwick was almost gabbling in his excitement and anxiety. 'The police, Mr Holmes? Yes, they should be on their way. I have sent the assistant-manager off in a cab to Scotland Yard. Only the best is good enough for the Cambridge. And now, if you care to follow me, gentlemen,' he continued, leading the way from the foyer, 'Dr Watson may view the body and you, Mr Holmes – and may I say again how relieved I am to have your assistance? – can make a preliminary investigation.'

'Whose body is it, Mr Merriwick,' I asked.

'Didn't I say, sir? Oh, dear, dear, dear! What a dreadful omission!' Merriwick cried, rounding his eyes again with shock. 'It's Marguerite Rossignol, the French Nightingale.

Top of the bill, too! The Cambridge will never live down the scandal. To think that she should be strangled backstage in her own dressing room!'

'Marguerite Rossignol!' I exclaimed, the shock of it bringing me to a complete halt.

Taking me by the arm, Holmes urged me on.

'Come, Watson. Bear up, my dear fellow. We have work to do.'

'But, Holmes, only a quarter of an hour ago that exquisite creature was alive and . . .'

I broke off, unable to continue.

'Pray remember your Horace,' my old friend adjured me. '"*Vitae summa brevis spem nos vetat incohare longam.*"'[6]

Still dazed by the news, I followed as Merriwick led the way to the area behind the stage, down dusty passages, their bare brick walls and stone floors in shabby contrast to the plush and gilding of the front-of-house, and finally through a door into a large and dingy back region where the dressing rooms were situated.

It was crowded with people, stage-hands as well as performers, the artistes still wearing their costumes with wraps or dressing gowns thrown over their shoulders, and all of them chattering like starlings. In the midst of this disorder, I have a dim recollection of seeing some iron stairs leading to a shadowy upper region and, immediately

---

[6] The quotation is taken from the *Odes* of Horace and may be literally translated as follows: 'The span of our short life forbids us to embark on lasting hopes.' Dr John F. Watson.

in front of us and a little distance away, the stage-door with a small cubby-hole beside it, not unlike a Punch and Judy booth, through the open partition of which a man in a cap and muffler had thrust his head. The next moment, Merriwick turned into another, shorter passage, facing the stage-doorkeeper's little office, and, taking a key from his pocket, unlocked a door.

'The scene of the crime,' he whispered in a sepulchral voice, standing aside to let us enter.

At first, I thought the room had been ransacked, it was in a state of such disarray. Clothes were scattered everywhere – on a shabby *chaise-longue*, over the top of a folding screen which occupied one corner, while garments of a more intimate nature dangled down from an improvised line slung between two hooks.

To add to my initial bewilderment, the large looking-glass of a dressing table faced us as we entered, in which I caught a glimpse of our reflections, our black evening clothes very sombre in the midst of all this colourful confusion.

Still seated on a stool in front of this dressing table but slumped across its surface, amid a litter of jars, spilt powder and sticks of grease-paint, lay the body of a woman with cropped, dark hair; not Marguerite Rossignol, I thought with a surge of relief, even though she was dressed in the same lavender silk gown which the French Nightingale had worn for her performance.

Merriwick, I assumed, had made a mistake.

It was only when I saw, propped up beside her on the dressing table, the corn-coloured hair, still adorned with its aigrette plume and looking disturbingly like a severed head, that I realised the mistake was entirely mine.

Holmes, who had strode purposefully into the room, was bending down to examine the body.

'She has not been dead long,' he announced. 'She is still warm.'

He broke off with an exclamation of disgust to wipe the tips of his fingers upon his pocket handkerchief.

Coming forward, I saw that the pure white marble of the shoulders was smudged where Holmes' hand had brushed against the skin and that it was nothing more than a thick layer of white powder and grease-paint.

'And strangled, too, with one of her own stockings,' Holmes continued, pointing to the wisp of lavender-coloured silk which had been drawn tight about the throat. 'She is still wearing the other.'

Had he not drawn my attention to this fact, I might not have noticed, in my dazed condition, the feet which protruded from below the hem of the gown, one clad, the other bare.

'Well, well!' Holmes remarked. 'This is all distinctly relevant.'

But he did not say to what and immediately sauntered off, first twitching aside some curtains to reveal a heavily barred window before peering behind the screen, a brief examination which seemed to satisfy him for he said, 'I have seen enough, Watson. It is time we spoke to any potential witnesses to this tragedy. Let us find Merriwick.'

Merriwick needed no seeking out. He was waiting

for us outside in the passage, anxious to inform us that the theatre was now empty, the audience having been dismissed on his instructions with some specious excuse, and that he was entirely at our disposal. On Holmes' inquiry if we could question whoever had found the body, Merriwick conducted us to his office, a comfortably appointed room, and then departed to fetch Mademoiselle Rossignol's dresser, Miss Aggie Budd, who had made the fatal discovery.

Shortly afterwards, Miss Budd entered the room. She was a sharp-eyed, elderly Cockney woman, dressed in shabby black and so diminutive of stature that when, on Holmes' invitation she sat down on the straight-backed chair he indicated, her feet barely touched the floor.

'I suppose,' said she, not at all intimidated and regarding us with a pair of little, round, black eyes, as bright as boot buttons, 'that you'll want to know about 'ow I came back to the dressin' room and found Mademoiselle dead?'

'Later,' Holmes told her. 'For the moment, I am more concerned with what happened before that, when Mademoiselle Rossignol was still on stage. You were in her dressing room, I assume, waiting for her to finish her performance? At what point did you leave the room and for how long were you gone?'

The query was as much of a surprise to me as to Miss Budd who countered it with a question of her own which I, too, was anxious to ask although I would not have framed it in quite the same manner.

"'Ere!' she cried, her shrivelled features lively with suspicion. "'Ow did you know that?'

Holmes must have seen my expression of astonishment as well as hers for when he replied, he addressed us both.

'Oh, it was simply a matter of deduction,' said he, with a shrug. 'The carpet behind the screen is liberally sprinkled with white dust where no doubt Mademoiselle Rossignol's shoulders were powdered before she put on her gown. Three sets of footprints were discernible in the dust, all of them fresh. Two were small and belonged to women; yours, Miss Budd, I believe, and Mademoiselle Rossignol's. The other set of marks were much larger and were indisputably those of a man. Unfortunately, they are too blurred to offer any distinguishing features as to exact size or to any patterning on the soles. However, the inference is obvious. A man, presumably the murderer, entered the dressing room and concealed himself behind the screen after Mademoiselle's shoulders had been powdered. As I conclude from his surreptitious behaviour that he had not been invited into the dressing room, then he must have entered it when it was empty, that is, after Mademoiselle Rossignol had gone on stage and when you, Miss Budd, were also absent. Hence my questions. When did you leave the room? And for how long were you gone?'

Miss Budd, who had been following Holmes' explanation with keen attention, her bright little eyes fixed on his face, nodded her head in confirmation.

'You're a clever one! Not the official police, are you, dear? No, I thought not. They'd have trampled all over them footmarks without givin' 'em a second glance. Well, you're right, whoever you are. I did leave the room towards the end of Mademoiselle's performance to wait in the wings for 'er with 'er wrapper. It was to put over 'er gown when she came off. Filthy them wings are! She'd only got to brush up against somethin' to get covered with dust.'

'Was this an habitual routine?'

'If you mean – did I always do it? – then yes, dear, I did.'

'So Mademoiselle Rossignol had, I take it from your answer, played at the Cambridge before?'

'Lots of times. And always top of the bill.'

'When was the second occasion you left the dressing room, before your return and your discovery of Mademoiselle Rossignol's body?'

'That was later, after she'd come off stage. She sent me out for 'alf a pint of porter from the Crown next door, same as she always did. Liked 'er drop of porter, did Mademoiselle; said it kept 'er whistle wet. She told me she was goin' to start gettin' changed while I was gone 'cos she was due on at the Empire[7] at the end of the

---

[7] The Empire music-hall was situated in Leicester Square and was the haunt of notorious ladies of the town who paraded its promenade, known as the Empire Gallery. After protests from a certain Mrs Ormiston Chant, the management erected screens between the gallery and the auditorium which were torn down by a group of counter-protesters, objecting to what they termed 'Prudes on the Prowl', amongst whom was the then Mr Winston Churchill. The Empire was closed on 21st January 1927, after the final performance of *Lady Be Good* which starred Fred Astaire and his sister, Adele. Dr John H. Watson.

second 'alf, where she was sharin' top billin' with Jolly Jack Tarbrush, the Saucy Sailor. That's why she was on in the first 'alf 'ere. She'd worn that lavender-coloured dress there two weeks before and she 'ad a mind to put on 'er pink instead. Ever so careful, she was, about not wearin' the same gown too often. Anyways, out I popped to the Crown and when I came back, there she was – stone dead. Give me the shock of me life, I can tell you.'

'And how long were you gone on this occasion?' Holmes inquired.

'Not more than 'alf a tick.'

'How long exactly is half a tick, pray?'

'A few minutes; five at the most.'

'What did you do when you discovered Mademoiselle Rossignol's body?'

'What do you think, dear? I let out an 'oller and Badger, the stage-doorkeeper, 'eard me and came runnin' into the dressin' room. We 'ad a good look round just in case the murderer was still 'angin' about but we didn't find no one.'

'Where did you search?'

'Every bloomin' where,' Miss Budd snapped as if the answer should have been obvious. 'Be'ind the screen and the curtains, even under the dressin' table but there wasn't a blessed soul in the place.'

'What happened next?'

'Badger went off to fetch Mr Merriwick and, as I was took bad – the shock, you know, as I'd been with Mademoiselle for these past fifteen years – I 'ad to go outside meself. One of the 'igh-wire ladies, 'er in the silver spangles, took me into 'er dressin' room and gave me a whiff of smellin' salts to bring me round.'

'So Mademoiselle Rossignol's room was left unguarded?'

'Well, I suppose it was,' Miss Budd conceded. 'But as it was empty, except for poor Mademoiselle's body, I don't see it makes no odds. Anyways, Badger was back within minutes with Mr Merriwick and, as soon as 'e'd took a look round the door, he locked the place up and put the key in 'is pocket. And that's all I know.'

'Not quite, I think,' said Holmes. 'Had Mademoiselle Rossignol any enemies to your knowledge?'

Miss Budd coloured up immediately, two spots of bright red appearing on her withered cheeks.

'No, she 'ad not!' she retorted angrily. 'And anyone as says she 'ad is lyin'.' Scrambling down from the chair on to her tiny legs, Miss Budd scuttled away across the room, adding over her shoulder, 'I'm off! I'm not stayin' 'ere to listen to tittle-tattle.'

'Please be good enough to send Badger to me,' Holmes called after her.

Her only reply was the bang of the door as she slammed it shut behind her.

Holmes leant back in his chair with a chuckle.

'Quite an indomitable character and obviously fiercely loyal to her mistress. Well, if Miss Budd is not prepared to gossip, perhaps Badger will oblige us. You followed the logic behind my questions, Watson?'

'Yes, I think so, Holmes. The murderer must have entered the dressing room and concealed himself behind the screen while Miss Budd was absent, waiting to escort Mademoiselle Rossignol from the stage. As it was part of a regular routine, this surely implies that, whoever he was, he must have known of the habit and therefore is not someone from outside but is more likely to be found either among the performers or the theatre staff?'

'Well reasoned, my dear fellow! You are becoming so familiar with my deductive methods that I can see I shall have to look to my laurels. We may further deduce that, when Miss Budd left the dressing room on the second occasion to fetch the half-pint of porter, the murderer emerged from his place of concealment and proceeded to strangle Mademoiselle Rossignol with one of her own stockings. Do make a note of that fact, by the way. It is quite crucial to the investigation. There remains one vital question to which I hope Badger will supply the answer. At what point did the murderer leave the dressing-room? Ah, I think that may be him now!' Holmes broke off to exclaim as there came a knock on the door. 'Come!'

At this invitation, a lugubrious man in a cap and muffler entered, the same individual whom I had seen a little earlier looking out from the booth beside the stage-door. Although his hair was grey, his walrus moustache was dyed a rich mahogany shade from a liberal consumption of cheap shag tobacco and, I suspected from the odour permeating the air about him, of strong ale as well.

Badger had plenty to say on the subject of

Mademoiselle Rossignol's movements in answer to Holmes' first question.

'Yes, I saw 'er come off stage, sir, with 'er dresser,' he said, after giving a few preliminary wheezes like an old harmonium which is reluctant to produce its first note. 'I can see every thin' what goes on from that cubby-'ole of mine. Saw 'er go into 'er dressing room; saw Aggie Budd come out again a few minutes later to go off for her 'er ladyship's 'alf pint of porter and I saw 'er come back, too.'

'One moment, pray,' Holmes said, holding up a hand to stem Badger's flow. 'Let us go back to a point a little earlier. Did you see anyone enter the dressing room between the time Miss Budd left it to wait for her mistress and their return?'

Badger blew out his moustache as he considered this question.

'Can't say I did, sir. But I wasn't watchin' all that carefully at that particular time. There was too many of 'em comin' and goin'. Them seals, for one. I 'ates performin' h'animals!' Badger exclaimed suddenly in an unexpected outburst of rage. 'Leavin' their callin'-cards everywhere for others to clean up after 'em and needin' fish and raw meat at h'ungodly hours! It h'aint Christian! Give me h'acrobats any day!'

'Yes, quite!' Holmes murmured. 'But pray let us return to the subject, Badger. What happened after Miss Budd came back from the Crown public house?'

'Well, the next thing I knew, she'd let out this scream – blood-curdlin', it was, sir – and when I went to h'investigate, there was Mam'zelle lyin' stretched out across the dressin' table as dead as a mutton-chop.'

'I understand you and Miss Budd searched the room?'

'We did, sir.'

'But found no one?'

'No; and that's somethin' I've been cudgellin' my brains over ever since. 'Ooever did 'er in must 'ave vanished into thin h'air, 'cos 'e 'adn't come through that door to my certain knowledge and 'e wasn't anywhere in the room neither. So where was 'e? That's what I want to know?'

'A most pertinent question!' said Holmes. 'And one I shall make it my best endeavour to answer. Now what of Mademoiselle Rossignol herself? French, was she not?'

'French?' Badger gave a contemptuous sniff. 'There was nothin' French about 'er, unless you count the scent she used to squirt all over 'erself. Born Lizzie Biggs, she was, in Bermondsey. But talk about h'airs!'

'Hairs?' Holmes inquired, as nonplussed as I was by this enigmatic statement. 'You mean the wig she was accustomed to wearing?'

'That, too,' Badger replied almost as cryptically. 'But I was referrin' more to 'er manner. 'Oity-toity, sir. Treated the likes of me as dirt. Not that she 'ad anythin' to be proud of. I knew 'er, sir, and 'er comin's and goin's. Saw it all from that little cubby-'ole of mine.'

At this, he dropped one eyelid in a most suggestive wink, the implications of which were only too painful for it was indeed distressing for me to have to sit there listening in silence, while the unspeakable Badger

75

stripped from Mademoiselle Rossignol the last vestiges of womanly decency and dignity.

Holmes approached this delicate subject with circumspection.

'I take it, Badger,' said he, 'that you are referring to gentlemen?'

'If that's 'ow you wants to put it, sir. Gentlemen's 'ardly the word I'd use meself.'

'And did they by any chance include anyone among tonight's performers?'

'It's more a question of 'oo wasn't h'included. She'd 'ad 'er little fling with all of 'em at one time or another.'

'All of them!' I burst out, unable to remain silent any longer.

Badger turned a knowing glance in my direction.

'H'every one of 'em, sir; on and off, if you gets my meanin'.'

'Thank you, Badger,' said Holmes. 'I think Dr Watson and I have heard enough.'

As Badger touched his cap and shuffled from the room, my old friend turned to me with a concerned expression.

'I am so sorry, my dear fellow. These revelations have quite clearly distressed you. It is never pleasant to discover that someone one admires has feet of clay.'

I was deeply touched by his words. Although at times he could be selfish and inconsiderate, it was at moments like these, when Holmes was at his most kind-hearted and solicitous, that I realised what a true friend I had in him.

I was prevented from replying by the arrival of a message from Mr Merriwick, informing us that a Scotland Yard Inspector and his assistants were at that moment entering the building, an interruption for which I was profoundly grateful for my heart was still too full to allow me to speak.

By the time we had emerged from the manager's office and had made our way to the backstage area, the five uniformed police officers had already divested themselves of their wet capes, while one of their number, a short, lean man in plain-clothes, who appeared to be in charge, was standing with his back to us, deep in conversation with Mr Merriwick.

'Lestrade!' Holmes exclaimed, striding forward, at which the figure turned towards us and I recognised the sallow features of the Inspector whom I had first encountered during the investigation into the murders of Enoch J. Drebber and his private secretary, Joseph Stangerson.[8]

It was clear from his expression that Lestrade neither expected nor welcomed our presence.

'You, Mr Holmes!' he cried. 'And Dr Watson, too! What may I ask are you doing here?'

'We were among the audience when the murder occurred. The management has retained our services,' Holmes explained briskly. 'Your arrival is well timed,

---

[8] This case, published in 1887 under the title of 'A Study in Scarlet', was the first investigation in which Dr John H. Watson assisted Mr Sherlock Holmes. Dr John F. Watson.

Inspector. As far as Dr Watson and myself are concerned, the case is solved. All that remains to be done is to arrest the murderer, a task which you will no doubt perform with your usual sangfroid.'

The Inspector's astonishment was no less than my own.

'Solved!' I exclaimed. 'But, Holmes, I do not understand. What evidence have we discovered that reveals the murderer's identity?'

'Facts, my dear Watson. On what else can any successful investigation be based?'

Lestrade, his face expressing both incredulity and suspicion, intervened at this point.

'That's all very well but I need to know what facts you're referring to, Mr Holmes. I cannot go arresting suspects merely on your recommendation without knowing all the evidence and judging it for myself. You could be wrong.'

Holmes, whose self-assurance could at times be infuriating, smiled confidently, not at all put out by Lestrade's scepticism.

'In this particular case, you may take my word, my good Lestrade, that I am not. As for the evidence, you shall shortly be apprised of that. If you care to come with me to Mademoiselle Rossignol's dressing room, you shall not only examine the scene of the crime but I shall acquaint you with all the other information I have gathered from the lady's dresser and the stage-doorkeeper. And you will need to read this,' Holmes concluded, taking from his pocket his copy of the programme of that night's bill at the Cambridge. 'Do not trouble yourself with the second half of the performance. It is not relevant to the inquiry.'

Still looking bemused and clutching the programme in one hand, Lestrade followed as Holmes led the way to Mademoiselle Rossignol's dressing room and flung open the door.

'Now, Lestrade,' said he. 'Look about you carefully. Observe the screen placed across the corner where the murderer hid when he first entered the room. His footprints are clearly discernible in the spilt powder on the floor. Note the window which is heavily barred. Note also the body, lying slumped across the top of the dressing table with one lavender silk stocking about the neck and with one bare foot exposed below the hem of the gown. And finally note with particular care the way in which the train and skirts of the gown have been arranged.'

Both Lestrade and I looked most earnestly about us as Holmes enumerated these various items, Lestrade for the first time while I carefully re-examined each in turn, eager to discover what evidence I had failed to notice on my earlier visit to the room.

But none of them, neither the window, the screen nor the body, offered any further clues.

As for Mademoiselle Rossignol's gown, there was nothing about that either which might suggest the identity of the murderer although on this occasion, prompted by Holmes' instruction to note it with particular care, I remarked that its skirts and long train had been draped over the edges of the stool in order to preserve from creasing, I imagined, the layers of extravagant ruffles with which both were decorated.

As we were making this examination, Holmes continued with his explanation for Lestrade's benefit.

'We know from the statement given by Miss Budd, Mademoiselle Rossignol's dresser, that she left the room on two separate occasions, the first to wait in the wings for her mistress to come off stage which is when, I suggest, the murderer took the opportunity to slip inside unnoticed and to conceal himself behind the screen. The second occasion was when she went to the Crown public house on her mistress's instructions to buy half a pint of porter. On her return, she found Mademoiselle Rossignol dead. Let us pause there, Lestrade, and reflect on what evidence we have so far and what we may assume happened next.'

'Why, that's easy!' Lestrade exclaimed scornfully. 'The murderer came out from behind that screen and strangled Mademoiselle Rossignol.'

'Quite so,' Holmes replied. 'I think we are all agreed so far. Then let us proceed with the rest of the evidence. When Miss Budd returned from the Crown, she gave a scream on discovering her mistress's body at which Badger, the doorkeeper, came running to her aid. Between them, they searched the dressing room but found no one.'

Before Holmes could continue, Lestrade broke in impatiently, 'Then the man had already made his escape.'

'Aha!' said Holmes with a triumphant air. 'You were too quick to answer, my dear Inspector. Badger is prepared to swear that in the interval between Miss Budd's departure from the dressing room and her discovery of her mistress's body, he had the door to this room under constant surveillance and that nobody passed through it.'

It took a moment or two for the full significance of this statement to penetrate Lestrade's mind. Indeed, one could almost read his thoughts as his expression turned first to a mild surprise and then by degrees to absolute astonishment. At the same time, his glance darted about the room, passing first to the barred window, then to the door before finally coming to rest on the faded, velvet-covered panels of the folding screen.

'No,' said Holmes, interpreting these glances. 'The murderer was not concealed there. Badger and Miss Budd searched behind it as well as all the other possible hiding places, including the space below the dressing table.'

'Then, where?' Lestrade demanded. 'If the murderer wasn't in the room and he hadn't come out of it, where the deuce was he?'

'Exactly Badger's point although he expressed it rather differently. Had the man, he asked, vanished into thin air?'

'But that's impossible!'

Lestrade's sallow features were suffused with a dark red stain of mingled anger and bewilderment.

'It has long been my maxim,[9] Holmes remarked, 'that

---

[9] Mr Sherlock Holmes expressed a very similar idea in a slightly different form in 'The Adventure of the Beryl Coronet' in which he states: 'It is an old maxim of mine that when you have excluded the impossible, whatever remains, however improbable, must be the truth.' Dr John F. Watson.

when the impossible has been eliminated, then the key to the mystery must lie in the improbable, however unlikely that may seem. As neither you nor Dr Watson seems prepared to offer an explanation, then let us proceed with the rest of the evidence. We have considered the murderer's movements but we have not yet taken into account Mademoiselle Rossignol's. Tell me, Inspector, on your observation of the evidence, what was she engaged in doing when she so unfortunately met her end?'

Having been caught once, Lestrade was more cautious this time and his little dark eyes were full of suspicion.

'Come, come!' Holmes chided as the Inspector hesitated. 'Is the answer not obvious? The stocking used as a means of strangulation? The one bare foot? What further evidence do you require? She was changing her stockings which is probably why she failed to notice the murderer creeping up behind her.' He broke off to ask unexpectedly, 'Are you married, Lestrade?'

'I hardly see . . .' Lestrade began but Holmes waved the protest aside.

'No matter. It does not take much imagination even on the part of such a confirmed bachelor as myself to picture the scene and make the connection. But I see from your expression, Lestrade, that you have failed to do so. You, too, Watson. Well, well! You do surprise me. The answer is as plain as the proverbial pikestaff. In that case, may I draw your attention, my good Lestrade, to the last piece of evidence – the programme which you are holding in your hand? Does anything about the list of performers strike you as significant?'

Lestrade, who had opened the folded sheet, began to read aloud the names of the artistes printed upon it.

'"Wee Jimmy Wells, the Cheerful Cockney Comic: full of quips, jests and mirthful ditties. The Daring Dinos: the amazing high-wire . . ."'

He was interrupted at this point in his recital by a knock on the door and the appearance of Merriwick's head round the frame.

'Pardon me, Inspector,' said he. 'I have done as you requested and have asked all the artistes to assemble on the stage for questioning. If you care to come this way, sir. You, too, Mr Holmes and Dr Watson.'

As we followed Merriwick out into the passage, Holmes murmured to me under his breath, 'Hardly a necessary confrontation since we already know the name of the murderer but one with which I shall comply. After all, Watson, as this is a music-hall theatre, it seems entirely appropriate that the denouement should take place on stage.'

Then, raising his voice, he hurried after Lestrade who had gone ahead with Merriwick.

'Inspector, if I may be allowed to give you a word of advice? Make sure your constables are posted in the wings. Once he is named, our man may try to make his escape.'

'That's all very well, Mr Holmes,' Lestrade protested. 'But who am I supposed to arrest?'

Whether Holmes genuinely failed to hear him or

whether he preferred to pretend that he had not, I cannot say although I suspect the latter. Still in his exultant mood, my old friend strode forward and, pushing open an iron door, made his way across the backstage area, as much at home, it seemed, in this cluttered world of stored props and leaning pieces of unused scenery as he was among his books and scientific apparatus in our Baker Street lodgings.

If my illusions had not already been severely damaged, they received a further blow when I walked on to the stage. Without the footlights to cast their dazzle and with only a few harsh lights for illumination, the scene which presented itself was a bitter disappointment, so different was it to the magical display I had observed with so much delight from my seat in the stalls.

At such close quarters and in the bleak lighting, the charming back-cloth of the garden scene with its trees and blossoms was reduced to mere daubs and splashes of colour while the rose-decked bower, under which the French Nightingale had posed so enchantingly, was nothing more than a frail arch of trellis, covered with wilted crêpe flowers, their petals dusty.

The artistes who had taken part in the first half of the bill fared no better. They stood about on the stage in small groups, some still in their gaudy costumes of silk and spangles, a few already changed into their street clothes, and all of them looking strangely diminished, ordinary mortals against this shabby background of painted canvas and paper blooms.

With Holmes leading the way, we walked to the front of the stage to stand before the drawn curtains, our feet echoing on the boards. Meanwhile, the constables, on Lestrade's orders, posted themselves in the wings on either side to cut off the murderer's retreat should he attempt an escape.

But who was he? One of the two male high-wire performers, who were huddled together with their female colleagues, or the contortionist, a dressing gown flung over his shoulders and looking much smaller than he had on stage? Or was it the low comedian in a quite deplorable checked suit, or the man with the performing seals, on this occasion thankfully without his charges?

While I pondered on this, a whispered altercation was taking place between Holmes and Inspector Lestrade who was wagging the programme under my old friend's nose. Although I could hear nothing of the exchange, I could guess its contents from Lestrade's expression of baffled rage and Holmes' raised eyebrows and look of smiling insouciance.

'Which one is he?' Lestrade was demanding.

'Have you still not deduced the answer?' came my old friend's reply.

It was quite clear that Holmes, who himself possesses a strong propensity on occasions towards theatricality, was thoroughly enjoying the situation.

And then he relented. Taking the programme from Lestrade, he produced a pencil from his pocket and, with a flourish of the wrist, drew a heavy line under one of the names before handing the sheet back to the Inspector with a small bow.

Lestrade looked at the name, gazed at Holmes in surprise and, on receiving a nod of encouragement, cleared his throat and stepped forward.

'Ladies and gentlemen,' said he, 'it is not my intention to keep you here much longer. Having carefully examined all the evidence, it is now my duty to arrest the murderer of Mademoiselle Rossignol. That man is . . .' and here there was a pause as Lestrade glanced down at the programme as if to reassure himself of the name, 'Vigor, the Hammersmith Wonder.'

There were several seconds of silent disbelief, followed by a shuffle of feet as those nearest to the villain hurriedly distanced themselves from him, leaving him isolated in the centre of the stage.

He had flung aside the dressing gown and stood there, clad only in the leopard-skin leotard which he had worn for his performance, a suitable garment for there was something of the leopard in the strong but supple body, in the bunched muscles of his forearms and shoulders and in the fiercely glittering expression in his eyes as he backed away from us, crouching low, like a big cat brought to bay.

Before any of us could shout a warning, he had sprung, not towards the wings where the sturdy police constables stood guard, but straight at Holmes, Lestrade and myself where we stood on the edge of the stage in front of the drawn curtains.

It was Holmes' presence of mind which prevented

Vigor from leaping past us into the darkened auditorium. As he came bounding forward, Holmes seized one of the gauze side curtains and, dragging it down, flung it like a net about the flying figure.

I shall refrain from recording the many foul oaths and curses which the Hammersmith Wonder uttered before, with the help of the constables, he was finally subdued and led away in handcuffs. Suffice it to say that the reputation of the French Nightingale received a savage mauling, leaving those who witnessed the scene in no doubt about her moral character.

Even Lestrade, despite his experience of the criminal world, was shocked by this outburst.

'Quite uncalled for, in my opinion,' he remarked disapprovingly as we walked off the stage. 'She may not have been a lady but that doesn't excuse the language.'

'Nevertheless, you have your man,' Holmes pointed out.

'Thanks to you, Mr Holmes. But I'm far from clear,' Lestrade continued, coming to a halt by the stage-door, 'where the deuce Vigor hid himself in that dressing room. If Badger and Miss Budd are to be believed, they searched everywhere, even under the dressing table.'

'But not under the stool,' Holmes replied. 'As a contortionist, Vigor was trained to twist his limbs into the most unnatural positions. Once Miss Budd had left on her errand to the Crown and Mademoiselle Rossignol was alone, he came silently out from behind the screen, where he had already concealed himself, and crept up on her from behind, no doubt picking up the discarded stocking where it lay on the floor. As Mademoiselle Rossignol was engaged at the time in removing the other, she therefore failed to notice his approach.

'You may recall, Lestrade, my remark that it does not take much imagination, even on the part of myself, a mere bachelor, to picture the scene. What does a woman do when she removes her stockings? The answer is obvious. She folds back her skirts in order to make the task easier. But the skirts of Mademoiselle Rossignol's gown were not disarranged. On the contrary, they were most carefully draped over the edges of the stool.

'The question – why should this be so? – then posed itself, to which there was only one answer. It was to provide the murderer with a second place of concealment and one, moreover, which even a search of the room would not reveal. No one, not even the most diligent, was likely to disturb Mademoiselle Rossignol's body in order to look under her skirts.

'A second question followed the first quite logically. Who was capable of squeezing himself into such a small space? The answer to that was also obvious – Vigor, the Hammersmith Wonder, the only contortionist on tonight's bill.

'Vigor remained concealed under the stool until Badger and Miss Budd left to fetch the manager. Once they had gone, he emerged from his hiding place and slipped unseen out of the dressing room.

'As to motive, I hardly think you need me to explain that. Vigor's imprecations against Mademoiselle Rossignol made it quite clear that she had recently transferred her affections from him to Miro, the Islington Marvel, the man with the performing seals.'

Lestrade, looking suitably impressed as well as chastened, shook my old friend warmly by the hand.

'Thank you, Mr Holmes. I must admit that there were times when I doubted you could supply the answer to the mystery. You and Dr Watson are leaving now, are you? Then good-night to you both. I shall have to stay on here to supervise the removal of Mademoiselle Rossignol's body and then charge Vigor with her murder.'

Outside the stage-door, Holmes hailed a cab, remarking with an amused twinkle in his eyes as the hansom set off. 'No doubt you will write up the case, Watson. Your reading public will expect a colourful account from you, suitably embellished.'

'I may do so, Holmes,' I replied, with pretended indifference. 'It certainly has some unusual features. But the same can be said for so many of your other investigations that it is difficult to decide which ones merit publication.' .

In fact, my mind was already made up.

No account of the case will ever find its way into print.[10] I should not wish to pass on to my readers,

---

[10] Dr John H. Watson kept his word and refrained from publishing an account of the case although he makes a passing reference to it in 'The Adventure of the Sussex Vampire'. However, Mademoiselle Marguerite Rossignol is not named and he refers instead to Vigor, the Hammersmith Wonder, who is listed, among others, under the letter 'V' in Mr Sherlock Holmes' encyclopaedia of reference. Dr John F. Watson.

especially those admirers of the undoubted talents of Mademoiselle Rossignol, whom I still cannot bring myself to refer to as Miss Lizzie Biggs, any of my own lost illusions concerning the French Nightingale. It is better that they should remain in ignorance of the truth, as I wish it could have been so on my part.

I shall therefore confine myself to writing this confidential report entirely for my own benefit in order to keep on record the full details of the case and to remind myself of the wisdom of the old adage: All that glisters is not gold.

The Case of the Maplestead Magpie

Although the year '95 was an exceedingly busy period for Sherlock Holmes with such investigations as the tragedy of Woodman's Lee[1] and the case of Wilson, the notorious canary trainer,[2] engaging his attention, it was one particular inquiry, never brought entirely to a successful conclusion, which occupied much of my old friend's time and energy in the late summer and early autumn. It concerned a series of burglaries at country houses during which priceless family heirlooms were stolen by an exceedingly clever master-thief, who called himself Vanderbilt, and his accomplice, a professional safebreaker, known among the criminal fraternity as a yeggman.[3]

[1] Dr John H. Watson published an account of the case under the title of 'The Adventure of Black Peter'. Dr John F. Watson.
[2] These two adventures, which were claimed to have been written by Dr John H. Watson, were published in *The Secret Files of Sherlock Holmes* under the titles of 'The Case of the Notorious Canary Trainer' and 'The Case of the Itinerant Yeggman'. Aubrey B. Watson.
[3] See above.

Holmes had tracked the two villains down and arranged for their arrest by Inspector Gow of the Kent County Constabulary at the residence of a potential victim, where they were caught red-handed while attempting yet another burglary. However, he would not allow me to publish an account of the adventure in case it came to the attention of the man who had organised the thefts and whom Vanderbilt had refused to identify. Because of this unknown individual's obsession with collecting rare works of art, Holmes gave him the sobriquet of The Magpie. The Magpie had promised, should Vanderbilt be arrested, that a large sum of money would be waiting for him on his release from prison provided that his own name was not revealed.

It would not be an exaggeration to state that, in the months following Vanderbilt's arrest in June '95, Holmes himself became obsessed with the identity of The Magpie. Even while he was still engaged in hunting down Vanderbilt and his yeggman, he had already built up a mental dossier of the man and was convinced that he must be exceedingly wealthy but eccentric, with some shameful secret surrounding his birth or antecedents which persuaded him to collect these *objets de vertu*, once owned by eminent individuals, in order to compensate for his own lack of a distinguished pedigree.

Indeed, The Magpie had become so real to him that my old friend, not generally given to imaginative speculation, preferring facts to fancy, had gone to the length of picturing him alone in a room, gloating over these treasures as if they were his own.

At first Holmes' inquiries had been general and had consisted of asking his well-to-do acquaintances, many of them former clients, if they had any knowledge of such an individual. There, however, he had drawn a blank. In addition, he searched the newspapers for any references to wealthy art collectors which he pasted into a new cuttings-book given over entirely to this subject, while his encyclopaedia of reference for the letter 'M' had several pages devoted exclusively to Millionaires.

He also took to attending all the major sales at which family heirlooms were auctioned on the premise that, now that Vanderbilt and his yeggman were safely behind bars and the burglaries had consequently ceased, The Magpie might resort to legitimate means of acquiring those personal *objets d'art* which he might wish to add to his collection.

It was all to no avail. The identity of The Magpie eluded him.

There is a strong streak of obstinacy in Holmes' nature. Like a bull-dog, once he has set his teeth into a problem, nothing will persuade him to let go. To my certain knowledge, he refused several important and potentially remunerative cases that summer, including a request from Lady Buttermere to investigate the curious nocturnal activities of one of her footmen, so engrossed was he in his own inquiries.

It was in September '95 when, having exhausted all other lines of investigation, Holmes finally resorted to a direct appeal, a stratagem which he had been reluctant to employ as he considered it might betray his hand and rouse the suspicions of his unidentified quarry.

Consequently, he placed the following advertisement in *The Times* for the 9th of that month:

Titled gentleman, who prefers to remain anonymous, is forced to sell certain valuable and important family heirlooms, including miniatures by Cooper and Cosway, eighteenth-century English enamelled snuff-boxes and jewelled vinaigrettes. No dealers. Private buyers only. Apply in strictest confidence to Mr P. Smith,[4] Poste Restante, St Martins-le-Grand.

'That is all very well, Holmes,' I said, laying down the newspaper after my old friend had pointed the advertisement out to me, 'but, even supposing The Magpie replies, which you cannot guarantee, how will you know it is he?'

'Oh, I have every confidence he will answer,' Holmes replied nonchalantly. 'I have deliberately chosen small but rare objects which The Magpie appears to prefer to larger items. I have gone to the trouble of writing to the victims of Vanderbilt and his yeggman and, from their answers, have compiled a list of the stolen objects which includes miniatures and snuff-boxes as well as jewellery

[4] Mr Sherlock Holmes disguised himself as Mr P. Smith, a dealer in curios, in 'The Case of the Exalted Client'. *Vide The Secret Files of Sherlock Holmes*. Aubrey B. Watson.

caskets and other such personal items of particularly delicate workmanship. As for recognising our quarry, I am quite certain I shall have no difficulty in picking him out from among any other applicants. I know this man, Watson. I have, in a manner of speaking, lived with him for the past few months. Only let him write and I shall recognise his spoor upon the paper as surely as if he had left his footprint on a patch of freshly dug soil.'

'Then what of these valuable heirlooms?' I persisted. 'The Magpie will wish to examine them before he buys. How will you acquire enamelled snuff-boxes and miniatures, let alone jewelled vinaigrettes?'

'My dear fellow, do you imagine that I have laid my trap without first making sure that I have the bait to hand? You have not met Viscount Bedminster, I believe? Then let me simply say that he is a former client of mine who had the unfortunate experience of becoming entangled with a lady of dubious reputation. As at the time he had no money to speak of but a career of great promise before him, I waived the fee. However, since then he has inherited not only the title but also a house in Knightsbridge replete with *objets d'art*, never publicly displayed. He has agreed to lend me certain of these heirlooms which will constitute my bait. All that remains is to await a letter from The Magpie and the trap will be sprung.'

Over the next three days, Holmes visited the Poste Restante in St Martins-le-Grand both mornings and afternoons, returning on each occasion with a small bundle of letters which, after perusing them, he threw impatiently to one side. None was from The Magpie.

Between these daily excursions, he fretted with impatience and became, in consequence, most difficult to live with, prowling restlessly about the sitting-room and sending away his meals virtually untouched.

Mrs Hudson was at her wits' end.

For my part, I absented myself from our lodgings as often as I could, either taking solitary walks in Regent's Park or retreating to my club in order to escape for a few hours from my old friend's black mood which seemed to permeate the whole house.

It was on the third day that his efforts were at last rewarded.

I returned from a game of billiards with Thurston, a fellow-member, to find Holmes standing at his desk, in the act of opening the latest batch of letters, the floor about him strewn with discarded envelopes and sheets of writing paper.

'No success?' I inquired as I entered, considerably cast down at the thought of spending the evening alone with Holmes in his present bad humour.

'It is extraordinary,' he replied peevishly, 'although the advertisement states quite positively "No dealers", how many of those rapacious gentlemen, no doubt hoping for a bargain, have written, trying to pass themselves off as private collectors.' Breaking off to tear open yet another envelope, he quickly scanned its contents, his brow contracted while I quietly retreated to a seat by the fire from where I observed his features with some anxiety, assuming from his expression that this last letter was from another dealer.

Then suddenly his countenance cleared and, waving the sheet of paper like a banner above his head, he gave a great shout of exultation.

'Watson, The Magpie has taken the bait!'

'Let me see!' I cried eagerly, scrambling to my feet from my chair.

The letter, which was written on good quality paper, bore no address, only the previous day's date, and read:

Dear Mr Smith,
Like yourself, I prefer to remain incognito. However, as a private individual who has devoted many years to collecting works of art, I am most interested in examining those family heirlooms which you have for sale. Kindly write to K. Wesson, Poste Restante, Charing Cross, making the necessary arrangements as to place, date and time for such an inspection.

There was no signature.

I was a little disappointed by this curt, businesslike communication although Holmes, who was chuckling and rubbing his hands together, seemed delighted by it.

'You see!' he exclaimed. 'It bears all the marks of The Magpie. No private address and no name, apart from Wesson. Smith and Wesson! Pistols for two, one might say. The man has a sense of humour, Watson. I am looking forward exceedingly to making his acquaintance.'

'But where, Holmes? You can hardly arrange the meeting to take place here.'

'Of course not, my dear fellow. That would be the height of folly. We shall meet at Claridge's Hotel where I shall engage a suite of rooms for you.'

'For me?' I exclaimed, somewhat alarmed at the prospect.

'I can hardly be expected to confront him myself. My features are too well known from the illustrated papers.'

'But couldn't you wear one of your disguises?'

'Quite out of the question. I shall have to be on hand to follow him or any agent he sends in his place. The Magpie is clever enough to employ such a ruse. You noticed, of course, the postmark on the envelope?'

'No; I am afraid I did not.'

'It was West Central. But do not be taken in by that either, my dear fellow, and assume he lives in London. It is easy enough to bring a letter to town and to post it in some convenient pillar-box. Now, to work! There is plenty to be done. I must write to The Magpie, engage the rooms at Claridge's and call on Freddy Bedminster to collect the *objets de vertu*. And you, my dear Watson, must begin your studies.'

'What studies?' I inquired.

'Into Bilston enamels, silver hallmarks and the art of the English miniaturist. I have the necessary volumes of reference here. Before you meet The Magpie or his agent, you must be fully conversant with the subjects.'

Seating me down at the table, he placed several large

books of art in front of me, before, having hurriedly written a reply to The Magpie's letter, he bustled out of the room.

It was well over an hour before he returned, late for dinner, much to the discomposure of Mrs Hudson who had to keep the meal hot for him, although she was considerably mollified, after his earlier abstinence, by his appetite once the dishes were brought to the table.

'Everything is arranged, Watson,' he said, cutting with enthusiasm into the steak and kidney pudding. 'The letter is posted, the rooms engaged at Claridge's for the day after tomorrow and I have the Bedminster family heirlooms in that morocco case. You shall examine them after dinner. How have your studies progressed?'

'Quite well, Holmes,' I said cautiously, a little daunted by the task he had set me. 'You know I have a limited knowledge of art and am quite hopeless at remembering dates.'[5]

'I shall assist you,' Holmes assured me which was exactly what I had feared. I was not sure if Holmes in this ebullient mood would be any easier to live with than he had been in his former low spirits, especially as I should have little opportunity of escaping for a few hours to my club until my part in the investigation was completed.

After dinner, he brought the morocco case to the table

[5] Dr John H. Watson's inability to remember dates may explain the discrepancy in the dating within the published canon of certain events and investigations, quite apart from the theory put forward by my late uncle, Dr John F. Watson, which is printed in the Appendix. Aubrey B. Watson.

and, opening it up, displayed the curios it contained which even I had to admit were particularly fine. They consisted of several tiny, silver bottles, cunningly hinged to contain fragments of aromatic sponge and fashioned into ingenious shapes, from a miniature book to a rosebud, and all of them elaborately chased and decorated with seed pearls or minute gems; four enamelled and gold-mounted snuff-boxes, their colours as brilliant as the precious stones; and lastly, two miniature portraits, one of a gentleman in a powdered wig, the other of a young lady.

I have to confess that it was the latter portrait which I found the most appealing. Half-turned, she gazed out of the oval frame directly at the observer with a smile of such winsome charm that it was irresistible. Tendrils of fair hair fell about her shoulders, the delicate skin tones of which were enhanced by a strand of pearls about her throat and the lacy folds of her bodice.

'I see,' Holmes remarked with an amused air as I picked the portrait up in order to study it more closely, 'that you are running true to form, my dear fellow, and that it is the young lady who has caught your attention.'

'She is charming, Holmes.'

'Indeed she is. Her name, by the way, is Lady Amelia Bedminster and she is an ancestress of the present Viscount. However, her beauty probably owes as much to paint as it does to Nature which is so often the case in real life although, in this instance, we have the skill of Samuel Cooper, the miniaturist, to thank rather than the rouge-pot. His dates, by the way, are 1609 to 1672.

Pray note the tiny monogram, S.C., in gilt, the sign of this particular artist. The portrait is painted on vellum, known by the expert as a "table", and is executed in gouache, that is opaque colours thickened with honey and gum. Ivory, on which the second portrait was painted, was not introduced until the early eighteenth century.'

So began a catechism such as I had not had to endure since my school-days when I was constrained to repeat aloud Latin declensions or the dates of English kings and queens during question and answer sessions which, at the time, had seemed interminable.

Holmes employed much the same methods. Sitting opposite me at the table, he held up each individual object in turn as he subjected me to a lengthy cross-examination regarding its date, the techniques employed in its manufacture and the merits of its workmanship. If I failed to answer correctly, I was sent back to the volumes of art.

In the course of the next two days, I learnt more about silver hallmarks, the dating of Bilston enamelware and the techniques of the miniaturist than I had ever needed to know before or since.

Nevertheless, his method was successful for, by the time we set off for Claridge's Hotel to keep the eleven o'clock appointment with the man calling himself Wesson, I was confident that I was as knowledgeable about the Bedminster heirlooms as any expert.

Holmes had insisted that I dress with extra formality for my part as the agent of the titled gentleman wishing to sell the family treasures. I had, however, refused the goatee beard he had proposed although I was prepared to accept a monocle which hung on a ribbon about my neck and which added, I thought, a suggestion of artistic interests.

Holmes, who was to follow Wesson once he had left the hotel, was also disguised and was wearing a black waxed moustache and a dark ulster, in the capacious pockets of which he carried other means of changing his appearance, should the need arise.

The suite he had chosen at Claridge's consisted of a drawing-room with a communicating door into a bedroom where Holmes was to conceal himself in order to overhear my interview with Wesson. Both rooms also had entrances opening from the corridor.

In the half-hour we had to wait before the expected arrival of Wesson at eleven o'clock, Holmes put me through a last catechism in which I repeated once more the prices on each item, which he had set deliberately high in order that Wesson would hesitate to complete a purchase there and then.

I was to refuse to accept a lower figure and was to appear anxious to come to an agreement at a later date, after I had consulted the anonymous titled gentleman on whose behalf I was negotiating the sale. Any further correspondence between us was to be conducted, as before, through the Poste Restante addresses.

'And please remember, Watson,' Holmes concluded, 'to make it clear when Wesson is about to leave so that I shall have plenty of warning to follow after him.'

At this moment, there came a knock upon the door and

with a murmured, 'Good luck, my dear fellow,' Holmes withdrew into the adjoining bedroom, leaving me alone.

In those last few seconds, I felt all my former confidence desert me.

Would I be able to remember that the initials W.I. stood for the silversmith, David Willaume, senior? Or that the turquoise and claret-coloured enamels had first been introduced into the Bilston manufactory in 1760?

However, drawing myself upright, I summoned up as assured a voice as I could and called out, 'Come!'

At that, the door opened and Wesson entered the room.

I was disappointed at that first acquaintance with him for he was not at all what I had expected.

He was a small, thin, pale-faced man with sharply pointed features which put me in mind of a ferret and, like a ferret, he darted quick, suspicious glances about the room from little, restless eyes.

If he were The Magpie, he failed totally to live up to my conception of a millionaire, even an eccentric one.

'You are alone, Mr Smith?' he inquired in a voice which had the unpleasantly Cockney overtones of a minor clerk.

'Of course,' I replied, assuming an indignant manner. 'The transaction is entirely a private affair, conducted between the two of us. My client insists on complete secrecy.'

'Then what is through there?' he demanded, pointing to the communicating door.

It was then that I decided on a bold move. Raising my voice so that Holmes could not fail to hear me, I replied, 'It leads to a bedroom. Do you wish to examine it, Mr Wesson? You are perfectly at liberty to do so. Pray, sir, allow me to demonstrate that it is quite empty. I should not wish you to suspect that any third party is privy to our conversation. It is essential that there should be perfect trust between us.'

Stalking over to the door, I flung it open, fervently hoping that my lengthy protestation would have given Holmes time to find a hiding place.

I was greatly relieved to find the room empty with no indication where Holmes might have concealed himself, whether under the bed, inside the wardrobe or behind the heavy curtains which were draped over the window.

'You see, there is no one there,' I announced.

Wesson had the grace to look abashed and muttered something about the need for total privacy as I led the way back into the drawing-room where I invited him to sit down in the armchair which Holmes had carefully placed so that it had its back to the door. As I shut it behind me, I took care not to engage the catch.

However, by the time I had seated myself opposite Wesson and had placed the morocco case on the low table between us, I saw that the bedroom door had silently opened an inch or two.

As soon as I lifted back the lid of the case, Wesson became much too engrossed in its contents to notice what was happening behind his back. Although he tried not to appear eager, his little, black eyes became fixed on each packet as I lifted it out, unwrapped it and laid the object it contained on the table. Thus exhibited, with the light from the window glittering on the facets of the gems and on the painted surfaces of the miniatures and the snuff-boxes, they made a most tempting display.

If Wesson were not The Magpie but merely his agent, he nevertheless showed an expert knowledge of *objets d'art*. Taking a jeweller's eyeglass from his pocket, he picked up and carefully examined each curio in turn, while I, not to be outdone, demonstrated my own expertise by commenting on the exquisiteness of the enamelling or the delicacy of the gouache.

I need not have troubled myself. Apart from asking the price of each individual item, Wesson merely grunted before replacing it on the table and turning his attention to the next, subjecting it to the same minute scrutiny.

It was only when the last heirloom had been thoroughly examined that he offered any remark.

'The prices are very high,' he said.

I gave the answer which Holmes had prepared for me when we had rehearsed together.

'The objects are unique. They would probably fetch far more at a public auction but my client prefers a private sale. He might, however, be prepared to lower his prices if you were willing to purchase the whole collection and not merely a few individual items. I should, of course, have to consult him first before we could reach such an agreement.'

Confident that this offer would be accepted, I began to wrap up the objects one by one, intending to replace them in the morocco case, when Wesson shot out a skinny hand and grasped me by the wrist as I picked up the miniature of the young lady by Samuel Cooper.

'Not that one,' he said roughly. 'I'll take it with me. You will want to be paid in cash, I suppose?'

With that, he took out a pocketbook, opened it and counted out the banknotes on to the table and then, while I watched horrified, he quickly wrapped the miniature in its wadding and paper.

Holmes had not prepared me for this contingency and, as the miniature disappeared inside the pocket of Wesson's topcoat, I could think of nothing to say. Nor was there any opportunity. Rising hurriedly to his feet, Wesson made for the door, remarking over his shoulder, 'Tell your client that I shall write to him again.'

The next moment, the door had closed behind him.

To say that I was dumbfounded is hardly an exaggeration. For several moments, I stood there unable to move, knowing that there was nothing I could do to retrieve the situation. Wesson had gone and with him the priceless heirloom which had been in the Bedminster family for generations.

Holmes had trusted me and I had let him down.

It was with an exceedingly heavy heart that I packed up the remaining treasures and took a cab back to Baker Street where I sat alone by the fire, constantly turning over in my mind what I should say to Holmes on his return.

I have never known the hours pass so slowly. The afternoon and then the evening dragged by as I waited for the sound of his familiar footstep upon the stairs and listened to the clock striking the hours. Ten o'clock came and went, then eleven and still there was no sign of my old friend.

At midnight, I went at last to bed, exhausted by mental torment, although I slept only fitfully, my mind still in an anguish of self-recrimination.

It was almost half-past three before Holmes eventually returned. Although I had dropped into an uneasy slumber, my senses must still have been alert for I was aware of a cab drawing up outside the house, followed shortly afterwards by the sound of his latchkey in the street door.

In a second, I was wide awake and, lighting a candle, I put on my dressing-gown and slippers and went downstairs to the sitting-room to find Holmes, disguised with a brown beard and a flat cap, in the act of filling a glass of whisky with soda water from the gasogene.[6]

'My dear fellow!' said he, as I came creeping round the door. 'Did I wake you? I am most dreadfully sorry.'

'It is I who ought to apologise,' I said humbly. 'I am afraid, Holmes, that I mishandled the business with Wesson very badly. To think that I allowed him to walk away with the Cooper! What on earth can I say or do to

---

[6] A gasogene was an apparatus for use in the home, consisting usually of two glass globes, connected by a tube, which contained water and chemicals. It was used to produce aerated or soda water. *Vide* 'The Adventure of the Mazarin Stone' and 'A Scandal in Bohemia'. Dr John F. Watson.

make up for my mistake? If you wish me to apologise in person to Lord Bedminster . . .'

'Oh, that!' he said, with a dismissive wave of his hand. 'Do not trouble yourself in the slightest about it, Watson. We can easily retrieve the miniature from The Magpie whenever we wish. A whisky and soda?'

I was so greatly relieved by my old friend's cheerful insouciance that it was not until I had sunk down into an armchair by the fire, the embers of which Holmes had coaxed into a blaze, that the full purport of his remark struck home.

'You mean that you have discovered The Magpie's identity?' I asked.

'Of course,' he replied, handing me a whisky and soda. 'What else was the purpose of our little excursion to Claridge's Hotel?'

'Then who is he?'

To my utter astonishment, Holmes began to chant in a singsong voice, as if repeating a well-known nursery jingle or a childhood tongue-twister, 'Are you feeling low? Is your pulse too slow? Then let Parker's little pink pills perk you up.' Seeing my bewildered expression, he burst out laughing. 'Surely you are familiar with the advertisement, Watson? It appears regularly in all the popular penny newspapers. I am surprised, in fact, that Parker's Pills have not put you and your colleagues out of business long ago, for they are claimed to have such efficacious results in the treatment of a host of ailments, from insomnia to headaches and from neuralgia to muscle fatigue, to say nothing of the tonic effect they have on the blood, the liver, the kidneys and the digestive system generally.

'Well, my dear fellow, I have discovered that The Magpie is none other than Parker himself, retired now from active participation in the business but still no doubt enjoying part of the profits from his most lucrative trade in little pink pills. It is astonishing how gullible the general public is over patent medicines. It will spend a small fortune on such restoratives when a decent bottle of brandy would do them twice as much good at half the price.

'However, to return to The Magpie. You realised, of course, Watson, that Wesson was merely his agent? But you are probably unaware of who exactly Wesson is. He is none other than Arty Tucker, short for Arthur but a particularly apt sobriquet in this particular instance as he is a notorious dealer in stolen antiques and works of art. I first made his acquaintance several years ago when I recovered the Duchess of Melton Mowbray's collection of jewelled Renaissance stilettos. Unfortunately, I was not then able to lay my hands on Arty himself.

'Incidentally, may I congratulate you on the cool manner in which you dealt with his request to examine the bedroom at the hotel? I could not have handled the situation better myself.'

'Oh, it was nothing, Holmes,' I said with an offhand air although I was secretly delighted with the tribute. 'Where exactly were you concealed?'

'I merely retreated to the passage outside the bedroom

where I waited until I judged it safe to return. Such a precaution is typical of Arty, however. It is why he has succeeded in evading the law for so long. Following him after he left the hotel was as difficult as tracking a fox through a dense thicket. Although he had no reason to suspect I was on his trail, he changed cabs three times before eventually alighting at Victoria station where he caught the slow train to Chichester which stops at Barton Halt.

'There he took the only station fly, forcing me to await its return before I could discover his destination from the driver. He had been instructed, he informed me, to take his passenger to Maplestead Hall, a journey of about eight miles, where the man paid him off. That was all the driver could tell me.

'I was therefore obliged to hire the same fly and, once the horse was rested, repeat Tucker's journey in order to discover the whereabouts of his employer, for it was quite obvious that Tucker, who was acting as The Magpie's agent, was, at that very moment, reporting back to him on the transaction at Claridge's Hotel as well as handing over to him the Samuel Cooper miniature.

'Having arrived at the gates of Maplestead Hall, which was where Tucker had alighted, I rather foolishly dismissed the fly at the suggestion of the driver who quite mistakenly believed that I would be able to hire another vehicle at the local hostelry, the Dun Cow, for the return journey to Barton Halt. I am afraid, Watson, that the man was over-sanguine. The hospitality at the tavern does not extend as far as transport although it supplied an excellent supper of jugged hare and, once I had bought pots of ale for the customers in the public bar, a fund of information regarding the owner of Maplestead Hall. There is no better place than the tap-room of an inn to hear the neighbourhood gossip.

'It was there that I discovered our quarry's true name and the origins of his wealth. He is, moreover, a bachelor and a recluse. No one in the village has ever seen him for it appears he shuns all publicity. This would account for the lack of information about him in the newspapers.

'The time being then nearly eleven, I paid my bill and took leave of my new-found acquaintances before setting off for Barton Halt where I caught the last train. Hence my late arrival at Baker Street.'

'On foot, Holmes? But you said it was eight miles from the station to Maplestead!'

'Oh, I hardly noticed the distance. At the time, it was nothing more than an evening stroll, made even more delightful by the thought that we shall soon have the pleasure of clipping The Magpie's wings. However, I am willing to admit now to a trifling weariness. I shall sleep for a few hours, Watson, and then tomorrow – or, rather, *this* morning, for it is now nearly four o'clock – you and I shall catch the 9.25 from Victoria to Barton.'

Despite his exertions of the previous day and his lack of sleep, he was the first to rise and was already dressed and seated at the table, reading the *Daily Telegraph*, when I joined him for breakfast.

When Holmes is engaged on a case, there seems to be no limit to his energy. He can exist without rest or food although, on this occasion, he was enjoying a hearty meal of eggs and bacon. It is as if his mind is like a prodigious dynamo, charging the body with such tremendous power that he can perform feats of endurance beyond any ordinary mortal. It is only when he lacks intellectual stimulus, which his mind seems to need in order to maintain his physical vitality, that he sinks into a torpor and will spend days lounging about the sitting-room, lying on the sofa or seeking what solace he can from playing melancholy airs on his violin.

On that particular morning, it was I who suffered most from the lack of sleep the previous night.

As soon as breakfast was over, we set off by cab for Victoria station, Holmes carrying in his pocket the list of family heirlooms which had been stolen from various country houses during the criminal career of Vanderbilt and his yeggman.

I was concerned about Holmes' intentions regarding The Magpie for he had not, to my knowledge, informed either Inspector Lestrade at Scotland Yard or the Sussex Constabulary of his discovery of the man's identity. Nor was either of us armed. Was he proposing to confront the man without the assistance of the official police? It seemed to me unwise for The Magpie, whom we knew had consorted with professional burglars, could be a dangerous and cunning opponent.

However, Holmes adroitly avoided my questions and

we spent the journey discussing his most recent interest, the identification of human remains by means of their teeth which he considered could be put to considerable use in scientific detection.[7]

It is not my habit to force a confidence and I was therefore no better informed of Holmes' designs for The Magpie at the end of the journey than at the beginning.

Once arrived at Barton Halt, we took the station fly for the eight-mile drive to Maplestead Hall, a large residence, built only in the past thirty years or so but designed in the once-fashionable Gothic style and surmounted by so many turrets and battlemented towers, covered with heavy ivy, that it appeared of much more ancient construction and might have been lifted bodily from some Rhenish escarpment to be deposited in the quiet Sussex countryside.

Instructing the driver of the fly to wait, Holmes alighted and I followed him up the steps to the massive front door where he rang the bell.

The summons was answered by an elderly butler who, after taking my old friend's card, inspected it solemnly and then handed it back.

'Mr Parker does not receive visitors,' he informed us.

---

[7] As an orthodontist, I find Mr Sherlock Holmes' insight into the potential usefulness of this particular branch of detection quite remarkable. Forensic odontology is now an important part of forensic medicine, employed in the identification of dead bodies as well as in providing evidence for the successful prosecution of criminals who have left their teeth-marks at the scene of a crime. Aubrey B. Watson.

'I believe he will see us,' Holmes replied.

Turning the card over, he wrote a few words on the back and returned it to the butler who again examined it before inviting us into a large hall, hung with tapestries, where we were confronted on all sides by suits of armour, standing guard like grim sentinels. Here we were told to wait.

'What did you write on it?' I asked curiously when the butler had departed.

'Only three words,' Holmes replied, 'but enough, I think, to lure our bird down into the open from whatever solitary nest he occupies. They were Vanderbilt, Smith and Wesson.'

On the butler's return, we were conducted down several corridors, guarded by more suits of armour, and finally into a large drawing-room furnished with the most splendid antique furniture that I had ever seen, the walls so thickly hung with paintings that it resembled more an art gallery than part of a private residence. Even my untutored eyes could discern among the collection work by Rembrandt, Velasquez and Titian. At a modest estimate, the paintings alone must have been worth a fortune and that was not to take into account the many pieces of sculpture, porcelain and silver which also adorned the room.

In the midst of this display of exquisite objects, the very pinnacle of man's artistic achievements, the figure of The Magpie seemed an aberration of Nature and, on seeing him, my first sensation was of enormous relief for he was not the master-criminal I had imagined.

He was seated in an invalid-chair before the fire, a small, twisted, grotesque shape, his hands resting like white claws on the rug which covered his knees, his head as bony as a skull. He was wearing tinted spectacles which heightened this effect, making his eyes appear as black, empty sockets.

'Mr Holmes, Dr Watson, pray be seated,' he said, his voice nothing more than a harsh whisper. 'I am suffering from a wasting disease which makes it impossible for me to rise to greet you.'

There was no self-pity in either his tone or his manner. He was merely stating a fact and, as Holmes and I sat down facing him, I could not help feeling, as a medical practitioner, a surge of belated compassion for this man for whom death could not be far away.

Neither could I think of him as anything other than The Magpie, an apt sobriquet for he had about him the look of some gaunt, wasted bird, reduced by age and disease to a few brittle bones.

'Ever since the arrest of Vanderbilt, I have expected your arrival, Mr Holmes,' he continued. 'Even so, I fell into your trap. But the bait was so tempting, I persuaded myself there was no danger. A Bedminster family miniature and a Cooper, too! It was irresistible. I have longed for many years to own a Bedminster heirloom. I assume that, since you are here, you will wish to examine my collection? Very well, Mr Holmes. You and Dr Watson shall have that privilege although no one, not even Vanderbilt, has seen it in its entirety.' One of the claw-like hands was raised to point to the far side of the room. 'If you care to propel me over to that door, I shall open my Aladdin's Cave for your inspection.'

While I took charge of the invalid-chair, Holmes went ahead to hold back a tapestry curtain which hung in front of the door. Here we paused while The Magpie took a large key from his pocket, inserted it into the lock and turned it. There was no handle and the door swung silently open on oiled hinges, revealing the chamber which lay beyond.

I use the word 'chamber' although it is an inappropriate term to describe the room for it more closely resembled a temple. Stone pillars supported a groined ceiling, painted with reclining figures of gods and goddesses, the shafts forming large, arched niches which extended on either side. It was unfurnished apart from a sumptuous Persian carpet on the marble floor and the huge, glass-fronted cabinets which filled every recess.

The Magpie had spoken of his Aladdin's Cave and it was a suitable epithet for the first impression was of entering a treasure trove of ivory, crystal, porcelain, precious metals and jewels.

Each cabinet was full of small, exquisite *objets d'art*, from jewelled snuff-boxes to painted fans and from silver goblets to gold caskets.

At a gesture from The Magpie, we halted in front of one of these cabinets where, in pride of place on the central shelf, stood the miniature which only the day before, to my enormous chagrin, Wesson had put in his pocket before walking out of the drawing-room at Claridge's Hotel.

Opening the door of the cabinet, The Magpie took it out, looking round at us over his shoulder, his mouth stretched into a ghastly parody of a smile.

'Beautiful, is it not?' he asked. 'Such superb workmanship! I have always loved small objects, more especially since I have started to lose my sight and now cannot see anything unless I can hold it close up to my face, like this.' Clutching the miniature in one emaciated hand, he carried it to within a few inches of his eyes and scanned it eagerly. 'Look at her smile and the soft curls of the hair! I was starved of beauty as a child. I was a foundling, abandoned when only a few days old in a churchyard and brought up in a workhouse where I was surrounded by ugliness and poverty, a deprivation which bred in me a deep hunger for beautiful things which I have spent a lifetime trying to satisfy. There was only one item of beauty which brought a little joy to that cheerless upbringing. You will smile, gentlemen, when I tell you what it was. It was a tiny gold locket with a seed pearl in its centre which was worn by the workhouse matron on Sundays, a trivial enough ornament but to me it seemed to glitter like the sun. I vowed then that one day I would be rich enough to own such an exquisite object.'

'And you have more than succeeded,' Holmes remarked, indicating the cabinets full of treasures which surrounded us on all sides.

'Through my own efforts,' The Magpie retorted, a flush of faint colour staining the white, hollow cheeks. 'At twelve, I was put to work for a chemist, sweeping the floors of his shop and washing his galley-pots, and I might have risen no higher. But because I was industrious and eager to learn, my master began to instruct me in the skills of mixing medicines and potions. It was then that I learnt the trade which later was to make my fortune and it was also then that I began to indulge my hobby of collecting which, as the years passed and I became more wealthy, has meant more to me than family or friends. Look at them!' he interjected, pointing a quivering finger about him. 'There they all are! The friends I never made, the women I never married, the children I never had! But far more precious to me than flesh and blood because they are perfect and incorruptible.

'I should explain, Mr Holmes,' he continued, turning his black spectacles in my old friend's direction, 'that not all these objects are stolen. Most of them have been acquired legitimately at sales and auctions or through dealers. It was at an auction that I met the man you know as Vanderbilt. He impressed me at once with his expert knowledge of art, particularly of the type I was interested in buying. He began by advising me on what to purchase and then, as my health began to fail, by acting as my agent and bidding on my behalf. Like many of those associated with the art world, not all his transactions were strictly legal. During his career as a dealer, he had handled both stolen and forged works of art. It was he who suggested there were other means of acquiring what I so much desired to own by less lawful means. Pray do not misunderstand me. Although I left the arrangements of such acquisitions entirely to him, I was not unaware of the methods he used.'

'Such as burglary and theft?' Holmes suggested pleasantly.

'Oh, yes, indeed,' The Magpie conceded. 'I do not wish to gloss over the unpleasant truth for which I accept full responsibility. As you so rightly say, it was nothing less than burglary and theft.'

'It was Vanderbilt, I assume, who introduced you to Arty Tucker, alias K. Wesson?' Holmes interposed. 'Were you also aware that he is a notorious dealer in stolen antiquities and works of art?'

'Yes, Mr Holmes. I do not deny that either. I have made many strange acquaintances during my career as a collector, not all of them honest. Tucker may be a criminal but he is as knowledgeable about *objets d'art* as any expert you will find at any of the great auction houses and the commission he charges for his advice is considerably less. And now, Mr Holmes, what action do you propose taking? I am not foolish enough to suppose that you have come here merely to inspect my collection. I assume you have informed the police and that I can expect their arrival at any moment?'

Instead of replying to The Magpie, Holmes turned to me.

'Watson,' said he, 'would you please be good enough

to find the butler and ask him if he would let you have two strong cardboard boxes, a roll of cotton wadding and some tissue paper?'

When I returned with these items, I found Holmes had carried in a table from the drawing-room which he had placed in the centre of the treasure chamber and on which were displayed those heirlooms which had been stolen by Vanderbilt and his accomplice over the past three years. Holmes was in the act of ticking each one off against the list he held in his hand while The Magpie sat watching silently from his invalid-chair, his hands resting quietly on the rug, his expression inscrutable.

'. . . and the jewelled prayer book, once owned by Mary Queen of Scots and the property of Sir Edgar Maxwell-Browne,' he concluded, putting the sheet of paper away in his pocket. 'That is the last heirloom accounted for. Ah, Watson! I see you have the boxes and the other items I requested. If you would assist me in packing up these treasures, then we shall take our leave.'

There was no sign from The Magpie until we had almost completed the task. I was in the act of wrapping up the Cooper miniature of Lady Amelia Bedminster and placing it in the last box when Holmes crossed the chamber to where The Magpie was sitting in order to return the money which Arty Tucker had paid for it. It was only then that we were aware of The Magpie's response to our actions.

As Holmes placed the banknotes in his hand, he gave a strange, harsh cry, similar to the croak of the bird after which he was named, and, letting the money fall to the floor, covered his face with his two claw-like hands.

'Come, Watson,' said Holmes quietly. 'It is time we left. On the way out, we must find the butler and alert him.'

The last glimpse I had of The Magpie was of him sitting there alone in his Aladdin's Cave, the open doors of the cabinets indicating where Holmes had removed part of their contents, the floor about his invalid-chair scattered with the fallen banknotes like so many dead leaves.

'Will you inform the police, Holmes?' I asked, once we were in the fly on our way back to Barton Halt, the boxes at our feet.

'I think not, Watson,' Holmes replied. 'What good would it serve? The man is clearly dying and would not long survive a prison sentence. On some occasions, justice is better served than the law, as I believe is so in this case. The owners will regain their stolen possessions while The Magpie will be punished by losing them. You, too, I am afraid, will also suffer, my dear fellow, in consequence.'

'How is that?' I asked.

'By being deprived of the opportunity to publish an account of the case. Not one word of it must ever appear in print. Certain of The Magpie's victims might insist on charges being brought against him if they knew his true identity and that I cannot allow.'

I have given him my promise and have kept to it even though, only a month after our visit, a notice appeared in the obituary columns in all the London newspapers announcing the death of Joseph Parker, the millionaire, at his home in Maplestead Hall.

There was, however, a sequel to the story. When his will was published, it was discovered that the whole of his valuable art collection, thereafter known as the Parker collection, was left to the nation, and that large premises had been acquired in Kensington in which it was to be placed on permanent display, free of charge to the general public.

I occasionally visit it when I am in that part of London and have an hour or so free to wander through the galleries of paintings and sculptures. But it is always in the rooms set aside for the cabinets containing the *objets d'art* that I pause the longest to examine those tiny, exquisite treasures of gold and silver, ivory and crystal, once so beloved of The Magpie for his exclusive delight and now enjoyed by so many.

Seeing them there on public display, I feel that he has at last paid his debt to society.

The Case of the Harley Street Specialist

In my account of the adventure of the Devil's Foot which took place in 1897, I described how the health of my old friend, Sherlock Holmes, began to suffer from the heavy load of investigations he had undertaken and how his specialist, Dr Moore Agar of Harley Street, recommended that he should lay aside all his cases and seek a complete rest.

I also briefly referred to the dramatic manner in which the eminent doctor was first introduced to Sherlock Holmes, adding that I might one day publish a full account of it.

As so many members of my reading public have pressed for further details of the case, I was tempted to put pen to paper and consequently I have written the following narrative. However, while Holmes, who has read it, has no objections to its publication, apart from his usual criticism that I have placed too much emphasis on description and not enough on facts, Dr Moore Agar has refused to give his permission for professional reasons.

I can understand his prohibition. As a well-known Harley Street specialist, he has his reputation to consider and, while the case casts no stigma on his good name as a highly regarded medical practitioner, the very fact that details concerning himself and, in particular, one of his patients should be made public has caused him to withhold his consent.

Although I have offered to change the names and to make any other alterations to the manuscript that he might see fit, he has remained adamant.

Naturally, I am disappointed. The case has several unusual features and illustrates, I believe, not only Holmes' great deductive skills but also his tenacity in following an inquiry through to the end. However, in the face of Dr Moore Agar's obduracy, I have no other alternative than to place this narrative in my dispatch box, among my other confidential records, in the hope that one day, possibly on the death of the protagonists, the full account of the adventure may be published.

It began one September morning, about eighteen months after Sherlock Holmes had returned to London after an absence of three years, following his extraordinary escape from death at the hands of Moriarty at the Reichenbach Falls. My wife having died in the mean time, I had moved back to my old lodgings in Baker Street.

We had not long finished breakfast when Dr Moore Agar was shown upstairs. He was a tall, portly gentleman with a fine brow and a magnificent head of grey hair; very dignified in his bearing and forthright in his manner.

No sooner had he presented his card than he came straight to the point.

'It is not my custom, Mr Holmes, to consult private detective agents. However, I wish to retain your services regarding a matter which is causing me considerable unease.'

'Pray, be seated, sir,' Holmes said. He had lit his after-breakfast pipe but, on seeing Dr Moore Agar's expression of disapprobation, he knocked it out into the coal-scuttle before sitting down opposite his client. 'I take it,' he continued, 'that, while you dislike the smell of tobacco, you will have no objection to my old friend and colleague, Dr Watson, being present at the interview?'

'Not at all,' Dr Moore Agar replied. 'And I apologise if my disapproval of your lighting up your pipe made itself apparent. What a man does in his own home is his business entirely. However, as a doctor, I do indeed condemn the habit of smoking as being injurious to the general health. Having said that, I shall now pass on to the business which brought me here.

'You should understand, Mr Holmes, that I have a private apartment over my consulting rooms in Harley Street. At about ten o'clock last night, my doorbell was rung and the maid showed a gentleman upstairs. He introduced himself as Josiah Wetherby but presented no card, his explanation being that he had left home so hurriedly that he had omitted to bring his pocketbook. I should add that he spoke with an American accent and was in a highly agitated state. He requested that I should immediately accompany him to his house in order to treat his daughter who had been taken ill.

'In view of the lateness of the hour and the fact that I had never seen the man before, I demurred. Could he not, I asked, consult his own doctor? He explained that, as he had not long been in this country, he had not yet acquired a personal physician but, having heard of my reputation, he desired my services.

'In the end, I reluctantly agreed and accompanied him downstairs to a carriage which was waiting outside my door. No sooner had we seated ourselves inside it than it started off at a brisk pace but to what address I have no idea, Mr Holmes, as the blinds were drawn over the windows. After a journey lasting about an hour, we drew up outside a house in a dimly lit street. I was hastily taken inside and up the stairs to a room on the first floor where a young woman was lying in a bed.

'I examined her and found that her breathing was slow and irregular and that she was extremely drowsy, symptoms which made me suspect that she was suffering from the effects of a narcotic analgesic.'

'Cocaine, do you suppose?' Holmes put in quickly. 'Did you observe any needle-marks upon her arms?'

Dr Moore Agar gave him a long, shrewd look as if he had deduced from the too-eager question that my old friend's interest and knowledge derived from personal experience as was indeed unfortunately the case.[1]

'No; in my opinion, it was not cocaine, Mr Holmes. Nor did I perceive any marks on her arms which might have suggested that the narcotic had been injected into the bloodstream. I am more inclined to believe that the drug was morphine[2] and was introduced orally as a solid, perhaps as a powder or in tablet form. Mr Wetherby's anxiety to explain that the young lady was subject to these attacks of extreme drowsiness tended to confirm my suspicions.

There is indeed a medical condition known as narcolepsia[3] but I am convinced that the patient was not suffering from it.

'As Wetherby refused to allow his daughter to be admitted to hospital, his excuse being that she had an

---

[1] Mr Sherlock Holmes was regrettably in the habit of injecting himself with a 7 per cent solution of cocaine. He also on occasions used morphine. Despite Dr John H. Watson's attempts to persuade him to discontinue this practice, he was still indulging in it from time to time as late as 1897. I draw this conclusion from Dr Watson's veiled reference to Mr Sherlock Holmes' breakdown in health being 'aggravated, perhaps, by an occasional indiscretion of his own'. *Vide* 'The Adventure of the Devil's Foot'. Dr John F. Watson.

[2] Morphine is derived from the milky substance exuded from the seed capsule of the opium poppy, *Papaver somniferum*, which is then collected and dried. Morphine was first isolated from opium in 1806 by a German chemist, F. W. A. Serturmer. Dr John F. Watson.

[3] Narcolepsy or narcolepsia is a nervous disease, the symptoms of which are bouts of recurring drowsiness. The first reference to the disease by name is in the *Lancet* on 28th January 1888. Dr John F. Watson.

aversion to such places, and as her condition was not serious, I recommended an immediate intake of caffeine in the form of strong, black coffee which would act as a stimulant upon the system and allay the symptoms.

'I should add, Mr Holmes, that, apart from these circumstances which I have already described, there were two others which caused me further misgivings. The first was the marked differences in any physical resemblance between the young woman and Wetherby who claimed to be her father. The other was the absence of servants about the place, apart from a woman who Wetherby said was his housekeeper and who remained in the room while I examined the patient. It was she who went to make the coffee I had recommended which I administered myself.

'After I had completed my treatment and my patient was showing signs of recovery, I was again hurried out of the house to the carriage by Wetherby who accompanied me on the return journey to Harley Street where I was left outside my front door.

'I hardly slept last night, Mr Holmes, I was so uneasy in my mind. The young woman's drugged state, Wetherby's furtive manner, the fact that there appeared to be no servants in the house apart from the housekeeper, all suggested that I had been drawn unwittingly into some highly suspicious affair. At first, I contemplated going to the police but I have so little information to offer, no positive identification as to who these people are, no address, not even the faintest idea where the house is situated except it must be somewhere in London.'

'But you have some evidence,' Holmes pointed out. 'You met the man who described himself as Josiah Wetherby. You say he is an American. What is his appearance?'

'He was a tall, heavily built man; in his fifties, I should estimate, with a full, dark beard turning grey; well-dressed but rather coarse in his manner; hardly a gentleman.'

'Did you notice any distinguishing features? I myself usually remark on a person's hands.[4] They are often highly revealing as to their owner's social standing and employment.'

Dr Moore Agar looked astonished.

'How perspicacious of you, Mr Holmes! I did indeed take note of his hands. They were scarred and rough-skinned as if he had been used in the past to heavy, manual labour. His face also had a weather-beaten appearance, suggesting he had worked in the open air.'

'Excellent!' Holmes cried. 'You see, we are already making progress! What of the young lady?'

'She was fair-haired and fine-featured, which made me doubt that Wetherby was her father. As for the housekeeper, I can tell you nothing except that she was a short, stout, middle-aged woman. She did not speak while I was attending the patient so I have no knowledge of her accent or her social background.'

'And the house?'

---

[4] In 'The Sign of Four', Mr Sherlock Holmes remarks that, among other details, it is 'by a man's fingernails' and 'by the callosities of his forefinger and thumb' that a 'man's calling is plainly revealed.' Dr John F. Watson.

'As I saw so little of its exterior, I cannot describe it in detail except that it was a large, detached villa set back from the road and that there was a bay window to the right of the front door.'

'The colour of the door?'

'Black.'

'Was there a knocker?'

'Yes, indeed there was! It was in the shape of a dolphin. Really, Mr Holmes, it is quite astonishing how much detail I absorbed without being aware of it myself. There was, now I recall it, a number on the gate. It was thirty-two.'

'Can you remember any other details, however unimportant they might seem?'

'No; except I recollect there was a path of red and black tiles leading up to the front door. I could see nothing of the garden; the street lighting was so poor. However, I happened to notice that a large quantity of fallen leaves had blown up against the step as if from a nearby tree. When I returned home last night and prepared myself for bed, I discovered one of them stuck to the sole of my boot. I have brought it with me in case it should be useful to your inquiries as, trifling though it may be, it is the only material evidence I can offer you.' Taking out his pocketbook, Dr Moore Agar extracted an envelope from it which he handed to Holmes. 'I am not familiar with the species of tree from which it came.'

Holmes looked briefly inside the envelope before laying it to one side with the remark, 'It may indeed be of use,

Dr Moore Agar. In my experience, it is often on the most trivial-seeming data that the success of an investigation may depend. Pray continue. If there is nothing more you can tell us about the exterior of the house, let us pass on to its interior.'

'Apart from the young lady's bedroom, I saw only the hall, the staircase and the upper landing and these only briefly as Mr Wetherby hurried me up the stairs so quickly that I had little opportunity to look about me. Moreover, the lighting was exceedingly dim. However, I had the impression that the house was rented. There were few personal possessions about the place, not even in the patient's own room. The general furnishings were old-fashioned and shabby. The blind was drawn down over the window and there was a chest of drawers standing . . .'

'The details of the furniture are of less consequence than the position of the young lady's room,' Holmes broke in. 'Where precisely was it?'

'At the front of the house and to the left of the door.'

'Thank you, Dr Moore Agar. That is most useful information. We come now to the journey itself to this unknown address. You say it lasted about an hour. Have you no idea which route you took?'

'I have already told you, Mr Holmes, that the blinds in the carriage were drawn,' Dr Moore Agar replied, somewhat testily. 'I could see nothing.'

'Quite so. But that should not have prevented you from obtaining some impression of your journey. When you accompanied Mr Wetherby from your house, in which direction was the carriage facing, south towards Cavendish Square or north towards Regent's Park?'

'Towards the park.'

'And when the carriage started off, which way did it turn?'

'To the left and then soon afterwards to the right.'

'So you were still proceeding in a northerly direction?'

Dr Moore Agar seemed to grasp the purpose behind Holmes' questions for his heavy, rather severe features suddenly became quite animated.

'You are quite right, Mr Holmes! You were recommended to me by a colleague as being the best private inquiry agent in the country and I can now appreciate why you have gained such a reputation. As a matter of fact, my curiosity was aroused by the singularity of Wetherby's request and I paid particular attention to the first part of the journey. Allow me a few moments to consider.' There followed a silence in which Dr Moore Agar contemplated his beautifully polished boots, chin in hand, before his brow cleared and he continued, 'We seemed to travel along a relatively straight route for some distance. For part of the way, it was a main thoroughfare, for I recall seeing lights behind the drawn blinds and was aware of our carriage overtaking other vehicles. We then turned off to the right and began a long, slow climb up an incline which lasted some considerable distance and which grew steeper as we progressed. Somewhere along it, we turned off to the left.' Dr Moore Agar's brief animation passed as he concluded, 'I am afraid, Mr Holmes, that is all I can recollect. We took several more turnings after that but whether to the left or to the right, I cannot now recall. Mr Wetherby engaged me in conversation and my attention was taken off the journey.'

'No doubt deliberately,' Holmes remarked. 'No matter. I believe I may have enough information.'

'You mean you may be able to find the house?'

'I shall certainly do my best to trace it this very day,' Holmes replied, rising from his chair and holding out his hand. 'I shall call on you at Harley Street as soon as I have any definite information. I take it you will have no objections if the official police are called in at some later stage in the investigation should the case prove to be a criminal matter?'

As soon as Dr Moore Agar had given his assent and had departed, with many protestations of gratitude, Holmes settled down in his chair, refilling and relighting his pipe with every sign of satisfaction.

'Despite Dr Moore Agar's strictures on the evils of tobacco,' said he, puffing away contentedly, 'there is nothing like the smoke from a strong shag to clear one's mind and stimulate one's thoughts.'

'So you really think you can find this unknown address?'

'I believe I can at least locate the immediate area. There were several clues in Dr Moore Agar's account of the journey, including the length of time it took. If you care to hand down my gazetteer which contains a large-scale map of London, I shall begin my research. As I know nothing about Nature, I shall assign the leaf which the doctor so thoughtfully brought with him to you for study, Watson. I believe there is a volume somewhere on the shelves which deals with the subject. It has never afforded me the slightest pleasure to tramp about the countryside, exclaiming over the beauties of bird, beast and flower.'

I have commented before on the strange gaps in Holmes' knowledge[5] and, as I fetched the volumes of reference, handing the gazetteer to Holmes, I could not resist remarking,

'I am surprised at your lack of interest, Holmes. After all, Nature is a study of botany which is a branch of science. Think of osmosis and the dissemination of seeds.'

'I would rather not, my dear fellow. Given the choice, I should much prefer to inspect a footprint than a foxglove. Or if you insist on forcing the foxglove upon me, then it would be its medicinal properties which would engage my attention and the effects of digitalis on the human heart.'

From an illustration in that section of the reference book devoted to deciduous species, I had no difficulty in identifying the leaf as coming from a beech tree, a discovery which I communicated to Holmes who was still

[5] In 'A Study in Scarlet', Dr John H. Watson describes Mr Sherlock Holmes' knowledge of Botany as 'variable' and states that he 'knows nothing about practical gardening' although it is typical of Mr Sherlock Holmes' changeable nature that elsewhere in the published canon, notably in 'The Adventure of Black Peter', he expresses a desire to walk in the woods and 'give a few hours to the birds and the flowers'. Dr John F. Watson.

poring over the map which he had spread out upon the table.

'And I,' said he, 'believe I may have traced the greater part of the route which Dr Moore Agar took last night.' As I joined him, he continued, placing a long finger on the page, 'Harley Street is here, Watson, and the carriage was facing towards the park. When it started off, it turned to the left, almost certainly into Marylebone Road, before turning again, this time to the right into, I believe, Park Road. Now, according to our client, it then continued on a straight route for some considerable distance. This would have taken it into Wellington Road which leads through Swiss Cottage to Finchley Road, the main thoroughfare where Dr Moore Agar was aware of lights and other vehicles. Somewhere along that road, the carriage turned again to the right and began to climb a long hill. This could answer the description of Belsize Lane or any of these other turnings which lead eventually to the steeper incline of Heath Street in Hampstead. As it was here that the carriage turned to the left, it will be in this area,' he concluded, his finger resting on a portion of the map which indicated a series of side roads to the south and west of Hampstead Heath, 'that we shall find the house we are looking for. As soon as I have made a large-scale copy of this particular portion of the map, our hunt shall begin.'

We set off shortly afterwards by hansom, Holmes giving the driver precise instructions as to the first part of our journey which followed the route he had indicated in the gazetteer.

Having reached Hampstead and the cab having gained the top of the steep hill which was Heath Street, Holmes ordered the cabby to turn to the left.

We now found ourselves in a residential district, comprising quiet side roads, many lined with large houses, any one of which could have answered Dr Moore Agar's description of the unknown residence he had visited the night before.

It was here that our knowledge of our client's exact route failed us and our real search began. With his copy of the map in his hand, Holmes called out to the driver to turn either left or right as we traversed the area, following a logical pattern of my old friend's devising.

After we had taken several such turnings, the little flap door in the roof of the hansom flew open and a bleary eye appeared in the aperture.

'What h'exact h'address is you lookin' for, guvn'r?' inquired the cabby.

'It is more a matter of finding a beech tree than a precise road,' Holmes replied. 'Drive on! I shall tell you when to stop.'

For a moment, the eye continued to regard us suspiciously.

Then, 'A beech tree!' came a disgusted voice, the flap was slammed shut and the cab continued on its way.

We found the tree in the seventh or eighth turning. By that time, I had lost count of the number of roads we had driven down although Holmes kept a record, ticking off each name on the map he had prepared.

It was situated in Maplewood Avenue and stood on the right-hand side in the garden of a tall, brick villa, very similar to the others which lined the road.

Holmes rapped on the roof and, after the cab had drawn up and my old friend had paid off the driver, we stood waiting until the hansom had driven away before Holmes gave me my own instructions.

'We shall walk casually past the place, Watson, without staring at it or paying it any undue attention. However, do please take a note of those distinctive details which Dr Moore Agar mentioned, such as the red and black tiled path and the dolphin-shaped knocker.'

The house did indeed possess these features but, as we strolled past the gate, I noticed, to my great disappointment, that the number affixed to it was twenty-three.

'We should have kept the cab, Holmes,' I remarked as we passed down the road. 'Dr Moore Agar specifically stated that it was number thirty-two. It is the wrong house.'

'I think not,' Holmes replied. 'You may have remarked, Watson, that the figures were made of brass and were screwed into place, thus making it easy for them to be removed and replaced in reverse order. What you evidently failed to notice, but which I took particular pains to observe, were the scratch marks on the heads of the screws, tiny but quite fresh, which suggest that this is indeed what occurred.'

In fact, I had not noticed such a trifling detail although

I was not in the least surprised that Holmes should have done so. Not only are his powers of observation remarkable but he has the keenest eye-sight of any man I know.

'In addition,' Holmes continued, 'the exterior of the house answers in every particular the description given to us by Dr Moore Agar. However, one problem remains. How are we to contrive to see inside the place? Before we can involve the official police in the investigation, I must have some data to prove we have found the correct address. Neither Lestrade nor any of his colleagues will be impressed when the only evidence we have to offer them is a beech leaf.'

'Could we not approach the house on some pretext or other?' I suggested.

'What have you in mind?'

In truth, I had nothing in mind although, casting my mind back quickly to another investigation in which we had successfully impersonated two clergymen in order to gain entrance to one particular residence,[6] I said, 'Could we not pretend we are collecting on behalf of some charitable organisation?'

'No, no! That would not do at all!' Holmes sounded impatient. 'Supposing no one answers or we are turned away on the doorstep? We shall have seen no more of the place than the porch or, at best, the hall. That will hardly

[6] Dr John H. Watson is referring to an earlier adventure, an account of which, under the title of 'The Case of the Exalted Client', was published in *The Secret Files of Sherlock Holmes*. Aubrey B. Watson.

satisfy Lestrade. We must be certain that Wetherby and the young lady, his supposed daughter, are indeed in residence.'

While we had been discussing the matter, we had emerged at the top of Heath Street and were walking down the hill past some small, rather nondescript shops which lined the road when an empty hansom passed us. Holmes hailed it and, bundling me unceremoniously inside, gave the driver our Baker Street address, calling out, as the cab drew away, leaving him standing on the pavement, 'I shall see you later, my dear fellow!'

I was, I confess, not only bewildered by this sudden and unexpected turn of events but also somewhat annoyed and it was with considerable impatience that, after arriving at Baker Street, I waited for Holmes to return and explain his extraordinary behaviour.

It was more than an hour later, however, before he came bursting into the sitting room to fling a large brown paper parcel down on to the table.

'There, Watson!' said he with a triumphant air. 'Our problem is solved! We shall return to Maplewood Avenue this afternoon where we shall not only see inside the house but, if I am not mistaken, also make the acquaintance of Mr Josiah Wetherby.'

'How shall we contrive that?' I asked, my curiosity quite overcoming my earlier exasperation.

'By the simple method of disguising ourselves as window-cleaners.'

'Window-cleaners, Holmes?' I protested. 'But I can

hardly pass as a window-cleaner dressed as I am. I shall need clothes . . .'

'They are here,' he replied, laying a hand on the parcel.

'. . . not to mention special equipment such as buckets and ladders. How shall we acquire those?'

'They are already spoken for,' he replied. 'As we walked down Heath Street, I noticed the entrance to a small yard with a sign advertising a window-cleaning firm. I thought it might arouse the owner's suspicions if the two of us approached him. That is why I so rudely hustled you into the hansom, for which I apologise most sincerely, my dear fellow. He is a certain Joseph Smallwood who runs the business with the assistance of his son, young Dorian. In consideration of a fee, two guineas to be exact, Mr Smallwood senior agreed to lend me his hand-cart, his window-cleaning equipment and also a set of his working clothes, Mr Smallwood being of approximately the same height and figure as yourself. Oh, I can assure you, Watson,' Holmes continued, seeing my dubious expression, 'that although Mr Smallwood may be a tradesman in a very minor capacity, he is quite clean in his person and a thoroughly respectable citizen, being, as I understand from my conversation with him, a sidesman at St John's in Church Row. As for my own disguise, I have plenty of clothes in my wardrobe amongst which I have no doubt I shall find something suitable for the occasion.

'I also visited the house agents in the area and discovered the very one, Nichols and Allison's, which handled the lease of twenty-three Maple wood Avenue. On the pretext that I had heard this particular property had been on the market and that I was most anxious to rent it myself, should it ever fall vacant, I learnt some very pertinent information from the junior partner, Mr Allison.

'It appears, Watson, that the present occupant has taken it on a very short lease, one month to be exact, and that he is due to move out at the beginning of October, in one week's time. I think we may deduce from this fact that, whatever nefarious business Mr Wetherby may be engaged on, he expects to have it completed by that date. It also means that time is short and that we have not long before our bird flies the coop. Hence my anxiety to return to Hampstead this afternoon without delay.'

As soon as luncheon was over, we put on our disguises. Mine consisted of a flannel shirt, a waistcoat, a pair of corduroy trousers, very worn about the knees, and an old jacket, also showing signs of wear on the elbows and cuffs. Despite Holmes' assurance that Mr Smallwood was approximately my size, he must have been considerably stouter than I about the waist for the trousers had to be held up by means of a strong leather belt which Holmes produced from his collection of suitable accessories. As for the boots, they were several sizes too large and, although crumpled paper stuffed into the toes made them an adequate fit, they were far from comfortable.

It is extraordinary what a change of clothes will do to a man's apparent social standing. Dressed in this attire and with Mr Smallwood's cap upon my head, I saw, when I looked in the long glass in Holmes' bedroom, that my appearance was completely altered from that of a respectable member of the professional classes to that of a workman of the lower orders; not a comfortable experience when one considers that mere outward appurtenances such as one's boots or the cut of one's coat can bring about so fundamental a change.

Holmes appeared to suffer no such qualms. From his extensive wardrobe of disguises, he had selected garments very similar to mine with the addition of a red-spotted kerchief which he knotted casually about his neck.

It was on my insistence that we wore our topcoats over this shabby apparel. As a respectable doctor, I was sensitive about appearing in public in Baker Street, where neighbours might recognise me, dressed as I was. Holmes, who is quite oblivious to the opinions of others, had no such misgivings. Indeed, I have known him come and go from our lodgings dressed in all manner of disguises from a Nonconformist clergyman to an old woman.

However, he acquiesced in my demand and, with our working men's attire decently covered, at least as far as our lower legs and feet, we took a cab to Mr Smallwood's yard in Hampstead where the proprietor of the window-cleaning business, Mr Smallwood himself, a cheerful, rotund man, was waiting for us, together with the equipment of his trade.

It was piled on to a hand-cart and consisted of two

lengths of ladder which could be assembled together to form one long one, a collection of various polishing-rags and wash-leathers, and two buckets, half-full of water, swinging from hooks on the back. As if the cart were not conspicuous enough, along both sides were painted the words *Jo Smallwood & Son*, *Potter's Yard*, *Heath Street* in large, white letters.

Leaving our topcoats in the care of Mr Smallwood and watched by both Smallwoods, father and son, who appeared to find much to their amusement in the situation, Holmes and I trundled the cart out of the yard and up the hill towards Maplewood Avenue.

I cannot say, in all honesty, that I enjoyed the experience, unlike Holmes who entered into the spirit of the occasion with great gusto, to the extent of tipping his cap at a rakish angle and whistling the tune of a rather vulgar music-hall song, made popular among the lower classes by Marie Lloyd.[7]

By the time we reached Maplewood Avenue not only was I in considerable discomfort from Mr Smallwood's boots but my arms were aching so much with the effort of pushing the loaded cart up the steep incline that I was twice forced to ask Holmes to slow down his pace.

It had been arranged between us that I should hold the ladder while Holmes mounted the rungs to look in

---

[7] Marie Lloyd (1870–1922) was a popular music-hall artiste who first appeared at the Eagle Music-Hall in 1885 at the age of fifteen under the name Bella Delmare. Shortly afterwards, she adopted the name by which she was made famous. Dr John F. Watson.

at the rooms while he wiped the windows and, recalling Dr Moore Agar's statement, that the bed-chamber where he had examined the young lady was in the front of the house and to the left of the door, it was at this window that Holmes chose to start his activities.

However, even as we placed the ladder in position, I could see that our efforts had been in vain. The blind to that particular window was drawn firmly down, excluding any possible glimpse of the interior.

I was about to point this out to Holmes but he had already climbed the ladder, bucket in hand, with great nimbleness and dexterity, as if quite used to this employment, and had begun to wash over the panes.

Hardly had he finished the upper portion of the window when the front door flew open and a man appeared in the porch.

There was no doubt in my mind that he was Josiah Wetherby for, with his full, dark beard and coarse complexion, he closely resembled the description which Dr Moore Agar had given to us. It was also clear that he was extremely angry.

'What the devil are you doing?' he demanded in a strong American accent, coming out on to the doorstep and addressing Holmes on the top of the ladder.

'What does it look like, guvn'r?' Holmes riposted, continuing to wipe over the glass with his wash-leather.

'Come down at once!' Wetherby demanded, his face scarlet with rage. 'I gave no orders for the windows to be cleaned.'

Holmes gave a last polish to the pane before descending the ladder.

'This is number twenty-three, ain't it?' he asked, his face expressing bewilderment. 'Mr h'Atkinson's 'ouse? I 'ave a standin' h'arrangement with Mr h'Atkinson to clean 'is winders back and front every last Friday of the month and that's today.'

'Mr Atkinson must have been the previous tenant,' Wetherby said, still angry but mollified a little by this explanation. 'I had no idea of such an arrangement or I would certainly have cancelled it.'

'Then you don't want your winders cleaned, guvn'r?' Holmes asked.

'No, I do not, either now or in the future! Leave immediately!'

'That's all very well,' Holmes said, assuming an aggrieved air, 'but when we've gone to the trouble of pushin' this 'ere cart all the way up from Potter's Yard, it don't seem right we're to be sent away h'empty-'anded.'

Anxious to be rid of us, Wetherby took a florin from his pocket which he handed to Holmes with the command, 'Now clear off and take your d-d ladder with you.'

Holmes touched his cap but before he could reply, Wetherby had gone inside the house, slamming the front door after him although I could see him standing at the bay window, glaring out at us as we loaded up the cart and pushed it up the path.

I waited until we had reached the pavement before voicing my disappointment.

'What a waste of time and effort, Holmes! With the blind down over the window, you cannot have seen anything.'

Holmes laughed out loud.

'On the contrary, my dear Watson, I had an excellent if limited view through a small slit in the fabric which I had expected to find from Dr Moore Agar's description of the room. He said it was shabby. I have observed before that, when furnishings have been neglected, it is invariably the blinds, which are in daily use, that are the first to suffer from wear and tear.'

'What did you see?' I asked eagerly.

'Enough to convince me that Dr Moore Agar was correct in his fear that some illegitimate business is being conducted on those premises. I saw a bed on which was lying a young, fair-haired woman who answered the doctor's description and who appeared to be asleep. Seated on a chair beside the bed was a middle-aged, stout woman, the housekeeper without a doubt, who seemed to be keeping guard over her. But whether it will be enough to satisfy Lestrade is another matter.'

'But surely, Holmes, if it is a case, as you suspect, of abduction, Lestrade will not hesitate to apply for a search warrant?'

'Lestrade is a man of little imagination and excessive caution, a combination of qualities which does not readily lend itself to swift and decisive action. He will, I am sure, raise all manner of objections. To him, the situation may appear perfectly innocent – a case of a respectable

American citizen with a sick daughter who, for reasons of her health, has to be kept in a darkened room with a woman servant in attendance.'

'What can be done then?'

'Leave it to me, my dear fellow. I know a bait which will persuade Lestrade to swallow our hook.'

He would say no more on the subject and, as soon as we had left the hand-cart at Small wood's, we returned by cab to Baker Street where, having changed into his own attire, he immediately left again to call on Dr Moore Agar at Harley Street, his intention being to proceed from there, accompanied by the doctor, to Scotland Yard to lay the case before Inspector Lestrade.

After I also had changed into my own clothes, I waited impatiently for my old friend's return, anxious to know if he had persuaded the Inspector to act positively in the affair.

He was gone for more than two hours but I could tell by the manner in which he banged the front door behind him and came running jubilantly up the stairs that his efforts had been successful.

'The hook has been taken!' cried he, striding into the room. 'Lestrade has agreed to apply for a warrant which will be signed by a magistrate later this evening. He has also agreed that you and I, Watson, shall be present when the premises are searched and that Dr Moore Agar shall be on hand as well in case the young lady needs further medical attention.'

'What was the bait you used, Holmes?' I asked.

'Wait and see, my dear fellow!' said he, his deep-set eyes sparkling with mischief.

It was ten o'clock that evening when, for the third time that day, we returned to Hampstead, on this occasion attired in our own clothes, stopping briefly on the way at Potter's Yard to return the parcel containing Mr Small wood's garments before proceeding to Maplewood Avenue.

On Holmes' instructions, the cab halted a little distance from number twenty-three to join a small group of other vehicles already drawn up including a four-wheeler containing Lestrade, a sergeant and two constables, and a brougham in which was seated Dr Moore Agar, accompanied by a nurse.

Leaving the doctor to wait, Holmes, the police officers and I approached the house on foot, the sergeant and one of the constables making their way to the back of the building to cover any rear entrance should an attempt be made by Wetherby and his female accomplice to make their escape.

At the time I thought this an unnecessary precaution as I did also the heavy walking-stick with which Holmes had armed himself.

There were a few lights burning in the house, one in the hall, one in the ground-floor room through the window of which Wetherby had watched Holmes and I depart with the cart, the last behind the drawn blind of the upstairs room where Holmes had seen the young woman lying in the bed.

While the rest of us waited in the porch, Lestrade knocked on the door, three heavy, officious-sounding thumps, which must have echoed throughout the house. There were a few moments of silence, followed soon afterwards by a rattle of bolts being drawn and keys being turned before the door opened a scant few inches on its chain and Wetherby's dark, bearded face appeared in the aperture.

'Who are you? What do you want?' he demanded.

I fear that in several of my published accounts of investigations with which the official police have been associated, I may have given the impression that the officers concerned were incompetent, Lestrade in particular. In comparison with Holmes' quick intelligence and scientific deductive methods, they have indeed at times appeared slow-witted.

However, when it is a matter of a formal arrest or, as on that occasion, the presentation of a search warrant, I doubt if even Holmes, consummate actor though he is, could have produced quite that combination of a dignified, not to say pompous, manner and the officially polite form of address.

'I have a warrant to search these premises,' Lestrade announced, 'so you will oblige me, Mr Wetherby, by removing the chain from the door and allowing entry to myself and my colleagues. And I should warn you, sir, that I have two other officers posted at the rear of the building.'

Wetherby appeared to acquiesce for, without any

149

protest, he withdrew his head, removed the chain and opened back the door to allow us to enter.

I was therefore astonished when Holmes, pushing Lestrade to one side, rushed ahead of him into the hall and brought down his walking-stick with considerable force on Wetherby's right arm.

'Now, Mr Holmes!' Lestrade protested. 'There's no need for any violence . . .'

He broke off, his mouth agape, as a Colt revolver fell from Wetherby's hand on to the tiled floor.

'You said nothing about Wetherby being armed,' Lestrade continued in an aggrieved voice when the man had been finally overcome and was led away in handcuffs by the two constables, still struggling wildly, his face distorted with rage.

'I suspected it from the bulge in his right-hand pocket when he came to the door this afternoon,' Holmes explained. 'However, a stick is as good a weapon as a firearm if used at the right moment. And now, Lestrade, pray let us proceed upstairs.'

Holmes led the way, making straight for the room where the young lady was incarcerated and where we found her still lying in a drugged state upon the bed. The housekeeper, who had been alerted to our presence by the noise of Wetherby's arrest, was cowering behind the door. She, too, was taken away for questioning and a constable dispatched to fetch Dr Moore Agar and the nurse.

In the mean time, Holmes and I wrapped the patient in

blankets after I had taken her pulse and pronounced her in no immediate danger.

Even in her comatose state, she was a most attractive young woman, with an abundance of fair hair and features of a refined nature, made even more delicate by the extreme pallor of her complexion.

When she had been carried downstairs to the waiting brougham to be driven to Dr Moore Agar's consulting-rooms in Harley Street, Lestrade, who had been examining the room with great suspicion, turned to address my old friend.

'And where, Mr Holmes, might I ask, is the forging press you said you saw when you looked through the window?'

Holmes' expression was most apologetic.

'I fear, Inspector,' said he, 'that I was mistaken. As I explained to you this afternoon, I only glimpsed the interior of the room through a tear in the blind. I am afraid that I took that wash-hand stand against the far wall for the printing press. You must agree that, with the jug and basin standing upon it, it would look remarkably like forging equipment if seen in the half-light. I do most heartily apologise for the mistake although your time has not been entirely wasted. You have made an arrest in a most serious case involving abduction and unlawful imprisonment.'

From the expression of heavy suspicion on Lestrade's face I deduced that he was not entirely convinced by this explanation although there was nothing he could do for

Holmes was careful to preserve his look of genuine regret.

It was not until we were inside the cab and on our way back to Baker Street that he burst out laughing.

'You see now, Watson, what my bait consisted of?' he asked.

'Indeed I do but I fear Lestrade suspected you had deceived him and did not take kindly to it.'

'Oh, he will come round eventually. Even if he has lost a forger, he has gained an abductor, for which he will, of course, win all the credit. There is no doubt in my mind that, as in the case we investigated a few months ago in Surrey,[8] the young lady is the heiress to a considerable fortune which Wetherby was attempting to seize into his own hands.'

In this assumption, Holmes was not altogether correct.

About a week later, we received a second visit from Dr Moore Agar who called to inform us that the young lady, a Miss Alice Maitland, was recovering in a private clinic in Kent and had sufficiently regained her health to be able to give an account of herself and her abductor whose real name was Victor Rouse.

It appeared that Miss Maitland was the only daughter of Henry Maitland, a Californian gold prospector who, together with his partner, Rouse, had once owned a small

[8] Mr Sherlock Holmes is almost certainly referring to the adventure of the Solitary Cyclist which occurred in April 1895. In that case Miss Violet Smith was abducted by Jack Woodley and forced into an illegal marriage with him in order that he might gain control of her fortune. Dr John F. Watson.
This dating would tend to confirm the supposition that the meeting between Mr Sherlock Holmes and Dr Moore Agar also took place in 1895. Aubrey B. Watson.

mine in a place called Lazy Creek which had been only moderately successful. Both men eventually took wives but, being of the opinion that a mining camp was no fit place to bring a woman or to raise a family – although of the two, only Maitland had a child – they invested their modest capital in a small business in the nearby settlement, selling stores and equipment to the other miners.

Over the years, the store had prospered, Rouse taking charge of the sales side of the business while Maitland, an engineer of considerable talent, had, after the death of his wife, turned his attention to designing new machinery, in particular a drill for breaking into the ore-bearing rock.

The drill was still in its experimental stage, although a patent had been applied for, when Maitland was killed in a rock fall while he was testing it. In his will, everything, including his half-share in the store and all his papers and notebooks, was left to his daughter, Alice, who was then twenty-one years of age.

It was these papers, rather than the money, which his partner, Rouse, had wished to acquire, knowing that a large fortune could be made once the drill was successfully manufactured and sold.[9]

With this purpose in mind, Rouse had offered to take Miss Maitland on a trip to England, thinking that, if she

---

[9] Readers may be interested to compare this reference to the career of Howard Robard Hughes (1869–1924) who made his fortune by designing and manufacturing a new bit for an oil-drilling rig which was capable of penetrating hard rock. Dr John F. Watson.

were separated from her family and friends, he might persuade her to sign over her father's papers to him. As chaperone, he took with him his wife, Agnes, the same woman who had played the part of the housekeeper. The pretext for the journey was to give Miss Maitland a much-needed holiday and change of scene after her father's tragic death.

At first, they had rented a comfortable house in a fashionable district of London and the Rouses had gone to great pains to entertain their young guest, taking her on visits to the West End shops, theatres and art galleries.

But Miss Maitland had proved obstinate and no inducement would persuade her to sign any documents which would place her father's papers in Rouse's possession.

As the weeks passed and the date of their return passage to America drew nearer, Rouse had resorted to more desperate measures. If Miss Maitland would not part willingly with her father's documents, then she must be coerced into doing so.

Consequently, Rouse had rented the isolated house in Hampstead where Miss Maitland was taken late one night, having first been rendered unconscious by a sleeping-draught added to her wine at dinner. It was intended that she would be kept there in a drugged state, induced by regular intakes of morphine introduced into her food or drink, until a lawyer of dubious reputation could be found to draw up the necessary document which Miss Maitland, now dependent on the drug and with her mind clouded and her will broken, would sign without protest.

On their return to California, Rouse intended to tell any concerned friends that Miss Maitland had suffered a breakdown in health while in England and, with no witnesses to refute his story and with Miss Maitland's memory of the events far from clear, he might have escaped without detection.

'A remarkable story!' Holmes exclaimed when Dr Moore Agar had finished his account. 'When you next see Miss Maitland, pray convey to her my very good wishes for a complete recovery. She will, I assume, return to America, when she has fully regained her health?'

'That is her intention,' Dr Moore Agar replied. 'I understand that, once there, she will marry a young man who, like her father, is a talented engineer and who no doubt will develop and manufacture the drill. I shall certainly pass on your good wishes to her, Mr Holmes, and in return, I have to convey her gratitude to you and Dr Watson, together with these tokens of her regard.'

He handed each of us a small parcel the contents of which, when unwrapped, were revealed to be two silver cigar cases, engraved with our initials.

With a disapproving air, Dr Moore Agar remarked, 'I deliver them with reluctance, gentlemen. However, Miss Maitland chose them herself. As a token of my own gratitude, I felt I could make you no better offering than my own services. Should you ever be in need of medical attention, Mr Holmes, pray do not hesitate to pay me a professional visit. My fees will, of course, be waived.'

'That is most generous of you,' Holmes said. 'However, as my good friend, Dr Watson, will vouchsafe, I am generally in excellent health, although it is a subject which affords me no interest whatsoever. Nevertheless, should I ever require your services, I shall certainly call on you in Harley Street.'

Dr Moore Agar took a long look round the room, his glance passing from Holmes' rack of pipes and tobacco pouch to the tantalus of decanters standing upon the sideboard.

'A few words of advice before I leave,' he continued, rising to his feet and holding out his hand. 'If you wish to continue in the excellent state of health which you at present enjoy, allow me to recommend regular hours and meals, adequate fresh air and exercise, and an abstinence from all forms of drugs such as alcohol, tobacco and any others which you may from time to time indulge in. They are poisons to the system, Mr Holmes. Good-day to you, sir!'

Holmes waited until he had heard the street door close behind his client before he burst out laughing.

I was less inclined to be amused.

'He is quite right, you know, Holmes,' I said seriously. 'You should take more fresh air and exercise as well as giving up that most pernicious habit of yours, as I have long advised you.'

Holmes laughed even more heartily.

'Oh, come, my dear fellow!' he exclaimed. 'It was you,

not I, who complained about the effort of pushing the hand-cart up Heath Street.'

'That was entirely the fault of Smallwood's boots,' I protested.

'Then let us see which one of us can outwalk the other,' he rejoined, seizing his hat and stick. 'Twice round the lake in Regent's Park, Watson, and the one who loses shall buy the other a whisky and soda at the Criterion Bar!'

And with that, still laughing, he went bounding off down the stairs.

The Case of the Old Russian Woman

I

In 'The Adventure of the Musgrave Ritual', I described how my old friend Sherlock Holmes, although otherwise neat in his personal habits, had a horror of destroying documents and that, in consequence, they would gather in dusty piles about our sitting-room until he could find the inclination or the opportunity to put them away. To be fair to him, much of his time was taken up with more urgent matters, in particular his investigative activities although his chemical experiments, his books and his violin as well as many other interests too many to mention also claimed his attention. It was, therefore, very infrequently, perhaps only once a year, that he set about docketing and tidying away these accumulated papers.

Such a fit overtook him late one winter's afternoon before my marriage. The weather was so bitterly cold that we had not ventured out of doors all day but had stayed by the fire reading, I engrossed in one of Clark Russell's sea adventures, while Holmes was deep in the study of a volume of reference concerning the mathematical principles on which the Egyptian pyramids were constructed.[1]

He was mercurial by temperament and suddenly, at five o'clock, he flung aside the book and announced, 'Enough of Cheops, Watson. I am in need of something less cerebral to pass the time until dinner. What do you suggest, my dear fellow?'

I put forward my proposal a little diffidently, not at all expecting him to agree to it.

'Well, Holmes,' said I, 'could you not make a start in indexing some of your documents? You have been saying for months now that you ought to make the effort and, in the mean time, the piles have grown even higher.'

To my utter astonishment, he concurred at once.

'Well said, Watson! The room has indeed come to resemble the chambers of some over-worked barrister whose clerk has been on extended sick leave. I shall begin immediately.'

With that, he sprang up from his chair and disappeared inside his bedroom to return shortly afterwards dragging behind him a large tin box. Depositing it in the centre of the carpet, he knelt down in front of it and, throwing back the lid, began to empty it of its contents, neatly packaged up and tied with red tape, in readiness for it to receive all the other bundles of manuscripts which had

---

[1] If my late uncle's theory regarding the precise date of Dr John H. Watson's marriage is correct, then this event would have taken place in the winter of 1887/8. Aubrey B. Watson.

overflowed from his desk on to the floor and which no one was permitted to touch, let alone dispose of.

I, too, rose from my chair to look curiously over his shoulder, knowing that the trunk contained the records and mementoes of those earlier cases which Holmes had investigated before I became acquainted with him, only a few of which he had so far recounted to me.[2]

One small packet which he was in the act of laying to one side caught my attention. I had not seen it before and, as he set it down, I inquired, 'What is in that, Holmes?'

He looked up at me, a mischievous twinkle in his eyes.

'The relics of a most singular case, Watson, which occurred before your advent as my chronicler. Would you care to hear about it? Or would you prefer that I went on with the task of putting away my papers? The choice is yours entirely.'

I was torn between the two suggestions, as no doubt Holmes had intended I should be, but, in effect, I had little choice in the matter, curiosity proving stronger than the urge for tidiness, as Holmes had probably also been aware when he put his proposal.

I attempted a compromise by saying, 'If the account of the case will not take too long, Holmes, I should very much like to hear it. Perhaps there will be time to finish the more onerous task before dinner.'

---

[2] Mr Sherlock Holmes gave Dr John H. Watson accounts of two cases he had investigated prior to their meeting. One was 'The Adventure of the "Gloria Scott"', the first he undertook, the other 'The Adventure of the Musgrave Ritual'. Dr John F. Watson.

Abandoning the trunk in the centre of the room, we resumed our places by the fire, Holmes curling up in his favourite baggy armchair and watching with an expression of amused indulgence as I eagerly undid the piece of tape which held the bundle together and examined its contents.

They consisted of three items, a faded photograph of an elderly peasant woman wearing full skirts and with a shawl about her head and shoulders, a small, crudely executed painting on wood of a bearded, emaciated Saint, the gilt peeling from his halo, and lastly an official-looking piece of paper, well creased and thumbed, which was printed in Cyrillic characters and bore several stamps and signatures in the same script.

'Well, Watson, what do you make of them?' Holmes inquired after I had carefully examined these objects.

'They appear to be Russian,' I ventured. 'Whom did they belong to?'

'To a certain Misha Osinsky.'

'And who is he?'

'You are looking at him, my dear fellow.'

'You, Holmes!' I exclaimed, greatly surprised. 'I had no idea you had Russian connections.'

'Nor have I. The name, along with the photograph and the ikon, was given to me by a Count. As you may guess, they are mementoes of a case I once investigated on his behalf into the murder of an old Russian woman. No, not the one in the photograph. She was supposed to be my mother and was part of my assumed identity as Misha Osinsky.'

'How did you come to be involved?' I asked, quite forgetting the trunk and its scattered contents.

Holmes, who had been filling and lighting his pipe in a leisurely manner, settled back in his chair, the wreaths of smoke curling about his head.

'Like several other of my early cases, it came to me through an old fellow-student at University for, although I had but one close friend,[3] my name was already becoming known through the studies I was making into criminal research.

'Among these acquaintances was Sergei Plekhanovitch who was at the same college as myself and whom I met through a common interest in fencing,[4] one of the few athletic sports I indulged in. We used to practise together with the foils although we were not intimate; he was too sociable and fond of amusement for my tastes. However, he had a most interesting background, being the only son of Count Nicholai Plekhanovitch who had once owned extensive estates in Imperial Russia. Because the Count had liberal and democratic sympathies, he had fallen foul of the Tzarist authorities and consequently had sold up his land and had brought his family and his fortune to this country where he intended to raise his son in the English

[3] This was Victor Trevor through whom Mr Sherlock Holmes became involved in the case of the 'Gloria Scott'. Dr John F. Watson.

[4] In addition to fencing, Mr Sherlock Holmes was also skilled at *baritsu*, a form of Japanese self-defence, boxing, and in the use of the singlestick. *Vide* 'The Adventure of the Empty House', 'The Adventure of the 'Gloria Scott'' and 'A Study in Scarlet'. Dr John F. Watson.

tradition. There had been, I understand, an English great-grandmother, the daughter of a Yorkshire squire, and I like to believe that it was she who had passed on to her descendants that sturdy love of freedom and hatred of oppression which characterised the Plekhanovitch family.

'As you know, Watson, when I first came to London, I had lodgings in Montague Street, not far from the British Museum, and it was there that I received a visit one evening from Sergei Plekhanovitch.

'I found him greatly changed, and for the better, since I had last seen him at University where he had been chiefly known for his love of fashionable clothes and good company. In the intervening time, he had grown more mature and sober in his manner; perhaps as a result of the experiences he had to recount to me.

'I must break off my narrative at this point to explain to you, Watson, that I had had some little success with one or two investigations I had undertaken, principally into the affair of Lady Greenleaf's missing son. Indeed it was this case, as well as my former acquaintance with Sergei, which had persuaded the Plekhanovitchs to consult me.

'Would I, Sergei inquired, be willing to undertake an inquiry on behalf of himself and his father?

'The case he laid before me was so singular that I readily agreed. To sum it up briefly, it was as follows.

'Because of Count Nicholai Plekhanovitch's liberal sympathies, his house in Kensington had become the focal point for many Russian émigrés who came to him pleading for help and advice. On account of this, the

Plekhanovitchs had decided that, in order to assist their fellow-countrymen, they would rent a house in the East End of London, not far from the docks where the exiles had first disembarked and where they had a better chance of finding employment. The house would be used as a refuge for some of the more deserving among them where they could stay as temporary tenants until such time as they could find lodgings of their own.

'Count Plekhanovitch had placed an elderly but still active woman in charge of the household to act as housekeeper to the tenants. She was a former nurse to Sergei whom the Plekhanovitchs had brought with them from Russia, and she was devoted to them. They, in turn, were extremely fond of her and treated her as one of the family.

'Two nights before Sergei called on me at my rooms in Montague Street, this old woman, Anna Poltava, had been found murdered in her bed. It was this case which the Plekhanovitchs wished me to investigate.

'This was all that Sergei had time to tell me in the cab on the way to his father's house in Kensington although once we had arrived and were shown upstairs to the drawing-room, Count Nicholai Plekhanovitch, a tall, handsome man, with exquisite manners, was able to give me further details of the case.

'"It is a matter of honour, Mr Holmes," he explained in excellent English. "Anna Poltava was part of my household and a most loyal servant. I feel I must make every effort to find her murderer and bring him to justice.

That is why my son and I decided to call on your services. The official police, under Inspector Gudgeon, appear to have reached an impasse in their inquiries and admit themselves baffled."

'"Have they no evidence?" I asked.

'"Very little, it seems. They have one witness, a man called Moffat, a porter, who was passing the house on his way to Spitalfields market at about half-past three in the morning, the time when it is believed that the murder was committed. He saw a dark, bearded man, wearing a long black coat and with a wide-brimmed hat pulled down over his eyes, lurking at the entrance to an alleyway which leads to the yard behind the house. The description appeared to fit one of the tenants, a certain Vladimir Vasilchenko, who is also dark and bearded, but when Moffat was called in to identify him, he failed to do so. The man he had seen, he insisted, was shorter and of much slighter build. Inspector Gudgeon has therefore dismissed Vladimir Vasilchenko from the case. Indeed, I understand that the Inspector is firmly of the opinion that the murder was the work of an outsider, not one of the tenants."

'"On what grounds?"

'"On the evidence at the scene of the crime. Anna Poltava was found smothered in her bed on Monday morning, two days ago. Her room was on the ground floor at the rear of the house, its window overlooking the yard. From various marks and gashes on the outside of the frame, made apparently with a knife, it seemed the window was forced open by an intruder who, the official police assume, crept into the room while Anna Poltava was asleep and placed her own pillow over her face before making his escape by the same route, taking with him her purse containing, among other coins, two half-sovereigns which were intended for housekeeping expenses and the payment of the rent. Moreover, the door to her room was still found to be locked. It had to be broken open the following morning by some of the tenants when her absence was noticed."

'From his manner and his troubled countenance, I deduced that Count Nicholai Plekhanovitch was not convinced by this official explanation and when I put this suggestion to him, he immediately replied, "No, Mr Holmes, I am not! I grant it is plausible and would seem to cover the evidence and yet I cannot believe that it is the true explanation for Anna Poltava's murder."

'"You have your own theory?" I inquired.

'"Theory, yes, but I have no facts to support it apart from my own instinct in the matter."

'"Then pray expound it," said I. "If robbery was not the motive, what do you suppose was?"

'As you know, Watson, although I generally prefer facts to mere conjecture, I am not entirely averse to a little judicious imagination being brought to bear on a problem. It is one of my chief criticisms of Lestrade and his colleagues at the Yard that, although they may be thorough in a plodding, pedestrian fashion, they lack that spark of imaginative intuition which, if properly employed, can cast light into the darkest corners of a case.[5] Moreover, Count Plekhanovitch had knowledge of the persons concerned in the inquiry which I myself did not, at the time, possess. I was therefore curious to hear his ideas on the matter.

'"I am convinced," said he, "that the death of Anna Poltava was politically motivated."

'This seemed highly unlikely to me. Why should anyone wish to murder an elderly Russian servant-woman? When I expressed my doubts, Count Nicholai continued,

'"You must understand, Mr Holmes, that not all the Russian exiles who seek refuge in this country are private or even innocent individuals, such as Jewish immigrants escaping from the pogroms carried out against them by the Tzarist authorities or Liberals like myself who wish to live and raise their families in a more tolerant society. Among them are Revolutionaries, Nihilists and Anarchists, desperate and dangerous men – and women, too – who seek to bring about the violent overthrow of the Imperial Russian Government through acts of terror, murder and assassination, such as was carried out in St Petersburg in 1881 against Tzar Alexander II,[6]

[5] In 'The Adventure of the Three Garridebs', Mr Sherlock Holmes criticizes Inspector Lestrade and his colleagues for a 'want of imaginative intuition'. Dr John F. Watson.
[6] Tzar Alexander II was succeeded by his son, Tzar Nicholas II, who was murdered together with his family by the Bolsheviks in 1917. Dr John F. Watson.

or by Vera Zasulich[7] a year earlier in her attempt against the life of General Trepov. Mine is a tragic country, Mr Holmes, with a past that is dyed deep in blood and a future which will, I fear, be no less savage and bloody. You do not know how fortunate you are to be English and born into a democracy.

'"However, while I myself wish to see a democratic government established in my mother Russia, I am strongly opposed to all forms of violence. Therefore, when I come to select tenants for the Stanley Street house from among the many exiles who clamour for a place there, I am most careful in my choice. It is not an easy task. Although Sergei and I scrutinise their documents closely, it is quite possible that some of these may be false and that, despite our efforts, a criminal escaping from justice may have slipped through our net. Indeed I have reason to believe that an attempted assassin has taken refuge on the premises, disguised as an ordinary lodger. Or so rumours among the *émigré* population have informed me."

'"Man or woman?" I asked, my interest naturally quickened by this information.

'The Count spread out his hands in a hopeless gesture.

'"I cannot tell you, Mr Holmes. It could be either. This person, whoever it is, made an unsuccessful attempt on

---

[7] Vera Zasulich (1849–1919), who was acquitted of the attempted murder of General Trepov, was a founding member of the first Russian Marxist organisation, the Liberation of Labour. She was, however, opposed to the Bolshevik Revolution of 1917. Dr John F. Watson.

the life of the Chief of Police in Odessa a few months ago as he was on his way to dine at a restaurant. It was dark and the street was crowded. Someone fired a revolver at his carriage, missing him but fatally wounding the coachman. Witnesses to the incident could give no clearer description than that the assassin was well built and was wearing a black cloak. He, or she, then disappeared into the crowd and is believed to have escaped to this country. Whether or not that person is residing in the Stanley Street house is a matter of conjecture. But I thought you should be warned of the danger.

'"In addition to this, it is possible that a member of the Tzarist secret police, the Okchrana, may have penetrated the establishment, acting either as a government spy or as an *agent provocateur*, placed there, perhaps, because an assassin is indeed in the household. Who can tell? The Russian *émigré* community lives on rumour and speculation."

'"The waters do indeed seem exceedingly murky," I remarked.

'"Exactly, Mr Holmes! That is my point. Surely there is no need to muddy them further by introducing an extra suspect in the way of an intruder or the additional motive of robbery. Anna Poltava was a shrewd old woman who knew the tenants well. If there is an assassin among them or an *agent provocateur*, acting on behalf of the Okchrana, she, of all people, would have been aware of it. I believe she was murdered in order to silence her. In other words, it was a political killing. The purse was stolen merely to make it appear as a robbery. But I cannot convince Inspector Gudgeon. It is most foolish of him for, believe me, Mr Holmes, sooner or later your official police will have to face up to the very special problems presented by some of those among my fellow exiles.[8]

'"That is why I have asked you to investigate on my behalf although how you will set about the inquiry poses a problem. The tenants at Stanley Street are suspicious of foreigners, as they regard you native-born English. They have moreover, because of their experiences in Russia, an inbred fear of anyone in authority, and very few of them speak English. Consequently, they have been unwilling to co-operate with the police. I can only trust that you will succeed where Inspector Gudgeon has failed. Have you any suggestions, Mr Holmes, as to how you might undertake this inquiry?"

'I had indeed, Watson. Ever since Sergei Plekhanovitch had called at my rooms in Montague Street, I had been turning over in my mind this very question. Had the case involved a houseful of English lodgers or even French,[9]

---

[8] Count Nicholai Plekhanovitch was correct in his fears. The most serious incidents involving émigrés were the Houndsditch murders of three policemen in December 1910, followed by the siege of a house in Sidney Street to which the Scots Guards were called out and which the then Mr Winston Churchill attended as Home Secretary. Dr John F. Watson.

[9] Mr Sherlock Holmes had French connections, his grandmother being the sister of the French artist, Vernet. As he disguised himself as a French workman during his investigation into the disappearance of Lady Frances Carfax, it may be assumed he spoke French. Dr John F. Watson.

there would not have been any difficulty. But Russian!

'However, as you know, I can no more resist a challenge than a woman can a compliment. Indeed, I dare say a challenge may be looked on as a form of flattery. I am also of the firm opinion that any problem of a practical nature must, by its very predisposition, be open to a practical solution. If my ignorance of the Russian language was a handicap, why should I not turn it into an advantage?

'I therefore put the following suggestion to the Count.

'"Could I not be introduced into the Stanley Street household as a new tenant but one who is unfortunately a deaf-mute?" I said. "That would not only circumvent the language difficulty but I should also be resident in the house and therefore on hand to observe the lodgers' behaviour. And even if I do not understand them, I should at least be able to follow a little of their conversation by their gestures and expressions."

'The expression on the Count's own face was indicative of his response to this proposal. For a few seconds, it was one of total incredulity which, as the idea took root in his mind, changed by degrees to astonished relief.

'"A deaf-mute!" he exclaimed. "I do believe that you have the answer, Mr Holmes! Do you not agree, Sergei? We shall put the idea before Dmitri Sokolov at once." Going over to the fireplace, he pulled on the bell-rope, explaining to me as he did so, "Dmitri used to be my steward on my Russian estates. Here he acts as my general factotum. He speak good English and has been assisting the police at the Stanley Street house by translating the

171

tenants' statements. Ah, Dmitri! This is Mr Holmes, the consulting detective, who is to investigate Anna Poltava's murder. He has just put a most excellent suggestion to me."

'Dmitri Sokolov was a small man with a face that might have been stitched together from scraps of brown leather and the watchful eyes of some creature from the wild. He also had, as I was to discover later, the soul of a comedian. For many Russians, both laughter and tears are close to the surface and they are as easily moved to one as to the other.

'He listened in silence as the Count explained my proposal. Then he said, "He will need papers, your Excellency."

'"And clothes," I put in quickly. "I myself have nothing suitable."

'"Can that be arranged?" the Count asked with some anxiety.

'Dmitri gave a shrug as if the matter were perfectly simple.

'"Of course. In twenty-four hours, I shall see that everything necessary is supplied."

'He was as good as his word and the following day arrived at my Montague Street lodgings with those papers you hold in your hand, Watson, identifying me as Misha Osinsky. He had also thought to bring with him some of Misha's most treasured possessions, including the photograph of the old peasant woman, my supposed mother, and the small family ikon which the wretched young man refused to be parted from. There were clothes, too, in a shabby carpet-bag and the admirable Dmitri had also prepared a life-history for me which he recounted as I tried on my disguise.

'I was from a remote village in the Urals, chosen because none of the *émigrés* were from that region, and was not only a deaf-mute but, like many poor Russian peasants, also illiterate. This was to prevent anyone trying to communicate with me in writing. My mother, Luba Osinsky, was a widow but, before her marriage, had worked as a servant to the local landowner who took a paternal interest in the family. Because I, Misha, was being unwittingly used by the Nihilists as a courier, the landowner, a kindly man who, like Count Nicholai Plekhanovitch, had liberal sympathies and feared that my activities might become known to the authorities, had paid for passages to England for both my mother and myself. Unfortunately – and here Dmitri's face took on a most tragic expression, as if he himself believed the story to be true – my mother had died on the journey of fever. I had arrived in London, alone, starving and frightened, and had been taken by some Russian exiles to the Kensington house of the Count who, moved by my plight, had agreed to accept me as one of his tenants.

'While Dmitri was speaking, I had gone on with dressing myself in my disguise and, almost involuntarily as I listened to this sorry tale, I found myself assuming Misha's character, drooping my shoulders and dangling my arms so that, by the time he had finished and we gazed at my reflection in the glass, neither of us knew whether to laugh or cry at the pathetic figure I presented.

'As later events were to prove, this element of tragi-comedy ran like a *leitmotiv*, as Herr Wagner has called it, throughout the whole case. Another theme was the matter of disguises. I think I may say without any exaggeration, my dear fellow, that I have never before or since undertaken an investigation in which there were so many false identities or assumed appearances.

'My encounter that day with Dmitri soon descended into farce. It had been decided, in order to give credence to my place in the Stanley Street lodgings, that I should perform certain household duties. I see you smile, Watson, at the mere idea. I confess that the situation has its amusing side for I am the least domesticated of men. However, the tasks were simple and were quite within the scope of my limited capabilities. Dmitri threw himself enthusiastically into the task of instructing me in this new role, mouthing the Russian words for "broom" or "firewood", which of course as a deaf-mute I was not supposed to hear, with such ridiculous contortions of his leathery countenance and accompanied by so many elaborate pantomimic gestures that I was hard put to it not to burst out laughing and so ruin my "Misha" expression of a not over-intelligent peasant with a pathetic desire to please.

'The excellent Dmitri had also supplied me with a list of the lodgers and a short resume of their past histories so that I could acquaint myself with their names and backgrounds before I met them. There were fourteen of them and I shall not bore you with reciting them all. Suffice it to say at this juncture that the one I was most interested in was Vladimir Vasilchenko who had at first been suspected by the police and then dismissed by them from the case when the market-porter, Moffat, had failed to identify him.

'When I asked Dmitri for his own opinion of the man, he merely gave one of his eloquent shrugs and replied, "The witness might have been mistaken."

'Whether he meant to imply that Moffat had been wrong in failing to identify Vasilchenko or mistaken in his original description of the man, it was impossible to tell.

'According to Vasilchenko's papers, he was nothing more dangerous than a student of literature from Moscow University who had never been in trouble with the Tzarist authorities.

'The next morning, wearing Misha Osinsky's clothes and carrying his meagre possessions in the carpet-bag, I was taken by Dmitri Sokolov by cab to the house in Stanley Street and introduced to the tenants.'

II

'Are you familiar with Stanley Street, Watson, and the district in which it is situated? I thought not. It is not a part of London which offers many attractions to the casual visitor.

'Stanley Street itself is a long turning of shabby shops and houses between the Mile End Road and the Whitechapel area to the north and Commercial Road to the south, and runs through a part of the East End notorious for its numerous cheap lodging-houses, low "dives" and public houses as well as the many prostitutes who ply their squalid trade and whose services may be bought, I understand, for a few pence.

'Count Nicholai had said we English are a fortunate nation. Perhaps he is right. But, my dear Watson, it was hard to believe when I looked about me on that journey and saw on all sides the utter wretchedness and degradation of those streets. If there is a hell on earth, then surely it is to be found there in the barefoot children and the starving beggars, in men and women crammed ten or more to a room, in the homeless crouching in doorways and in the bands of urchins roaming the streets, like packs of dogs, stealing in order to eat and finding their beds at night under a costermonger's cart or a pile of rags.

'And yet there was a terrible animation about the place. It was like a dead creature from whose rotting corpse the maggots have come swarming and heaving into life from every putrid crevice. Day and night they thronged the pavements and the gutters, the air ringing with their cries and shouts, their screams and curses. Aye, and their laughter, too, for in that charnel-heap of humanity it was possible to hear the sound of laughter and singing.

'As I said to you at the beginning, it was a case which combined the elements of tragedy and comedy and I witnessed the same condition all about me. Here were drunken women brawling outside a public-house while, a few yards away, a little group of children were dancing and clapping their hands to an organ-grinder's tune.

'The house in Stanley Street teemed with the same life but at least it was clean if shabby. It was a tall, gaunt building of several storeys, each containing its complement of lodgers who had the privilege, rare in that part of London, of their own rooms, simply furnished, it was true, with little more than a bed and a cupboard in which to keep what few possessions they owned.

'The focus of the household was the basement kitchen. It was here that meals were served, where the samovar was kept constantly simmering and where the tenants tended to congregate in the evening about the fire. It was also here that I was first introduced to them by Dmitri.

'It would be tedious in the extreme to describe each in turn. Suffice it to say that four of them for various reasons roused my particular curiosity. One of them was, of course, Vladimir Vasilchenko, a tall, bearded man with a shock of black unruly hair and a most ruffianly appearance. Had one wished to describe a character who was the epitome of a Russian Revolutionary, one could have done no better than model him on Vladimir.

'There was one other man whom I came to suspect as a possible candidate for the murderer. This was Peter Tomazov, a shoemaker who, with his sick wife, occupied one of the attic rooms. There was an air of desperation about him and, not long after I joined the household, I had reason to believe he was stealing food from the kitchen. Had Anna Poltava, I wondered, also discovered this and had he murdered her before she could denounce him as a thief? He was, moreover, of slight build and, with the addition of a false beard, might have answered the description given by the witness Moffat.

'The other two were women and they came to my notice for quite different reasons, Rosa Zubatov because she was an example of the Russian "New Woman" movement[10] which I had read about. In the manner of

---

[10] The 'New Woman' concept was part of the Nihilist 'New People' movement, mostly favoured by young students. While the 'New Women' wore short hair, the 'New Men' wore theirs long. Blue-tinted spectacles, high boots and relaxed manners were adopted by both sexes. Dr John F. Watson.

that sisterhood, she had adopted the fashion of short hair and free manners, the latter to the extent of smoking black Russian cigarettes and refusing to help with the housework on the basis, so Dmitri informed me, that women should not be exploited domestically.

'Dmitri disapproved of her presence in the house. He was convinced she was a Nihilist and suspected her of being the assassin who had made an attempt on the life of the Odessa Chief of Police. However, according to the résumé of her background, she was a student from St Petersburg who had done nothing more subversive than distribute copies of a banned liberal periodical.

'With her short, blonde, curly hair and fair skin, she was a striking-looking young woman and attracted the notice of Vladimir Vasilchenko but, true to her "New Woman" beliefs, she spurned his attentions and he advanced no further than indulging in long discussions with her late at night by the kitchen fire which, judging by their earnest gestures and unsmiling faces, were political in nature. There is nothing quite like politics, Watson, to take all the humour out of a conversation.

'The other female lodger who came to my attention, or who rather forced her presence upon me, was Olga Leskova, a fat jolly woman. Since Anna Poltava's murder, she had been put in charge of the cooking under Dmitri's direction. Although I was accepted by the other lodgers with varying degrees of tolerance, it was she who took me under her wing. She seemed to consider I was too thin and tried to fatten me up like a goose for Christmas.

She was constantly setting plates of bortsch or pancakes filled with sour cream in front of me which she urged me to eat with much nudging of my shoulder and smacking of her lips. She also had the most trying habit of shouting at me in Russian at the top of her voice in the belief that she would eventually penetrate my supposed deafness. By so doing she nearly caused me an actual loss of hearing. Under this double onslaught, it was only with the greatest difficulty that I managed to maintain the inane smile which I had assumed as part of my character as Misha.

'On the subject of this disguise, let me say in parenthesis that, although it was not the most elaborate I have ever assumed, it was the hardest and most wearisome to maintain, depending as it did not upon such devices as wigs and makeup but on the day-to-day preservation of a certain expression which I dared not let slip in the company of others.

'Have you ever observed a totally deaf man, Watson? There is about his features a look of vacancy which, as soon as anyone approaches, becomes both anxious and eager, as if, as he scans the faces of others, he is straining to understand what they are saying. Moreover, he responds to nothing audible. A sudden loud knock upon a door, the crash of fallen china, an outburst of angry voices, are nothing to him. So I, too, had to control my own involuntary reactions to any unexpected noise.

'To return to my narrative. In addition to the lodgers I also had to keep up my assumed character in front of the police who, for the first few days of my tenancy in Stanley Street, remained on the premises concluding their investigation into the murder. The weather was wet and windy and, from time to time, they sought shelter from the elements in the kitchen, there to enjoy the quite unofficial pleasures of a seat by the fire and a pipe of tobacco.

'Having been told by Dmitri that I was a deaf-mute, they made no effort to lower their voices in my presence and I was therefore able to overhear some of their conversations.

'Inspector Gudgeon, a thick-necked, bullying man with too high an opinion of himself, was convinced, as Count Nicholai had informed me, that the murder was the work of an outsider and his suspicions were directed at one particular gang of ruffians, the Masons, so-named after their leader, a dangerous and cunning villain called Jed Mason. The gang's forte was burglary, mostly of business premises although they had been known on occasion to rob private houses, and they were not averse to attacking the householder if disturbed. At least one murder could be laid at their door, that of the elderly proprietor of a coffee house who had been bludgeoned to death. Mason, who was known to disguise himself, had since disappeared from his usual haunts.

'From Gudgeon's remarks, I understood that Mason, if wearing a false beard, could have answered the description given by Moffat, the porter.

'Because Anna Poltava's bedroom was out of commission, having been sealed off by the police while

181

they continued their inquiries, I was given a room opening off the kitchen, little bigger than a cupboard. Here a folding bed was set up for me and there I stowed Misha's pitiable possessions, taking care to place the photograph in a prominent position so that it was visible to anyone passing the doorway. The ikon was put to more practical use to cover up a small hole I had bored in the plaster partition between the kitchen and my room. It was a most uncomfortable billet but, as later events were to prove, was in an advantageous position for I was able to watch through my spy-hole the comings and goings of the various lodgers and to witness in particular the behaviour of one certain individual which was to prove decisive in the solution of the case.

'On my third day at the Stanley Street house, the police withdrew, Inspector Gudgeon announcing to Dmitri that their investigation of the immediate scene of the crime was finished although they would be continuing their inquiries elsewhere, presumably into the whereabouts of Mason. I was therefore at liberty to inspect Anna Poltava's bedroom which I did within the hour of their departure, taking with me a broom as if I had been sent by Dmitri to prepare the room for a new tenant.

'How exceedingly unobservant the official police are, Watson! If ever I were to be placed in charge of their training – which God forbid! – the cornerstone of my instructions to them would be "Look about you." For at most scenes where a crime has been committed there will be some clue which will point to the manner in which it has been carried out if not to the identity of the actual perpetrator.

'No sooner had I stepped inside Anna Poltava's bedroom than I saw at once that her murder was not the work of an intruder but of someone inside the house and that Inspector Gudgeon was wasting his time seeking the Mason gang.

'Facing me was a window which looked out into the backyard and, dangling loose against the frame on the right-hand side, was a length of broken sash-cord.

'Have you ever tried to push up the lower sash of a window of which the cord is broken? It is extremely difficult to do and impossible to achieve silently. And yet Gudgeon was prepared to believe that Anna Poltava's murderer, having forced open the window and climbed in over the sill, had smothered her as she lay in bed, before making his escape by the same route, taking her purse with him.

'You will recall, Watson, that Count Nicholai had informed me that part of Anna's duties was to act as concierge to the tenants and to admit them into the house after the doors were locked at eleven o'clock. If she could be roused from sleep by someone knocking at the door, she would certainly have been woken by the sound of her window being forced open a mere few yards away from her bed. Having established to my satisfaction that the murderer must be one of the lodgers, I then examined the room more carefully for other clues which Inspector Gudgeon and his men had also overlooked. Working on the premise that the murderer had not entered through the window, I therefore turned my attention to the only other means of access, the door.

'Even without the aid of my pocket lens, I was able to discern fresh scratches upon the escutcheons of the lock where someone, presumably working in the dark, had made several attempts to insert a picklock. There was also a smear of oil round the keyhole, suggesting that the murderer had first made sure that the wards would yield silently when the lock was finally and successfully picked. Moreover, I discovered on examining the back door, as I went out into the yard, ostensibly to fetch coal, that the lock and bolts on that, too, had been recently oiled.

'The bed was immediately inside the door, to the left. Anyone entering the room had only to stretch out an arm, take the pillow from under the old woman's head and press it down over her face. It would have been the work of a moment, giving her no opportunity to cry out and rouse the household.

'After removing the purse to make the motive for the crime appear robbery, the murderer had then left the house by the back door, faked the marks of entry on the outer frame of the window with a knife and then had loitered about at the entrance to the alleyway where he was seen by the witness, Moffat.

'I admit I was still puzzled by this last piece of evidence. Why had the murderer troubled with this stratagem, rather than returning immediately to the house? It seemed superfluous to his needs unless it was to suggest that the murder and robbery were the work of an outsider. Was it to throw suspicion on Vladimir Vasilchenko? If that had been his intention then it had been singularly unsuccessful for Moffat had failed to identify him. Or was it to confuse the police into hunting for a bearded man?

'My own suspicions were later to fall on Vasilchenko despite Moffat's assurance that he was not the man he had seen. Eye-witnesses are notoriously unreliable and moreover Moffat had glimpsed the man only briefly in the feeble light of a gas lamp. It was possible that he had been mistaken and that the man he had seen had indeed been Vasilchenko.

'It was Vladimir's subsequent behaviour which inclined me to think he was guilty for reasons which I shall shortly explain.

'One of my duties was to collect up the dirty linen and deliver it to a local washerwoman and then to distribute the clean laundry to the various rooms. Because of my supposed deafness, Dmitri instructed me by means of his system of signs, the only form of communication that we could use in front of the others, not to enter unannounced but to knock on the door and wait until the occupant opened it before handing over the clean linen. This task fell on the Monday morning, after I had been in the house for four days. Most of the tenants answered promptly but Vladimir Vasilchenko kept me waiting outside for several moments. Despite my assumed disability, my hearing is, in fact, particularly acute and I was aware, even through the closed door, of a series of hurried and furtive movements inside the room of papers being rustled together and a drawer being opened and closed. When Vasilchenko came at last to the door, a little out of breath and relieved, or so it seemed to me, that his visitor was only the deaf-mute peasant from the Urals, it was quite obvious what activity he had been so surreptitiously engaged in. The chair set carelessly to one side at the table where he had risen hastily from it, the ink-well with its lid still open and the fresh ink stains on the fingers of his right hand indicated quite clearly, even though the papers had been put away, that he had been engaged in writing.

'As I handed over the bed linen and gave him the foolish, vacant grin which I had assumed as part of my disguise, I considered what these documents he was so anxious to conceal might be. Was Vladimir Vasilchenko an *agent provocateur*, introduced into the household by the Okchrana in order to report on his fellow-lodgers? Or was he the Nihilist assassin who had attempted to shoot the Odessa Chief of Police and who was now writing seditious pamphlets in order to bring about the violent overthrow of the Imperial Russian Government?

'Either explanation might have provided a motive for the murder of the old woman. As for opportunity, his room was on the first floor, immediately above Anna Poltava's. It would have taken him no more than a few minutes to commit the crime and return to his bed.

'The following day, I had the opportunity to observe Vladimir Vasilchenko more closely. I had been sent by Dmitri to chop firewood in the coal-shed which stood in a corner of the yard when I saw Vasilchenko leave the house by the back door. His manner was so furtive that I decided to follow him. Moreover, a bundle of papers was protruding out of his pocket.

'So intent was he upon his errand that he failed to notice either me or Rosa Zubatov who, moments after Vasilchenko had disappeared down the short alley which led into Stanley Street, also emerged from the back door of the house, a shawl about her head and shoulders, and who, to my astonishment, set off in pursuit, for what purpose I could not guess unless, like me, she suspected him of Anna Poltava's murder and was carrying out her own investigation.

'I fell in behind them. We made a curious procession as we turned into Commercial Road, Vasilchenko striding along at the head of it, a striking figure with his black hair and beard, Rosa Zubatov lurking about twenty paces behind him on the other side of the street, her shawl drawn close about her head, and I bringing up the rear.

'One of the secrets of a successful disguise, Watson, is the ability to alter one's appearance in an instant without having to resort to a change of clothing or the adoption of other outward devices. The easiest transformation is in the style of one's physical stance and bearing. As the deaf-mute, Misha, I had adopted an awkward, shambling gait which seemed appropriate for his character. By merely pulling back my shoulders and assuming a brisk manner, I threw off Osinsky's personality and assumed that of an alert young working man, dressed in a cap and shabby clothes.

'Indeed, Vladimir looked back over his shoulder several times as if fearful of being followed but failed to observe me a few yards behind him among the other passers-by who thronged the street.

'His first destination was a cheap eating-house a little further down Commercial Road, a favourite meeting-place for Russian *émigrés*, where he went to the counter and bought himself a large brandy which he drank straight down as if to give himself courage. Rosa, meanwhile, had halted on the other side of the road and appeared to be intent on studying a pawnbroker's window. I decided on a bolder approach. Sauntering past the open door of the eating-house, I was able to observe Vladimir's actions more closely. Although I could not see exactly what coin he handed over to pay for the brandy, from the amount of change he received, I deduced that it was almost certainly a half-sovereign. You will no doubt recall, Watson, that there were two half-sovereigns in the purse which was stolen from Anna Poltava's bedroom on the night of her murder.

'I truly believed that I had my man. For how else was Vladimir Vasilchenko in possession of so large a sum of money when he appeared to have no means of earning it?

'My suspicions were further aroused when, on leaving the eating-house, he turned into a nearby side-street and entered a small, shabby shop, ostensibly a second-hand clothes' dealer's from the various articles of apparel displayed in the window or hanging from hooks outside the door. However, from the events that followed, I had reason to believe that the premises served merely as a cover for a more clandestine enterprise.

'As soon as Vasilchenko disappeared inside the shop, Rosa crossed the street and walked past, glancing in at the window as she did so before continuing on down the road, leaving the way clear for me to make my own examination of the premises which I did in a more leisurely manner, using the hanging clothes as concealment.

'I observed Vladimir deep in conversation with the second-hand dealer. Soon afterwards they were joined by a third man who emerged from a back room and who, from his leather apron and his ink-blackened hands, I took to be a printer, a deduction which was proved correct when Vladimir, reaching into his pocket, took out the bundle of papers and handed them over to this man who examined them, nodded as if satisfied and carried them off to the back room.

'Vasilchenko then turned towards the street door as if about to depart. I, too, took my leave and hurried ahead of him back to the lodgings where fortunately no one had noticed my absence. By the time Vasilchenko entered the yard, I had resumed my task of chopping firewood. He passed me without giving me a second glance.

'I was now convinced that not only had I identified the murderer but that I knew his motive. Anna Poltava, whom Count Nicholai had described as a shrewd old woman, had discovered Vasilchenko's contact with the clandestine printer and he had killed her in order to silence her. The Count was correct. It had been a political crime.

But whether Vladimir was an Okchrana spy or a Nihilist subversive had yet to be proved. As for Moffat's inability to identify Vladimir, I put that down to his unreliability as a witness.

'I believe I may have expressed to you before, my dear Watson, that in the business of detection one never ceases to learn.[11] I was then a mere novice but it was a lesson which was brought home to me most forcibly that very evening.

'As I have explained, my room opened off the kitchen and by applying my eye to the spy-hole I had made in the wall I was able to observe the behaviour of the other tenants without their knowledge. That same evening, having made up my mind that Vladimir Vasilchenko was guilty, I heard someone enter the kitchen and, hoping that it was Vladimir whom I could keep under further observation, I took down the ikon and prepared to keep watch.

'To my disappointment, it was only the young woman, Rosa Zubatov. Taking a chair, she sat down upon it by the fire and proceeded to light one of her Russian cigarettes.

'Have you ever observed a woman lighting a cigarette, Watson? It is not a common sight, I confess, although smoking has become more fashionable among young ladies, especially those members of what is known as the "fast set" who make up the Prince of Wales's rather raffish group of friends and who even include, I understand,

---

[11] In The Sign of Four', Mr Sherlock Holmes remarks that the science of detection can only be learnt through 'long and patient study'. Dr John F. Watson.

other men's wives. When women do indulge in the habit, they in variably strike the match *away* from their persons. Men generally do the opposite. You may take my word for it if you have not yourself observed the distinction.

'As Rosa Zubatov lit her cigarette, I perceived that she struck the match towards her.

'It was enough.

'Within seconds, I was out of my room and into the kitchen to seize her by the hair, much to her consternation and the amazement of Vladimir Vasilchenko who had that moment entered and who thought I had gone suddenly mad.

'As she fought me off and Vasilchenko struggled to pull me back by the arms, bellowing like a bull in Russian, I was left clutching in one hand a wig of blonde, curly hair which a moment before had adorned the head of the fair Rosa, revealing a short, military-style crop.

'The effect on Vladimir Vasilchenko was instantaneous. With a great shout of "Spic!", which I learnt later was the Russian for "spy", he changed sides at once and joined me in attacking Rosa Zubatov, wrestling her to the ground where he held her in a bear-like embrace.

'Our mingled cries and exclamations brought Dmitri and the others running and it took several moments of confused explanation in both Russian and English before they grasped the situation. Peter Tomazov, the shoemaker, who spoke a little English, was immediately dispatched to fetch Inspector Gudgeon. In the meantime, Dmitri had succeeded in rescuing Rosa Zubatov from Vladimir's clutches and had placed her on a chair where she sat, silent and defiant, while Vladimir went on haranguing both her and the assembled company, Dmitri translating for my benefit.

'Rosa Zubatov was, it seemed, Ilyich Rodzyanko, a member of the Tzarist secret police who had been sent to spy on Vladimir Vasilchenko which was not his real name either. He was, in fact, Boris Golenski, the former editor of a Nihilist periodical, calling itself *The People's Hammer*, which urged its readers to bring about the violent overthrow of the Tzar. Arrested for sedition, he had later escaped from the Peter and Paul fortress in St Petersburg where Ilyich Rodzyanko had been one of the Okchrana agents who had questioned him during his imprisonment which was how he had recognised her, or rather him, once the wig had been removed. Rodzyanko had been acting in disguise as an *agent provocateur*, his purpose being to persuade Vladimir to talk about his revolutionary activities during their late-night political discussions round the fire, hoping to trap him into naming some of his accomplices.

'What made Vladimir particularly furious was the fact that, since coming to England, he had abandoned his Nihilist principles as being far too dangerous and was attempting to dissociate himself from his past.

'"Then what," I inquired, "were the papers which he handed to the printer in Lukin Street?"

'When Dmitri translated my question, Vladimir looked most shame-faced.

'They were, he explained, a love story which he was

hoping to sell to a small publishing firm which produced a monthly periodical, completely non-political in its aims, for the Russian female *émigrés* in the East End of London. It was by this means that he earned his living, an employment which, for obvious reasons, he was anxious to keep secret from his fellow-lodgers. This accounted for the half-sovereign he had paid over in the eating-house. Incidentally, Watson, he was using the rather fanciful *nom de plume* of Princess Tatyana Ivanovna, thus adding yet another false identity to the many which bedevilled the case.

'Inspector Gudgeon arrived shortly afterwards with a uniformed sergeant and some constables. Had he not been such a dull-witted dog of a fellow and still stubbornly convinced that Anna Poltava's murder was the work of the Mason gang, I might have felt sorry for him for he was faced by several transformations which would not have disgraced a farce in which, in the final scene, disguises are thrown off and true identities revealed. Not only was I not a deaf-mute Russian peasant but the attractive Miss Rosa Zubatov, towards whom I suspected Gudgeon's interest had strayed during his investigation, had been unmasked as Ilyich Rodzyanko, an Okchrana male secret agent. Even so, when faced with the truth, he took a great deal of persuading.

'"But you can speak English!" he protested to me on more than one occasion.

'"Of course I can," I replied. "My name is Sherlock Holmes and I am a private consulting detective, called in by Count Nicholai Plekhanovitch to investigate Anna Poltava's murder."

'On the matter of Rosa Zubatov's, alias Ilyich Rodzyanko's, identity, he was even more nonplussed and it was not until her, or rather his, room was searched and the purse belonging to Anna Poltava was found, together with a long black cloak and a broad-brimmed hat, as well as a false beard and a set of picklocks, that he was finally convinced. Rodzyanko was then arrested and taken off to Commercial Road police station in handcuffs.

'I heard later that the market-porter, Moffat, was sent for and identified Rodzyanko, dressed in this disguise, as the man he had seen lurking at the alley entrance.

'Faced with this incontrovertible evidence, Rodzyanko then confessed to the murder of Anna Poltava. She, too, it seemed had, like me, become suspicious of Rosa Zubatov or rather Rodzyanko as I shall now call him to save further confusion, and had searched his room in his absence, disturbing his papers and thus arousing his suspicion. As only Anna Poltava possessed keys to all the rooms in the house, it was clear to him who had carried out the search. Fearful that the old woman would betray him, Rodzyanko decided to murder her in the manner I have already described, first picking the lock on her door and, having smothered her and taken her purse to make it appear a robbery, then faked the signs of a forced entry on the outer frame of the window. His purpose in waiting in the alleyway for a passer-by to observe him was to convince the police, as well as the inhabitants of the house, that the murder was the work of a bearded outsider.

'Thus the murder of the old Russian woman was satisfactorily solved.

'However, there remained a final mystery.

'You may be wondering, Watson, who, if anyone, was the Odessa assassin suspected of taking refuge in the Stanley Street household. Would you care to hazard a guess at that person's identity?'

'Oh, really Holmes!' I protested. 'I cannot imagine. There were a great many of them and Russian names are difficult to remember.'

'This one is not. Go on, my dear fellow. Pray indulge me.'

'Very well then,' said I, amused by the game. 'Whom shall I choose? Then let it be the shoemaker with the sick wife.'

Holmes laughed out loud with pleasure.

'You are wrong, my old friend. It was none other than Olga Leskova.'

'Olga? The fat woman who made you eat up your pancakes?'

'The very one! Can you imagine a more unlikely Nihilist? In the general confusion which followed my unmasking of Rodzyanko, no one noticed that she had quietly packed her bags and made her departure, fearful no doubt that her own identity would be the next uncovered. I learnt later from Count Nicholai that inquiries showed that she had taken passage to America where she disappeared from sight among the teeming millions of other foreign exiles. She is probably at this very moment running an eating-house in Kansas City or a Russian restaurant in the Bronx.

'And now, my dear Watson, if you care to assist me in packing up my trunk, I shall return it to my bedroom.'

'But, Holmes, what about the other papers?' I exclaimed, indicating the piles of documents which still stood about the room.

'Oh, there is no time to deal with those now,' Holmes declared airily. 'The maid will be coming at any moment to lay the table for dinner. Surely you do not expect her to do so with the contents of the trunk spread across the carpet?'

'But, Holmes . . . !'

My protests were to no avail. Holmes insisted and together we bundled up the documents, including the packet containing the false identity papers, the photograph and the ikon, and returned them to the trunk.

Although several months were to pass before Holmes finally found the time to clear the room of all his other records, I had at least the consolation of having heard from his lips the curious case of the old Russian woman.[12] even though I shall not be permitted to publish an account of it within the lifetime of Count Nicholai Plekhanovitch and his son, Sergei, who still continue their work among the Russian exiles and who wish to protect the interests of their fellow-countrymen.

---

[12] Mr Sherlock Holmes refers to this case together with several others in 'The Adventure of the Musgrave Ritual'. Dr John F. Watson.

The Case of the Camberwell Poisoning

Of all the investigations with which it was my privilege to be associated over the years of my friendship with Sherlock Holmes, few began with such dramatic abruptness as the one we were later to refer to as the case of the Camberwell poisoning.

It was, I recall, a little after eleven o'clock one evening in the spring of '87.[1] As my wife was away for a few days visiting a relative in Sussex,[2] I had called on Holmes earlier, having not seen him for several weeks, and, as the hours slipped by, we fell to reminiscing companionably over past cases, as we sat by the fire, in particular the theft of the Mayor of Bournemouth's regalia and the

---

[1] Readers are again referred to the monograph by my late uncle, Dr John F. Watson, printed in the Appendix. Aubrey B. Watson.

[2] This relative is almost certainly Mrs Watson's aunt whom she visited on at least one occasion (*Vide* 'The Five Orange Pips') although in some editions the relative is erroneously referred to as Mrs Watson's mother. Dr John F. Watson.

mysterious haunting of the Hon. Mrs Stukely Wodehouse.

Our conversation was interrupted by the sound of a vehicle drawing up in the street outside, followed soon afterwards by an urgent ringing at the front door bell.

'A client?' Holmes inquired, raising his eyebrows. 'I can think of no other reason for anyone to call at this time of night.'

Rather than allow Mrs Hudson or the maid to be disturbed, Holmes himself went downstairs to answer the summons, returning with a fair-haired, snub-nosed young man of about three and twenty, respectably dressed but without a topcoat, although the evening was chilly, and in a state of considerable agitation, his pleasant, rather nondescript countenance convulsed with an expression of despair.

When Holmes invited him to sit by the fire, he sank into the chair with a groan and covered his face with his hands.

After exchanging a glance with me over the top of his bowed head, Holmes opened the interview.

'I perceive,' said he, crossing his legs and leaning back comfortably in his own chair, 'that you are employed in an office, that you are a keen amateur cricketer, that you left home in great haste and that, although you arrived here by cab, the first part of your journey was conducted on foot.'

The words had their desired effect for the young man sat up instantly and regarded my old friend with great astonishment.

'You are quite right, Mr Holmes, although how the deuce you know all this is beyond me. I have heard of your reputation which is why I am here, but I never knew you had the gift of clairvoyance.'

'Not clairvoyance, my dear sir; simply observation. For example, you are wearing on your lapel a Camberwell Cricket Club badge with the letters CCC on a blue shield, easily recognisable to someone like myself who has made a study of such insignia. As for your haste in coming here and for making the first part of your journey on foot, the absence of a topcoat and the state of your boots give that away. There is fresh mud upon the soles.'

'Then how do you know I work in an office?' the young man inquired, looking more cheerful. 'I don't carry that on my lapel or my boots.'

Holmes laughed out loud.

'No, indeed! But you do on the middle finger of your right hand where I see there is a small callosity just above the first joint where a pen has constantly rubbed while your attire, although dishevelled, shows nothing of the bohemianism of the artist. Now come, sir, I have given away some of my professional methods. Will you now do me the courtesy of telling me who you are and what business has brought you here at this late hour? It is evidently a matter of some urgency which could not wait until the morning.'

The young man was immediately plunged once more into the depths.

'Urgent! I should think it is, Mr Holmes. I have been

accused of murder although I swear I am innocent . . . !'

'Pray, sir, let us approach the case from the beginning,' Holmes interrupted with a touch of asperity. 'Facts first, if you please. The protestations may come later. What is your name?'

Looking abashed, our young visitor made an effort to control his feelings.

'My name is Charles Perrott, Charlie to my friends, and I work as a clerk at Snellings and Broadbent, the stockbroker's in Cornhill. As both my parents died when I was young, I was brought up by my maternal uncle, Albert Rushton, and his late wife, my Aunt Vera, who were very good to me, took me into their own home and treated me like a son.

'Earlier today, when I returned from the office to my diggings, I found a message from my uncle, asking me to drop by at his house in Camberwell this evening, as he had an urgent matter to discuss with me. I called at about six o'clock and was invited into the study for a glass of sherry while my uncle explained to me that only that morning he had heard that his younger brother had died in Australia, leaving no family, and that consequently, he had altered his will, making me his sole heir. Under the terms of his old will, his brother would have been the main beneficiary. I ought to explain, Mr Holmes, that, before his retirement, my uncle was a successful wholesale greengrocer with a business at Covent Garden and was quite wealthy.

'I must confess that, while I was distressed for my

uncle's sake over the death of his brother – also an uncle although I had never known him as he had emigrated before I was born – I couldn't help feeling pleased at the news that I would inherit the largest portion of my Uncle Bert's estate which I knew amounted to as much as fifteen thousand pounds, not to mention the house and its contents. He had never made any secret of it and often talked openly about his will, even in front of the servants.

'Uncle Bert invited me to stay to dinner but I had to turn him down as I'd promised some friends I'd have supper with them and a game or two of billiards afterwards.

'I got back to my lodgings soon after half past ten and was getting ready for bed when there came a loud knocking on the front door and my landlady showed two men up to my room. They were police officers, Mr Holmes, come to tell me that my uncle was dead and they were arresting me on suspicion of murdering him!'

'Who were these officers?' Holmes asked.

'An Inspector Needham and a Sergeant Bullifont from the station in Camberwell Green.'

'Did either of these officers tell you how your uncle died or what evidence they had against you?'

'No, not a word, Mr Holmes. Inspector Needham handed me my jacket after the sergeant had searched the pockets and told me to put it on. I was in such a state of shock, what with the news of Uncle Bert's death, not to mention the accusation of murder, that I hardly knew what I was doing. It was while I was fastening up my jacket that the sergeant found something in the pocket of my topcoat. As far as I could see, it was nothing more than a scrap of paper, all crumpled up, but it seemed to excite the inspector and his sergeant. After they had examined it, Inspector Needham said, "Well, that's conclusive evidence, if ever I saw any," and the sergeant started to take a pair of handcuffs out of his pocket. It was then I decided to make a bolt for it.

'The bottom sash of the window was open to air the room. I'd smoked a cigar when I'd first got back to my lodgings and my landlady objects to the smell of tobacco smoke in the house. I knew the coal-shed roof was just below, so I made a dive round the end of the bed, jumped out of the window and made off across the garden. There's a back gate that opens into an alleyway. I ran down there, cut across some waste-ground and eventually came out in Coldharbour Lane where I hailed a cab. I'd heard of you, sir. The chief accountant at Snellings and Broadbent mentioned your name in connection with the Thisby fraud case. That's why I came to you. If anyone can prove my innocence, it's you, Mr Holmes!'

Holmes, who had listened to this account with the deepest attention, rose abruptly from his chair and took several turns up and down the room, plunged deep in thought, while Charlie Perrott watched him anxiously from his seat by the fire.

'Will you take the case, Mr Holmes?' he ventured at last.

'Oh, there is no question of my failing to do that! My present concern is over the immediate conduct of the investigation.' My old friend seemed to come to a decision for he suddenly exclaimed, 'Fetch your hat and coat, Watson! We are leaving at once for Camberwell. You, too, Mr Perrott. No, no! Pray do not object, sir. If I am to take you on as my client, you must allow me to proceed with this inquiry in my own manner and, as I see it, there is no alternative. Do you wish to spend the rest of your life running away from the law? Of course you do not! You will therefore return with us to your uncle's house where you will place yourself in the hands of Inspector Needham. On the way there, I shall further question you about your knowledge of this evening's events.'

Although Baker Street was almost deserted at that time of night, we had no difficulty in finding a cab and, once Perrott had given the driver the address, Laurel Lodge, Woodside Drive, Camberwell, and we had started off, Holmes opened the interview with a quite unexpected question.

'What do you know of poisons, Mr Perrott?'

'Poisons?' The man seemed utterly bewildered. 'Nothing at all! Why do you ask?'

'Yes, why, Holmes?' I interjected, as astonished as young Perrott by the question.

'Is it not obvious? Then let me explain. Your uncle has been murdered, Mr Perrott, presumably at home and at some time after you had left his house, subsequent to your visit. You are suspected of his murder but, as you were engaged with friends and therefore you have an alibi to cover the latter part of the evening, I assume the method of committing the crime was by some remote means, rather than in a personal confrontation such as stabbing or strangulation. As Inspector Needham seemed to regard the piece of paper found in the pocket of your topcoat of great significance, I further assume that he must have considered that it played some part in your uncle's death. Hence my query regarding poison, for what other means of murder could have been contained in so small a receptacle? Were you wearing the same topcoat when you visited your uncle earlier this evening?'

'Yes, I was.'

'And what did you do with it when you entered the house?'

'I hung it on the coat-stand in the hall.'

'You then proceeded to your uncle's study where you both drank a glass of sherry. Who poured the wine?'

'I did. But I don't see . . .'

'Pray allow me to continue, Mr Perrott. It will not be long before we arrive in Camberwell and I must acquaint myself with all the facts. I understand from your earlier remarks that you were familiar with the contents of your uncle's will. Who else would have benefited at his death?'

'There were some small legacies to three or four more distant relatives, several charitable bequests and sums of a few hundred pounds to each of the servants.'

'Ah!' said Holmes as if finding this information significant. 'And who precisely are they?'

'The cook, Mrs Williams, two maids, and the

coachman. They were to receive three hundred pounds each. Miss Butler, my uncle's housekeeper, was left five hundred pounds even though she has not been in the household as long as the others. It was in recognition of the care she'd taken in nursing my Aunt Vera before her death eighteen months ago. My uncle kept her on to run the house and to look after him as well. His own state of health hadn't been too good. He suffered from aneurism and so had to take care he did not put any strain on his heart. Miss Butler was also to inherit any residue from the estate.'

'Oh, really?' Holmes remarked with a negligent air before passing on to his next question. 'At what time did you leave the house, Mr Perrott?'

'I can't be sure but I think it must have been soon after seven. I got to the Red Bull where we were to take supper about ten past and it's a good five minutes' walk.'

'Where you met your friends? Very well. Now that accounts for your movements, but what of your uncle's? Did he have a nightly routine? Elderly gentlemen often do.'

'He dined every evening at half-past seven on the dot.'

'Alone?'

'No, usually in the company of Miss Butler.'

'How was the meal served?'

'I don't quite follow you,' Mr Perrott said. He seemed bewildered by this fusillade of questions.

With admirable patience, Holmes explained.

'I mean was the food served at the table from dishes or carried in from the kitchen on plates?'

205

'Oh, I see!' Perrott exclaimed, his brow clearing. 'No; it's served by Letty, the parlourmaid, who always waits in the dining-room to clear away.'

'Does Miss Butler have a role in this routine?'

'She pours the wine and supervises the meal generally.'

'Tell me about Miss Butler,' Holmes said, leaning back and folding his arms.

'I don't know a great deal except that she came, as I said, about two years ago, before my aunt died, to nurse her in her last illness and look after the house. Before that she worked as a housekeeper for a widowed doctor in Leamington Spa but had to leave when he remarried. She arrived with excellent references and runs my uncle's place like billyho.'

'I see. Now to return to your uncle's nightly habits. At what time would he retire for the night?'

'Usually at ten o'clock.'

'And was this also a routine?'

'Oh, yes. As soon as the clock struck ten, he'd say, "Time to climb the wooden hill to Bedfordshire." My aunt used to tease him about it,' Perrott replied, his bottom lip beginning to tremble like a schoolboy's at this homely recollection.

Holmes glanced out of the cab window.

'I see,' said he, 'that we are now in Camberwell and that we should soon be arriving at your late uncle's house. There are no more questions I wish to ask you, Mr Perrott. Rest assured that your case is safe in my hands and that, whatever evidence the official police may have against you, I shall do my utmost to prove your innocence.'

I, too, gazed out of the window at the familiar streets, partly to remind myself of the occasions when I had visited this same area on my first acquaintance with the young lady who was later to become my wife[3] but also, I confess, to avoid looking at Perrott who was sat facing us and who, now that the time of his arrest drew near, had once more become exceedingly nervous, his youthful, rather naïve features the very picture of despair.

Soon afterwards, we drew up outside a large but ugly grey brick villa, of the style built in the outer suburbs on the Surrey side of the river for prosperous tradesmen and their families. Its name, Laurel Lodge, was apt for the house was fronted by a dense hedge of that thick-leaved shrub, the heavy mass of which cast an air of gloom over the whole edifice.

Several lighted windows, both upstairs and down, and the presence of a uniformed constable on the front doorstep suggested that the police were still engaged on their investigation.

The constable seemed inclined to bar our way but, when Holmes produced his card and explained our

[3] Before her marriage to Dr John H. Watson, Miss Mary Morstan, as she then was, was employed as governess in the home of Mrs Cecil Forrester of Camberwell. It was in Mrs Forrester's house that Dr John H. Watson proposed to Miss Morstan. *Vide* 'The Sign of Four'. Camberwell is also associated with other cases which Sherlock Holmes and Dr Watson investigated. *Vide* 'A Case of Identity' and 'The Disappearance of Lady Frances Carfax'. Dr John F. Watson.

business there, he knocked on the door whereupon a heavily built sergeant opened it, took one astonished look at Perrott and then, quickly recovering himself, invited us into the hall where he told us to wait while he fetched the inspector.

We had but a few minutes' grace while the sergeant was upstairs for Holmes to ask one last question, less out of need, I felt, to obtain the information from Perrott than to distract his attention for he was looking wildly about him as if seeking for the means to make a bolt for it, as he himself had expressed it.

'I assume,' said Holmes, indicating a large hall-stand just inside the front door, 'that this is where you hung your topcoat?'

'Yes; that's right,' Perrott stammered in a faltering voice.

For at that moment, there came a heavy step on the landing and Inspector Needham came down the stairs, followed by the sergeant.

He was a tall, stoop-shouldered man with a drooping moustache which gave his features a lugubrious air despite his obvious delight at Perrott's unexpected reappearance.

'Well, well!' said he. 'This is a surprise, Mr Perrott. So you've decided to come back and face the music, have you? Very wise of you, sir, if I may say so. I take it that it was on the advice of Mr Holmes? I have heard of you, sir. You have quite a reputation among the police force even as far as Camberwell Green. I assume you have taken Mr Perrott as your client? Well, it won't do him much good because I intend taking him into custody here and now and sending him down to the station in the company of Sergeant Bullifont although where the deuce he'll find a cab at this time of night, I can't imagine.'

'You may take ours, Inspector,' Holmes said nonchalantly. 'As I assumed you would wish to arrest my client, I told the cabby to wait at the gate.'

I saw Inspector Needham and his sergeant exchange surprised glances at my old friend's cool manner as, under their curious gaze, he shook hands with Perrott and added a last remark or two of reassurance.

'Take courage, Mr Perrott,' said he. 'I have every confidence that this absurd charge against you will soon be dropped.'

These comforting words hardly seemed to convince the wretched Perrott for, as he was put into handcuffs and led away by Sergeant Bullifont to the waiting cab, he cast a last, despairing glance over his shoulder at Holmes.

When the front door closed behind them, Inspector Needham said in a jocular manner, 'Absurd charge, Mr Holmes! I am afraid you are not fully aware of all the evidence against your client.'

'No, I am not,' agreed Holmes. 'Perhaps you would care to inform me, Inspector, of the precise facts? I assume you have collected some data and that the case against Mr Perrott is not based entirely on supposition or circumstantial evidence.'

'If it's facts you want, I can supply you with plenty,' Needham replied and began to enumerate them on his fingers, holding up each in turn. 'Fact number one – the sherry glasses from which the accused and his uncle drank were fortunately not washed up with the other dishes after dinner. In the bottom of one of them, I discovered a whitish residue. That has still to be analysed but I have no doubt that it will prove to be poison, probably arsenic.'

'I am inclined to agree with you,' Holmes conceded. 'In a case such as this which appears to concern a will and the inheriting of money, arsenic is often employed as a means of murder. Indeed, it was so widely used in France in the eighteenth century to dispose of unwanted heirs and testators that it became known as the "*poudre de succession*" or "inheritance powder". The Reinsch test[4] will confirm it one way or the other.'

'You seem to be knowledgeable about poisons, Mr Holmes.'

Needham's attitude had changed from one of amused tolerance to cautious respect.

'Oh, I have merely dabbled in the subject,'[5] Holmes said airily. 'But, tell me, Inspector, how was it that the sherry glasses were so 'fortunately' not washed up?'

'The housemaid couldn't get into the study to collect them. The room was locked.'

'Under whose instructions?'

---

[4] The Reinsch test for detecting arsenic was devised by Hugo Reinsch, a German chemist, in 1842. Dr John F. Watson.

[5] Mr Sherlock Holmes is being unduly modest for, as Dr John H. Watson states in 'A Study in Scarlet', Mr Holmes was 'well up' in his knowledge of belladonna, opium and poisons generally. Dr John F. Watson.

'Mr Rushton's, I understand. He had left some important papers on the desk and he disliked any of the servants, even Miss Butler, the housekeeper, going into the room unless he himself was present. Now for fact number two, Mr Holmes,' and here a second stubby finger was stabbed into the air.

'The only other opportunity anyone else in the household had to poison Mr Rushton was during the evening meal. But no one, neither Miss Butler who dined with Mr Rushton, nor his cook and the maids who shared what was left over, suffered any ill effects whatsoever. And if you think someone other than Perrott could have slipped some poison into the decanter of wine, then you're wrong!' Inspector Needham sounded positively triumphant at producing this trump card. 'Miss Butler drank a glass of wine with her meal and the cook had confessed to taking a sip or two from it herself. Moreover, the decanter shows no sign of having been tampered with.

'And if that isn't enough, Mr Holmes, when my sergeant searched Mr Perrott's topcoat pocket, he found a small square of paper. It had been crumpled up but there were some grains of white powder still clinging to the folds. There is no doubt in my mind that it too, when analysed, will prove to be arsenic.'

'Quite,' Holmes murmured. 'But, in giving me your catalogue of data, Inspector, you have omitted one important fact.'

'What is that?'

'The last and most important one of all. Mr Perrott

himself has admitted he was to inherit a considerable sum on his uncle's death.'

Needham looked considerably taken aback.

So, too, I must confess, was I. The evidence against Perrott was damning enough without Holmes adding his own contribution which would tip the scales even further against our client.

'Well, there you are then!' Needham exclaimed. 'It is an open and shut case.'

'It would certainly appear so,' Holmes replied. 'However, with your permission, Inspector, I should like to examine some of that evidence for myself. I am sure you would not wish to obstruct me in my attempts to clear my client.'

'If it's the sherry glasses you want to look at, they are already packed up . . .' Needham began.

Holmes waved a negligent hand.

'Oh, I am not at all concerned with those. I am quite sure that, when analysed, the residue will be found to contain arsenic. No; it is the victim's bedroom I wish to examine. Has the body been removed?'

'It was taken to the mortuary about quarter of an hour ago.'

Even this information appeared not to discompose my old friend for he replied, 'No matter. Dr Watson and I shall be quite content with merely looking at the scene where the death took place. You surely have no objections, Inspector?'

'Very well, Mr Holmes. If you and Dr Watson care

to follow me, I shall show you the room. However I should explain,' Needham added over his shoulder as he preceded us up the stairs, 'that, although the symptoms pointed to poisoning, the victim died of a heart attack, brought on by a particularly severe attack of nausea. But that doesn't alter the fact that it was murder, Mr Holmes.'

'Of course,' Holmes murmured in agreement.

We had reached an upper landing. Here Needham turned to the left towards the front of the house where, throwing open a door, he announced, 'Mr Rushton's bedroom, gentlemen.'

It was a large chamber, furnished with the type of heavy, expensive mahogany pieces which were fashionable thirty or forty years before, including a wash-hand stand, its basin missing, and, just inside the door, a large, high bed which was mercifully stripped of its bedding so that the room presented no evidence that, not long before, Rushton had suffered there from the agonising symptoms of arsenical poisoning with all its attendant and unpleasant effects upon the bowels and stomach.

Holmes and I had remained in the doorway while Needham crossed the room to turn up two gas jets which had been left burning low over the mantelpiece. While he was thus occupied, Holmes, whose glance had been darting keenly about the room, took the opportunity to murmur to me under his breath, 'Try to distract Needham's attention for a few moments.'

There was no time for him to offer any further explanation. The inspector had turned away from his task and, with the room now brightly lit, we, too, advanced into the chamber, Holmes wandering off towards the night-table which stood beside the bed in order to examine a book which was lying on top of it together with a gold pocket-watch and chain and a small oil reading-lamp.

Picking up the volume to read its title, he gave me a small nod which I took to be my cue.

'As a medical practitioner,' said I, addressing Needham, 'I am interested in the effects of arsenical poisoning. I understand the symptoms generally begin within an hour of the toxin being introduced into the system. If Mr Rushton had taken the poison in the sherry wine, served between six and seven o'clock, he should have shown signs of it during dinner. I take it the ingestion of a heavy meal slowed down the onset of the symptoms?'

'I believe that is so,' Needham replied. 'According to Dr Livesey, Mr Rushton's own physician who was called in by Miss Butler, it is what must have occurred in this case. Mr Rushton had eaten a three-course dinner and, the stomach being full, the poison took much longer to have its effect.'

He broke off to inquire of Holmes, who had by now moved away from the night-table and was examining with apparent absorption a large and particularly ugly wardrobe against the further wall, 'Well, Mr Holmes, have you seen enough?'

'Thank you, yes, Inspector. I should now like to speak to Miss Butler. If that can be arranged to take place in the dining-room, I should be infinitely obliged to you.'

Needham shrugged but he seemed to treat the request with amused resignation rather than annoyance.

'If you think any good will come of it,' he replied, leading the way downstairs. 'Miss Butler has already given me a full account of what happened here this evening and I am perfectly satisfied with her statement. I must, however, insist on being present when you question her.'

'I have no objections, apart from one proviso,' Holmes replied. 'That is, I must be allowed to conduct the interview in my own manner.'

'As you wish, Mr Holmes,' Needham agreed, throwing open a door at the rear of the hall and standing aside to allow us to enter.

Like the bedroom, the dining-room was furnished in a heavy, old-fashioned style, on this occasion in dark oak, including a table, large enough to seat ten persons comfortably, and an elaborately carved sideboard.

'Yes, Holmes, what good will it do?' I asked when, the inspector having lit the gas jets and departed to fetch Miss Butler, we were left alone in the room. 'All the evidence so far only confirms Perrott's guilt. As Needham himself said, it is an open and shut case. Surely you are wasting your time in pursuing it?'

'The only shut part about it is the inspector's mind,' my old friend rejoined. 'Yours, too, Watson. And that surprises me, my dear fellow. We have already obtained some highly pertinent evidence.'

'Have we?' I was astonished. 'Exactly what, pray?'

I found myself addressing his back for he had again sauntered off, this time to examine the sideboard, first opening the drawers to look inside them in a cursory manner before shutting them and turning his attention to the cupboards underneath.

'Holmes, what evidence have we discovered?' I repeated, beginning to feel a little exasperated. Although our client's life was at stake, Holmes appeared not to be treating the case with much seriousness.

'Why, to a conspiracy, of course,' he replied, shutting the side-board doors and standing upright, one hand placed negligently in his pocket.

'A conspiracy!'

I was prevented from following up this astounding assertion by a light tap on the door.

'Come!' Holmes called out, at which a woman, Miss Butler, I assumed, entered the room, closely followed by Inspector Needham.

She came in almost silently, the only sound the rustle of her long black skirts as they brushed across the carpet and even that soft murmur of silk ceased as she paused just inside the room.

'You wished to question me, gentlemen?' she asked.

I can only speak for myself when I say that she was one of the most fascinating women I have ever encountered although, from the expression on my old friend's face, I could see that he, too, was brought up short by the sight of her.

She was not beautiful; beautiful is too commonplace

a word to describe her although, should I ever be asked to give an account of her physical appearance, I would be forced to fall back on a few conventional phrases. In figure she was slight; of age, about eight and twenty; of carriage, graceful.

Pressed for further details, I would be restrained to add that I was particularly struck by her pallor, a strange-seeming detail but that was one of my first and most lasting impressions.

She was dressed entirely in black, a plain, long-sleeved gown, cut high in the throat and unrelieved by any ornament, not even a brooch or a necklace. Against this sombre attire, her hands, which she held folded together in front of her, and the pale oval of her face stood out as if they had been cut, like cameos, from some translucent material, very simple and yet delicate in outline.

The only colour was in her hair and eyes and those, too, were pale, the hair a light gold and, like the gown, plain, being parted in the centre and smoothed back off the brow in two shining wings, while the eyes were a clear, almost transparent grey.

None of these epithets, however, convey the brilliant quality about both her hair and her eyes which shone as if they were lit by some strange, ethereal radiance.

Apart from these physical attributes, there was a calm and assured composure about her, almost an authority for so young a woman, and an overwhelming sense of a keen and highly intelligent mind.

I found it deeply disturbing.

Holmes quickly recovered, pulling forward a chair at the table and inviting her to sit down.

I must confess, however, that it was several more minutes after I, too, had seated myself that I felt able to give my full attention to the questions that Holmes was putting to her and even then my attention still strayed from time to time from her answers to Miss Butler herself.

She sat very still, her hands clasped together on the table and her pale, calm face turned in Holmes' direction, taking no notice either of me or of Inspector Needham who had seated himself next to me and who listened to the interview with the smiling air of a man who had heard it all before and who expects nothing new to come from it.

Holmes asked her first about Perrott's visit to the house earlier in the day and received confirmation from her of the time of his arrival and departure and also of the fact that it had been on Mr Rushton's orders that the study door was locked.

Holmes next asked her about the evening meal and it was at this point that I recovered myself and began to listen more carefully to her answers.

'We dined at the usual time, half-past seven,' Miss Butler said in a low, pleasant voice. Both her tone and manner were calm and unhurried. 'We were served by Letty, the parlourmaid. When the meal was over, Mr Rushton retired to the drawing-room while I remained behind to supervise the clearing of the table. After that, I went into the kitchen to speak to the cook, Mrs

Williams, about the following day's menus. I then joined Mr Rushton in the drawing-room, taking some sewing with me.'

'What time was this?' Holmes inquired.

He was observing her closely, leaning forward towards her across the table.

'A little before half-past eight. The clock in the drawing-room struck the half-hour not long after I had sat down. I had not been in the room more than ten minutes at most when Mr Rushton complained of feeling unwell.'

'Unwell? How precisely?'

'He said he felt nauseous. He also spoke of pains in the stomach and a burning sensation at the back of his throat. I suggested I called in Dr Livesey, who lives only a few doors away, but Mr Rushton declined. He said it was probably only indigestion, brought on by the acidity of the rhubarb pie we had eaten at dinner, and it would soon pass. But not long afterwards he said he would retire to bed, as he continued unwell.'

'The time?' Holmes demanded. He had taken out a small note-book and waited, pencil poised, for her answer.

Miss Butler regarded him calmly.

'I believe it was about ten minutes to nine but I did not pay particular attention. I accompanied Mr Rushton upstairs and waited in my own room while he prepared himself for bed before knocking at his door to inquire if he needed anything. As he was still complaining of nausea and of cramps in his legs, I went downstairs to the kitchen to ask cook to make up a hot-water bottle for him and also for a glass of warm water in which to mix a little bicarbonate of soda. The time was then soon after a quarter past nine.

'The mixture and the warmth from the bottle seemed to relieve the symptoms temporarily although he asked me to sit with him as he still felt very unwell. At about a quarter past ten, he requested that I bring the bowl from the wash-hand stand as he needed to be sick.'

'Was he?' Holmes inquired.

'Yes, he was,' came the quiet reply. 'Quite violently. As the pains in his stomach and legs also increased, it was clear to me that Mr Rushton was suffering from something more than mere indigestion. I rang the bell for Letty and told her to fetch Dr Livesey at once. He arrived within five minutes. It was while he was examining the patient that Mr Rushton had another severe bout of nausea which left him exhausted. A few moments later, he gave a gasp and collapsed against the pillows. Dr Livesey felt his pulse and said that he had passed away, in his opinion of a heart attack brought on by the severity of his sickness. As Dr Livesey insisted that the police were notified immediately, I sent Barnes, the coachman, to fetch them in the carriage. He returned with them about ten minutes later.'

'It all sounds straightforward,' Holmes remarked. 'You have made an excellent witness, Miss Butler. Indeed, there are only a few matters I wish to inquire into.'

'I shall do my best to answer them,' Miss Butler replied.

'Then can you tell me whether I am right in assuming

that the clocks in the house keep good time? Who is responsible for winding them?'

'Mr Rushton. He was most particular about that and allowed no one to touch them.'

'Not even yourself?'

'No; never.'

'And did this also apply to his own pocket-watch?'

Miss Butler widened her brilliant eyes.

'Certainly, Mr Holmes. I would not dream of interfering with it. It had belonged to Mr Rushton's father.'

'And this is Mr Rushton's watch, is it not?' Holmes inquired, producing a gold hunter from his pocket and laying it face upwards on the table.

Inspector Needham started up in his chair.

'Where did you get that, Mr Holmes?' he expostulated.

'From Mr Rushton's night-table,' Holmes replied coolly.

'But that's tampering with evidence!'

Ignoring Needham and with his eyes fixed on Miss Butler's face, Holmes slowly withdrew another object from his pocket, keeping it concealed in his palm until he had placed it beside the pocket-watch. It was only then that he opened his hand and revealed what had until that moment remained hidden.

It was a silver salt pot.

Although Needham and I both stared in bewilderment at this ordinary domestic object, the effect on Miss Butler was dramatic. She leapt to her feet so abruptly that the chair on which she had been sitting was sent crashing to the floor.

'You have searched my room without my permission!' she cried.

Holmes, too, had risen from the table and stood confronting her, his eyes not once leaving hers so that their mutual gaze seemed locked together as if in mortal combat.

Needham and I looked on in silence, watching their faces, hers so pallid that it seemed lit by some bright, cold, unearthly incandescence, his as austere and as watchful as a hawk's.

'No,' he said quietly. 'I have not searched your room, Miss Butler, but I suggest Inspector Needham does so immediately for I have no doubt that he will find hidden there the other salt pot which makes up the pair. There is only one more question I wish to ask you. How long have you been in the habit of consuming arsenic?'

For several moments we gazed at her without speaking, the only sound her frenzied sobbing.

It was Holmes who eventually spoke.

'I think, Inspector,' said he, his tone coldly implacable, 'that you have heard enough to charge Miss Butler with the murder of Albert Rushton.'

I prefer not to dwell on the events of the next half-hour. It has never afforded me pleasure to witness the mental agony of any fellow human-being, much less that of a woman and one, moreover, of Miss Butler's beauty and intelligence.

Suffice it to say that the first few minutes were anguished but that, after the formal arrest was made, she recovered her former composure and that, by the time a matron had been sent for from Camberwell Green police station, she had quite regained that air of calm self-possession.

In the mean time, Needham had searched her room and had found, hidden in her bureau, the second salt pot, the companion to the one which Holmes had produced from his pocket with such dramatic effect.

Accompanied by the matron, who carried a small valise containing some of the prisoner's clothes, and wearing a long black cloak, the hood drawn well up over her head so that it hid the pale gold hair and those pallid, delicate features, she passed down the stairs and through the door into the night while Holmes and I stood in the doorway of the dining-room watching her departure in silence, a form of tribute, at least on my part and I believe on his as well, to a most extraordinary woman.

Neither of us saw her again.

By the time our own cab had conveyed us to Camberwell Green police station, she had already been charged and taken down to the cells.

We were present when Perrott was released. He came into the small back room where we were waiting for Inspector Needham, smiling broadly, to wring our hands so vigorously and with so many protestations of undying gratitude that it became wearisome and both Holmes and I were relieved when he finally departed.

Soon afterwards, Inspector Needham joined us, his face haggard.

'It is a bad business, Mr Holmes.' he said, shaking his

head. 'It's the first time I have ever had to arrest a woman on a murder charge.'

'She has confessed?' Holmes asked quickly.

'Oh, yes. There was no question of that. But as I have not yet taken a full statement from her, I do not know all the details. Perhaps you could enlighten me, sir. If it had not been for you, the wrong person would have been sent for trial. What made you so sure young Perrott was innocent and she was guilty?'

'When Charlie Perrott first called on me and asked me to take the case,' Holmes began, 'I had very little evidence to prove his innocence. Indeed, most of the facts seemed to point to his guilt. He had motive in that he stood to gain substantially from his uncle's death. He also had the opportunity to administer the poison by means of the glass of sherry which he admitted he himself had poured for his uncle.

'But how and when had he obtained the arsenic? He had been at his place of employment all day and had not learnt that he was made his uncle's main beneficiary until he called at the house later in the evening in answer to a message.

'Besides, although a pleasant enough young man, he struck me as too naïve to plan anything as complex as murder by poison, always a premeditated crime necessitating careful forethought.

'I began to suspect a conspiracy. Someone in the household had deliberately contrived to cast suspicion on him and so to arrange the evidence that he appeared guilty. Although I had not yet met her, my suspicions fell on Miss Butler, the housekeeper, for reasons I shall shortly explain.

'I discounted the other servants. Under the terms of Mr Rushton's will, they inherited too little to make the risk worthwhile. Moreover, the average cook or housemaid would be no more capable of planning such a murder than Perrott himself. But Miss Butler was a different proposition.'

'Now wait a moment!' Needham interjected. 'Her legacy wasn't all that large. Five hundred pounds! That is hardly a motive either.'

'You have forgotten, Inspector, one very important clause in Mr Rushton's will. Apart from the five hundred pounds, she would inherit *any residue* from the estate. No doubt when Mr Rushton had the will drawn up, he intended it to cover any negligible sums of money which might be left over when the other legacies were paid. But, in effect, it meant that, should his nephew die or fail to inherit for any other reason, his part of the estate would automatically be assigned to Miss Butler, including not only a considerable sum of money, totalling fifteen thousand pounds, but the house and its contents. Now, under the law, no convicted criminal may benefit from the proceeds of his crime. If Charlie Perrott was found guilty of his uncle's murder, then Miss Butler would effectively take his place as the main heir. There is the motive, Inspector.

'There is no doubt in my mind that she knew the

contents of the changed will. Mr Rushton appeared to have made no secret of the various legacies included in it. It seemed more than likely that Miss Butler was aware under what terms she herself would have benefited.

'As for opportunity to implicate my client in his uncle's murder, Mr Perrott's topcoat was hanging on the stand in the hall in plain view of everyone. Nothing would have been simpler for her than to slip into his pocket a little square of crumpled paper which had once contained arsenic and in the folds of which some grains of the poison were still clinging. In addition, as housekeeper, she would have been told by Mr Rushton that his nephew had declined the invitation to stay to dinner; the way was therefore clear for her to proceed with her plan.

'All that remained for her to do once Mr Perrott had left the house and Mr Rushton had also vacated the study, was to slip into the room and add a little arsenic to the dregs of the sherry in one of the glasses, before leaving and locking the door behind her, thus ensuring that the housemaid could not clear away the used glasses. In her privileged position in the household, Miss Butler would have possessed keys to all the rooms in the house. Later, she announced to you that it was on Mr Rushton's orders that the study door was locked and, as Mr Rushton was dead, there was no one to refute her statement. By the time dinner was served, the evidence pointing to my client's guilt was already established.

'How she came by the poison is easily accounted for. Having acted as housekeeper to a doctor in Leamington

Spa before taking up her post in Laurel Lodge, she would have had access to arsenic, a common enough substance used by most medical practitioners for the preparation of Fowler's Solution, a frequently prescribed tonic.[6] That she did have such access was proved by the fact she was in the habit of taking arsenic.'

'Yes; she has confessed to that,' Needham said. 'But what made you aware of it?'

'Did you not observe the signs, Inspector? The pale skin and the shining eyes and hair? Used sparingly, it acts as a general stimulant upon the system. For this reason, the eating of arsenic is common among Austrian and Styrian peasants who regularly partake of minute quantities of the poison although the habit is much rarer in this country.[7] By this means, the arsenic-eater can build up a tolerance to the poison and can absorb quantities which would normally be fatal to any other person. It has

[6] Fowler's Solution contains 1 per cent Liquor arsenicalis. Dr John F. Watson.

[7] I call the reader's attention to the Maybrick case which occurred two years after the Camberwell poisoning. James Maybrick, who took regular doses of arsenic as a tonic, died of arsenical poisoning on 11th May 1889. His wife, Florence, who was accused of his murder, was found in possession of arsenic which she claimed she used in a cosmetic solution for her skin. Although she was found guilty and condemned to death, the sentence was commuted to life imprisonment of which she served fifteen years. Mr Sherlock Holmes may have had in mind an earlier case, that of Madeleine Smith, who was tried at Edinburgh in 1857 for the murder by arsenical poisoning of her lover, L'Angelier. She, too, claimed she had bought arsenic to use as a cosmetic. A verdict of Not Proven was returned. Dr John F. Watson.

also been employed, I believe, by certain foolish young women as a face-wash to improve the complexion.

'The crucial question was how had Miss Butler managed to introduce the poison to her victim? It had quite clearly not been added to either the food or the wine at dinner. The parlourmaid served the meal from dishes at the table and neither she nor the other servants suffered any ill effects when they shared the leftovers. Only one solution to the problem presented itself. The poison had to be present in some other ingredient which was on the table and to which the victim had access but not the servants. It also had to be white and of a similar texture to the arsenic otherwise the victim's suspicions might have been aroused. The answer was obvious. The poison was in the salt pot. This was why I insisted on interviewing Miss Butler in the dining-room. I wished to examine the sideboard in which the table silver would usually be kept. Any doubts I might have had about Miss Butler's guilt were dispelled when I observed that there was only *one* salt pot although there were two silver pepper pots in the cupboard. As we now know, the second was concealed in Miss Butler's room, her intention being to empty it of its contents and replace them with unadultered salt as soon as she had the opportunity.

'She was forestalled by Mr Rushton's sudden and unexpected death from a heart attack. Usually victims of arsenical poisoning linger for hours before finally succumbing to the dreadful symptoms. The police were immediately sent for and Miss Butler had no opportunity to empty the salt pot and return it to the dining-room.

'This brings us to the whole matter of timing. It was crucial to Miss Butler's plan that Mr Rushton should appear to suffer the first effects of arsenical poisoning not too long after he had drunk the sherry, thus casting suspicion on the nephew. As we had only her word that it was on Mr Rushton's instructions that the study door was locked, we also had to rely on her statement that he was first taken ill at about ten minutes to nine when he decided to retire to bed. The servants, shut up in the kitchen at the rear of the house, had no knowledge of what time, in fact, Mr Rushton went upstairs to his room.'

'But, Holmes!' I protested, perceiving a flaw in his reasoning. 'By a quarter past nine, Mr Rushton was so ill that Miss Butler came down to the kitchen for a hot-water bottle and a glass of warm water in which to mix bicarbonate of soda.'

Holmes raised his eyebrows at me.

'My dear fellow, of course she did!' said he. 'But once more we only have her word that Mr Rushton required such attention at that particular time.'

'Oh yes, I see, Holmes,' I replied, considerably dashed.

'Pray allow me to continue,' Holmes said with a pained air. 'It was Mr Rushton's habit to retire to bed at ten o'clock, a fact I learnt from his nephew. When we entered Mr Rushton's bedroom, I observed his pocket-watch lying on the table; no ordinary watch as I perceived from the key attached to the chain. It was a ratchet type and the patent of the well-known French watch-making firm of Breguet et fils.[8] The watch incorporated several other distinctive features, typical of Breguet's work, including a perpetual calendar on the face, a device for repeating the preceding hour as well as a gold engine-turned dial on the back showing the phases of the moon.

'But more important to the investigation, a Breguet watch has on the arbor[9] in the centre of the barrel a stopwork mechanism which allows the barrel to be turned only four full revolutions in thirty hours, the usual length of time a watch will run before it needs rewinding. This is to prevent the spring from being over-wound. As it would take two turns of the key to complete one full revolution of the barrel, it therefore follows that the key would have to be turned eight times for the barrel to be completely wound and the stopwork mechanism to come into play, preventing the barrel from being turned any further.

'I must confess, Inspector, that I asked my colleague, Dr Watson, to distract your attention for a few moments while I examined Mr Rushton's pocket-watch. The time then was a little before midnight but it required only one

---

[8] This famous French watch-making firm was first established in Paris in 1776 by Abraham Louis Breguet (1747–1823). In 1816, he was joined by his son, Louis Antoine (1776–1858). Breguet watches were famous for the beauty and originality of their designs. The ratchet, or 'tipsy', key was specially devised in order to prevent the barrel of the watch from being wound backwards, perhaps when the owner was intoxicated as the alternative name suggests. Dr John F. Watson.

[9] The arbor is the axle or spindle on which the barrel revolves. Dr John F. Watson.

half-turn of the key before the stop-work mechanism arrested the barrel, thus proving that the watch had last been wound up approximately two hours before, or if you wish me to be absolutely precise on the matter, one hour, fifty-two and a half minutes; in other words, at ten o'clock, the time Mr Rushton normally retired to bed. The mathematics involved are simple enough and I shall leave it with you to work them out for yourselves. As Miss Butler denied ever having touched the watch, it meant that Mr Rushton must have wound it up himself.

'But at a quarter past nine, if Miss Butler is to be believed, Mr Rushton was already in bed, suffering from nausea and cramps in the legs to such a degree that she went down to the kitchen for a hot-water bottle and a glass in which to mix bicarbonate of soda in order to relieve his symptoms. If that were so, he would hardly be in a fit condition to concern himself three quarters of an hour later with winding up his watch.

'In the light of the evidence, I think we may now revise the timing of the events which took place in Laurel Lodge and which led to Mr Rushton's unfortunate demise.

'He ingested the arsenic in the salt he added to his food during dinner soon after half-past seven but, because of the heavy meal he had eaten, a factor which can delay the onset of the symptoms of arsenical poisoning, as my colleague, Dr Watson pointed out and as you, Inspector, agreed, Mr Rushton did not begin to suffer any adverse effects until after ten o'clock, when he retired to bed at his usual hour, first winding up his watch, as was his habit.

Indeed, the initial symptoms did not strike him until a quarter past ten when he was taken ill and Miss Butler sent for the doctor. Death occurred, as we know, shortly afterwards from a heart attack.

'No doubt, Miss Butler will confirm these facts when you have taken a full statement from her,' Holmes concluded, rising to his feet and holding out his hand to Needham. 'Goodbye, Inspector. As you said, it is a bad business but one which is now closed.'

I felt that this last remark was a wry reference to Needham's earlier statement that, as far as he was concerned, it was an open and shut case.

As we left the police station and emerged into the street, I saw that it was a clear night and that, above the roofs and the clustered chimney-pots, the stars were very bright, burning in drops of pure, cold light which put me in mind of Miss Butler's own strange, ethereal radiance. Turning to Holmes, I put the question which, until that moment, I had dared not ask.

'She will be hanged, will she not?'

He turned on me a most sombre expression. Rarely have I seen him in so melancholy a mood.

'I fear so, Watson. She has confessed not only to Rushton's murder but to a conspiracy to bring his nephew to the gallows. Under such circumstances, there can be little hope of a reprieve. Nor does she deserve any mercy and I believe she herself will seek none. And yet I cannot help feeling that not all the blame should be laid at her feet and that she should not be alone when she mounts the scaffold.'

'Who else are you referring to, Holmes?' I inquired, quite nonplussed by his remark and assuming he must mean some accomplice whom we had not yet encountered.

'Society, of course!' he retorted. 'Consider her situation. Here is a young woman of undoubted intelligence and ability but of small fortune and even less opportunity to make her way in the world. For what do we – and here I speak of society in general of which you and I, Watson, are members – expect her to do with her life? Why, to marry, of course, and if that is not her inclination, to fritter away her talents acting as housekeeper or governess or a lady companion to others richer than herself but of less capacity. Had society allowed her to attain her full potential, it might never have occurred to her to turn to crime. She could have fulfilled herself in any profession she chose, as an ambassador, say, or a captain of industry or a politician, even reaching as high as the post of Prime Minister, absurd though that idea may seem.

'I want you to promise me that you will never publish an account of the case. The penny press will stir up enough scandal when it comes to court. I should not wish either your name or mine to be associated with such cheap sensationalism. Let her pass as decently as she can into oblivion.'

I had no hesitation in giving Holmes my word for I heartily concurred with his sentiments. Therefore, apart from a passing reference to the investigation in 'The Five

Orange Pips',[10] I have refrained from giving any further details, not even her name.

There was a melancholy sequel to the case.

Madeleine Butler was brought to trial and, having pleaded guilty to the charge of murder, was executed on 28th May, Ascension Day.

It was a black occasion for both Holmes and myself.

Although it was not in his nature to give any further thought to the protagonists in a case once an investigation was successfully concluded, for several years afterwards on the anniversary of the date when Madeleine Butler went to the scaffold, he was in low spirits as if still mourning the passing of that extraordinary woman.

---

[10] Dr John H. Watson includes the case among a list of other investigations which occurred in 1887, giving no names as he states here but referring only to the fact that, on winding up the dead man's watch, Mr Sherlock Holmes was able to prove that it had last been wound up two hours previously which was when the deceased had retired to bed. Dr John F. Watson.

The Case of the Sumatran Rat

I

Because the following case concerns matters which could affect the security of the realm, I know, even as I set pen to paper, that there is very little chance that I shall be given permission to publish this account and that it will have to be consigned, among other highly confidential reports, to my dispatch box in the strongroom of Cox and Co. of Charing Cross.

But as it was such a remarkable investigation, I cannot allow it to pass totally into oblivion and I shall therefore set down this record, if only for my own satisfaction and in the hope that at some future date, those in authority will grant leave for it to be placed before the public although this may never happen in my lifetime. As Holmes himself expressed it, the world is not yet prepared for a full account of the case.[1] However, even

---

[1] Dr John H. Watson indirectly quotes this comment almost word for word in The Adventure of the Sussex Vampire'. Dr John F. Watson.

in this secret report, I shall withhold or change certain facts pertaining to dates, names and, in particular, to scientific data.

Even I myself was not privy to the beginning of the case,[2] although I knew from its outset that Holmes was engaged on some urgent matter which took him away from our lodgings for days at a time and which, on his return, left him exhausted and careworn. He would either sit silently by the fire, smoking his pipe and staring into the flames, or would retire to his bedroom from where I could hear some melancholy air being played on his violin.

I also suspected that he had reverted to his habit of injecting himself with a 7 per cent solution of cocaine although, knowing my disapproval, he never employed the syringe in my presence.

Nevertheless, the symptoms were all too apparent in the intervals of feverish activity, followed by long periods when he seemed listless and drained of all energy.

At the time, my own health was far from good. The weather was exceedingly damp and consequently the wound I had received in my leg during the battle of Maiwand in Afghanistan had begun to ache with a dull but persistent pain which left me incapable of any

---

[2] Dr John H. Watson's ignorance of the beginning of this case is made clear in 'The Adventure of the Sussex Vampire' in which Sherlock Holmes has to explain to him how the firm Morrison, Morrison and Dodd of 46 Old Jewry and the ship "*Matilda Briggs*" came to be associated with it. Dr John F. Watson.

prolonged physical exertion and I was forced to lie with it up on the sofa.

It was during the second week of these secret and mysterious activities that Holmes confided in me.

I remember the occasion with great clarity. It was over breakfast one morning as we sat at table. He had left his food untouched, although he had drunk several cups of black coffee, and was sitting in his chair, watching me as I ate, an expression of brooding melancholy on his face.

Suddenly he said with great earnestness, 'Watson, you and I have worked together now on a great number of cases and I know I can trust you implicitly. I am presently engaged on an investigation of great secrecy in which I should be grateful for your assistance.'

I laid down my knife and fork.

'I shall be delighted, of course, to help you in any way I can, Holmes. What does this new adventure concern?'

'Adventure is hardly the word I would use, my dear fellow. It is nothing less than a monstrous conspiracy to blackmail the British Government which, should it ever be made public, would cause the utmost panic among the citizens of London and our other great towns. That is why I have not confided in you before. You have not been in the best of health and I did not wish to burden you with such an appalling secret. For secret it must remain. Not even a whisper of what I shall tell you must ever spread beyond these four walls.'

I had rarely heard him speak in so grave a tone or

seen him regard me with an expression of such sombre intensity and I replied with equal seriousness.

'You know you may trust me, Holmes.'

'Yes, I am aware of that, my old friend. Pray come with me. I have something I wish to show you.'

He led the way into his bedroom where, locking the door behind him, he crossed to his wardrobe which he opened with a key, precautions I had never known him take before in all the time of our acquaintance. Taking a wooden crate from the floor of the wardrobe, he carried it over to his bureau, removed the lid and, having felt about in the straw with which the box was packed, lifted out a large, sealed glass container in which some object was suspended in a fluid.

I went to stand beside him to take a closer look. It was then that I saw that the object was the body of a rat but of such gigantic proportions that I involuntarily took two or three paces backwards at the sight.

It was about the size of a terrier dog and was covered with a coarse, greyish-brown fur with a paler underbelly. Its snout was short and the muzzle was drawn back to reveal two wickedly sharp incisor teeth of an orange colour while the sturdy legs, though small in comparison with the rest of its huge body, were tipped with strong claws. It hung in the fluid, seeming to fix us with its evil little eyes through the glass, its scaly tail wrapped about it like some loathsome reptile.

'Hideous, is it not?' Holmes said.

'It is revolting!' I exclaimed. 'For God's sake, Holmes, where did it come from?'

'From Mycroft,[3] who in turn was given it by the Prime Minister. It was sent to him in Downing Street two weeks ago with an accompanying letter. All inquiries at present are directed towards finding where it originally came from. Have you ever encountered a more vile object, Watson? Then if you have seen enough, I shall immediately lock it away again. I must confess that I should prefer not to house it at all but Mycroft was of the opinion that it would be safer in my hands than in any of the Government offices.'

Replacing the jar inside the straw, he put the lid on the crate and carried it back to the wardrobe which he locked.

At his suggestion, we returned to the sitting-room where, in our absence, the breakfast table had been cleared and where we seated ourselves by the fire, Holmes first fetching from his desk, which was also locked, an envelope which he handed to me.

'This is the letter I referred to, Watson,' said he.

The envelope, which was unstamped, bore the words: *Most Urgent. For the Personal Attention of the Prime*

[3] Mycroft Holmes, Mr Sherlock Holmes' elder brother, ostensibly audited the books for some Government departments. However, he also acted on occasion as an unofficial adviser to the Government and Mr Sherlock Holmes once described him as 'the most indispensable man in the country', with powers of observation and detection which were superior to his own. *Vide* 'The Adventure of the Greek Interpreter' and 'The Adventure of the Bruce-Partington Plans'. Dr John F. Watson.

Minister, while the letter it contained carried no address, only a date of two weeks earlier and the following message:

Dear Sir,

Accompanying this letter will be a crate in which you will find the corpse of a giant rat, preserved in formaldehyde. After many years of the most painstaking research, I have now successfully bred several dozens of these creatures which I shall set loose into the sewers of London and several other of your cities should my terms not be met.

I desire that half a million pounds sterling shall be paid to me. However, as it may be difficult to obtain so large a sum, I shall give you and your Treasury a month from today in which to comply.

If you accept the terms, kindly place an advertisement to this effect in the *London Times* on Tuesday, 25th March. I shall then further communicate with you regarding the manner of payment.

I remain, Sir,
Your Obedient Servant,
The Pied Piper.

'This is quite appalling, Holmes!' I cried, laying down the letter. 'Half a million pounds! Why, it is a king's ransom. And by 25th March! But that means there are only ten more days left.'

'Exactly!' Holmes said grimly.

'How far have your investigations proceeded?'

'Not far enough, although we have made some progress. You noticed, I assume, several telling features of the letter?'

'You mean the absence of a stamp upon the envelope?'

'Yes; there is that. I shall refer to it later when I come to give you a brief account of what we have so far discovered about the villain who calls himself the Pied Piper. But what I had in mind was the character and background of the man. He is, I am convinced, not English although his command of the language is excellent. Note, however, certain stilted phrases such as "I desire" and the reference to the "London" *Times*. No Englishman would use such a term.

'In addition, although the language and the handwriting are those of a clerk, the man is highly intelligent. You remarked, of course, his choice of a *nom de plume* which suggests a mordant sense of humour. I believe also that he may bear a deep-seated grudge against the British Government. That, too, I shall explain later in greater detail.

'To return to more immediate matters, the letter and the crate itself. They were delivered to number ten Downing Street on 25th February. On receiving them, the Prime Minister immediately contacted my brother Mycroft who, as you know, Watson, has the full confidence of the Government over all matters covering the security of the realm or any highly confidential state affairs. He, in turn, alerted me and a certain Inspector Unwin of Scotland Yard. Unwin is an excellent man, intelligent, efficient and utterly trustworthy. He has gathered together a small group of fellow officers with whom I am working in liaison.

'So far we have followed several lines of investigation which seemed promising at the time but which unfortunately have come to very little. Allow me to give you a brief account.

'Unwin's men traced the carrier who delivered the crate and the letter to Downing Street. They were handed in at the firm's office in Holborn by a man whom the clerk described as short and sandy-haired, respectably dressed and wearing steel-rimmed eye-glasses but so insignificant in appearance that the clerk would not have taken note of him at all if it had not been the address to which the delivery was to be made. As he spoke with a faint foreign accent, I have no doubt that the man was the Pied Piper himself. He paid in cash and left no address.

'The rat itself afforded us a little more evidence. It was examined by a specialist who identified it as being of the species *Rodentia sumatrensis* and is, as the name suggests, indigenous to the Far East, in particular to the island of Sumatra[4] where it is known as the bamboo rat.

---

[4] In 'The Adventure of the Dying Detective', Sherlock Holmes claims he is dying of a 'coolie disease' from Sumatra, an infection he caught from an ivory box. He also investigated the case of the Netherland-Sumatra Company, an account of which has not yet been published. *Vide* 'The Adventure of the Reigate Squire'. Dr John F. Watson.

Although it is the largest of the subgenus *Rhizomys*, it does not normally grow to such gigantic proportions as the specimen in the jar. In the wild, it inhabits extensive burrows and is reported to be particularly vicious, with a savage bite. Moreover, it has a life-span of up to four years.

'This led us to make inquiries at the London docks about any ships which had called there recently from the Far East and we discovered one which appeared to fit our requirements. It was a cargo vessel which also carried a few passengers, among whom was a sandy-haired man in eye-glasses who called himself Van Breughel and who had boarded the boat at Padang, taking with him some personal luggage and, what is more pertinent to our investigation, several large metal crates with mesh sides which appeared to contain livestock. Van Breughel insisted that they were placed in a convenient part of the hold where he could have easy access to them in order to feed whatever creatures they contained which, I am convinced, were the very same rats he has threatened to introduce into the sewers.

'Unfortunately, by the time we made our inquiries, the boat had already unloaded, taken on board a new cargo and departed on its return voyage to the Far East so we have been unable to contact its captain.

'However, we learnt a little more from the dock officials. It seems that when the vessel came to be discharged, a fault was found in the lifting gear and, as the crates were too cumbersome to be manhandled out of the hold, they would have to be left *in situ* until one of their own engineers was free to repair the mechanism of the hoist.

'On being informed of this, Van Breughel became extremely angry and, declaring that his cargo might perish if it were left any longer on board the vessel, insisted that an engineer from a private firm be immediately sent for in order that the lifting gear might be mended without any further delay.

'Consequently, a Mr Dodds from an engineering assessors in Old Jewry arrived at the docks to repair the mechanical fault in the equipment and the crates were subsequently lifted from the hold.

'I interviewed Mr Dodds who had good reason to remember Van Breughel. Using the excuse that, as he had recently arrived in this country he had not yet opened a bank account nor had he enough money on him to pay in cash, Van Breughel asked for the bill to be sent to an address in Hertfordshire which proved, on later inquiry, to be false. Mr Dodds was, however, sufficiently suspicious of his client to take a keen interest in his behaviour and, fortunately for us, he observed the crates being loaded into the back of a large, covered van, bearing neither the name nor the address of any firm or business, but which was driven by a thick-set, swarthy-looking man. We therefore know that Van Breughel, alias the Pied Piper, has an accomplice.

'Mr Dodds also observed Van Breughel getting into a

cab with a large valise which he seemed reluctant to entrust to the van driver and overheard him telling the driver to take him to Charing Cross, which further aroused Mr Dodds' suspicions as the trains for Hertfordshire depart from St Pancras, not Charing Cross.

'To cut a very long story short, Unwin, his men and I made inquiries at Charing Cross and discovered that our quarry caught the 5.15 train to Chatham. Once again, it was his reluctance to part with money which made him conspicuous. A porter at Charing Cross, who carried his valise to the train, remembers the man for the smallness of the tip he gave him. Further inquiries along the line at every station at which the train halted on its route to Chatham established the fact that he alighted at Wellerby, undertipping another porter who carried his valise to a nearby hotel, the Maltby Arms. Here our quarry dined and was again remembered for the paucity of his remuneration by a waiter who reported that he was collected by a swarthy-looking man, the same individual, I am convinced, who was in charge of the van although on this occasion he was driving a gig. The two men then drove off together.

'It is here that our inquiries have foundered and where I shall need your assistance, Watson. All of this happened five days ago and since then neither Inspector Unwin, his assistants nor I have been able to discover any trace of either Van Breughel or his accomplice. No one in the area of Wellerby appears to have any knowledge of them.

'It is to be assumed that they are engaged in breeding more specimens of that hideous sample in the glass jar, for the letter refers to several dozen of the creatures, and that therefore they must have premises somewhere, presumably in the countryside, where such activities may be carried out without arousing the suspicions of their neighbours. But where exactly? That is the crucial question. It could be anywhere within a ten-mile radius of Wellerby; possibly even more. It could take weeks, even months, to scour such a wide area, examining every farm and small-holding, and we have a mere few days.

'To be frank with you, Unwin and I have reached an *impasse*. That is why I have confided in you, my dear fellow, now that your health has improved, so that, by using you as sounding-board, I may clear my own mind.'

'Have you made inquiries of land-agents in the area?' I suggested, deeply concerned not only by the gravity of the situation but by my old friend's obvious fatigue and low spirits. 'If this man, the Pied Piper, has only recently arrived in this country, he may have rented property . . .'

'Yes, yes!' Holmes said impatiently. 'That was the first thought to cross my mind. All premises which have been leased or sold over the past ten years have been inquired into and visited but none of them is the one we are seeking. Either the Pied Piper or the driver of the van must own whatever premises they are using, or they have made private arrangements to rent them.'

For several moments, I was silent as I considered the problem. Having had one suggestion so abruptly dismissed, I was reluctant to put forward any others without first giving them careful thought.

Meanwhile, Holmes had got to his feet and was restlessly pacing up and down the room.

It was then that an idea came to me so suddenly that I found myself uttering it out loud without thinking. 'Straw!' I exclaimed.

Holmes stopped in his tracks and turned on me an incredulous expression.

'Straw? What on earth are you talking about, Watson? The only straws in the case are those that Unwin and I find ourselves clutching at so desperately.'

'No, not straws, Holmes. Straw. If the Pied Piper and his accomplice are breeding rats, they will need bedding and probably a large quantity of it as well. Unless they have stocks of it themselves from growing their own corn, which seems unlikely, then they must buy it from a local farmer or dealer.'

'My dear fellow!' Holmes exclaimed, striding across the room to wring my hand. 'I do believe you have the answer. Straw! Of course! Whatever put such an idea into your mind? It is positively scintillating.'

'As a boy, I used to keep pet mice,' I said modestly. 'I recall having regularly to buy bedding for them; hay in that particular instance.'

'Pet mice? What a revelation! Although I have known you for a good many years, I was unaware of such a fascinating detail concerning your youth.'

In an instant he had changed, throwing off his exhaustion as if it had been an old coat and emerging a new man, fresh and invigorated, full of animation and energy.

Fetching his hat and stick, he announced, 'I shall go out at once and purchase all the Kentish newspapers. Straw! It is a stroke of genius!'

With that he was gone, bounding eagerly down the stairs.

He was back within a quarter of an hour, flourishing two newspapers, his expression jubilant.

'I do believe our luck has changed, Watson. I was able to acquire the *Wellerby Gazette* and the *Wellerby Chronicle* as well. Here, my dear fellow,' tossing me one of the newspapers, 'take the *Chronicle* and search through the pages of advertisements. And, remembering Van Breughel's reluctance to part with money, I suggest we look for a dealer offering the cheapest straw on the market.'

There followed several minutes of silence, broken only by the sound of rustling as Holmes and I turned over the pages of our respective newspapers.

It was Holmes who found the advertisement.

'Listen to this!' he exclaimed. '"Bargain Offer. Hay, straw, manure going cheap while stocks last." I believe we have found it!'

'Is there an address?'

'Yes; Armitage, Blossom Farm, Lower Bagnell. I

know the village. I passed through it when Unwin and I were making our inquiries. Pack a valise, Watson! We are leaving immediately. And do not forget to bring your service revolver with you. We may have need of it.'

Galvanised into action by Holmes' energy, I hurriedly threw a few things into an overnight bag, including my pistol, and within ten minutes we were in a cab and on our way to Charing Cross station, stopping briefly at a post office to allow Holmes to send a telegram to Inspector Unwin, who was presently engaged on inquiries in London, to inform him of our departure.

It was only when we were on the train on the way to Wellerby that I had the opportunity to ask the question to which I had been eager to know the answer ever since I had first seen the dreadful specimen inside the jar.

'Tell me, Holmes,' I said, 'how is it possible that the Pied Piper managed to acquire such a monstrous creature? Is it an aberration of Nature? Or is it the product of some fiendish scientific experiment?'

'I am convinced that it is a devilish combination of the two,' Holmes replied, his face grave. 'You have heard no doubt of Darwin?[5] Since his book was published in 1859 on the origin of the various species,

---

[5] Charles Robert Darwin (1809–1882) was famous for his theory of evolution which he based on observations made during the voyage of HMS Beagle, on which he served as naturalist, to the South Pacific, in particular the Galapagos Islands. Dr John F. Watson.

our ideas of evolution have been turned upside down, causing such a furore inside the established church that the dust has not yet settled. And yet it makes perfectly good sense to believe that it is by a process of natural selection that the animal kingdom – of which we must count ourselves members, Watson – should pass on to the succeeding generations those characteristics which are advantageous to their survival, rather than those that are not. But is the name Mendel[6] familiar to you?'

'No' I replied. 'I have not heard of him.'

'Few people have. He was an Austrian priest and botanist who, in the 1860s, carried out a series of experiments in the monastery gardens into the cross-fertilisation of the garden pea and discovered a constancy in height of the plants, for example, or the colour of the flowers. From these tests, he developed a theory that the alternative characteristics observed in the plants, both in the parents and their descendants, are caused by the presence of paired elements of heredity which obey simple rules, one half being transmitted by one parent, the other by the second. In other words, Watson, the off-spring inherit half their characteristics from the female plant, the other half from the male.

---

[6] The experiments of Gregor Johann Mendel (1822–1884) into the hybridization of garden peas led to the development of the science of genetics. It was extremely perspicacious of Sherlock Holmes to recognize the importance of Mendel's paper on the subject. Most scientists at the time ignored it. Dr John F. Watson.

'In 1866, Mendel published his results in an article entitled "*Versuche über Pflanzenhybriden*" or "Experiments with Plant Hybrids" which I happened to come across a few years ago in the British Museum library.

'Once one applies Mendel's discovery to mammals rather than garden peas, and combines it with Darwin's theory on natural selection, one grasps its relevance to such an animal as the bamboo rat which can reproduce itself within twenty-two days and give birth to a litter of up to five young. If one takes a larger than average male bamboo rat and mates it with a larger than average female, the off-spring themselves will be bigger than normal. If one then breeds from the largest of their offspring, their descendants will in turn be of increased size. And so one continues until eventually, over many generations, one can, by selective hybridisation, produce a rat which is several times larger than the original breeding pair and which is less selective in its feeding habits than those in the wild. Normally, as their name suggests, they live mainly on bamboo although they will eat other vegetable matter.

'I believe that is what has happened in this case. By careful mating, Van Breughel has developed a strain of the *Rodentia sumatrensis* of which we have so far seen only one dead example. What the living specimens must be like, I shudder to contemplate. It also defies the imagination to envisage the consequences should such creatures be let loose into the sewers. They would

251

overrun our cities, bringing God knows what pestilence with them. Think also of the terror they would inspire!

'As for the future, the prospect is alarming. While such theories could benefit mankind in the struggle against hereditary diseases or in the breeding of improved strains of plants in order to feed our increasing population, in the wrong hands they could lead to the restructuring of matter itself and to the reproduction of every kind of evil which haunts our planet.'

'I don't quite follow you, Holmes,' I said.

'My dear fellow, think of typhoid! Or cholera! Or bubonic plague! If some mad biologist were to breed a particularly virulent form of any of those infections and let it loose into a population, the results could be catastrophic. He could hold not just the British Government to ransom, as the Pied Piper is presently attempting, but the whole world!

'Which brings me to my theory that the Pied Piper bears a grudge against our Government. Sumatra is owned by the Dutch.[7] Why has he not turned his blackmailing threats against them? It would seem logical. But rather he has singled out this country. If ever this case is brought to a conclusion, we may discover the reason behind his choice of victim.'

'You think that we may finally solve this case then, Holmes?'

---

[7] Sumatra was formerly held by the British. It was handed by them to the Dutch in 1824 in exchange for Malacca. Dr John F. Watson.

'We must, my dear Watson,' he replied gravely. 'If we do not, I cannot tell what the consequences may be.'

For the rest of the journey, we were both silent, each of us contemplating this dreadful prospect.

On our arrival at Wellerby, a small market town, we took the station dog-cart to Lower Bagnell, a picturesque village some five miles distant. Fortunately, it possessed a public house, the 'Barley Mow', which let out accommodation and, having booked a room for two nights and deposited our luggage, we hired the publican's trap and set off immediately for Blossom Farm, two miles away, Holmes taking the reins.

He already had his story prepared and, as we rattled into the farmyard and drew to a halt, he jumped down to address Armitage who had come out of a barn to greet us.

He was a red-faced, corpulent man, slow of speech but shrewd of manner and he eyed Holmes warily as he approached.

We were, Holmes explained, looking for some acquaintances of ours who, he believed, owned a farm or a small-holding in the district. One was a short, sandy-haired man in eye-glasses, the other broad and dark-featured. Had Mr Armitage any knowledge of them?

'Londoners, bain't you?' Armitage asked, looking us up and down with the countryman's suspicion of strangers. 'Yes, we are.'

'Stayin' locally?'

'In Lower Bagnell.'

'How long for?'

'Two days.'

'Ah!' said Armitage and fell silent.

I could see that Holmes was growing impatient at this catechism but he contained his exasperation and continued, 'I am most anxious to trace these men for personal reasons. If you have any information about them, Mr Armitage, I should be happy to make it worth your while.'

Armitage immediately became more loquacious.

'Yes, I know one of 'em,' he said. 'The dark 'un. Comes 'ere regular, 'e do, buyin' straw. Milk, too, and eggs.' He cocked a knowing eye at Holmes. 'Owes you money, do 'e?' On receiving Holmes' confirmation, Armitage grinned triumphantly. 'I thought 'e might. Wanted to run up a bill with me, 'e did. But I told 'e, no money, no goods. So 'e pays me on the nose afore I lets 'e load up 'is van.'

'Do you know where he lives?' Holmes inquired.

Armitage again fell silent, an expression of bovine stupidity overtaking his features. But, as soon as Holmes produced a half-crown from his pocket, he recovered his power of speech, like a mechanical piano set in motion by the insertion of a penny.

'Can't tell 'e the address,' he said, 'but when 'e drives off, 'e goes that way.' A dirty thumb was jerked to the left.

'Thank you,' Holmes said, trying to hide his disappointment that, despite the half-crown, Armitage had given us no more specific information than this. 'You have been most helpful. I should be grateful if you did not mention any of this to the man concerned.'

'Bain't none of my business,' Armitage replied with a shrug.

He waited, deliberately I suspected, until Holmes had climbed back into the trap and had taken up the reins before he added, 'I'll tell 'e somethin' else though. 'Is 'orse is allus fresh. Bain't come more'n two or three miles at most.'

'My dear sir, you have my eternal gratitude!' Holmes called over his shoulder as the trap moved off.

As soon as we were out of earshot, he burst out laughing.

'A cussed old devil but observant nonetheless, Watson. Two or three miles north of here! That should make the search easier.'

As events were to prove, he was far too sanguine. It was growing dusk before we finally found the place after several weary hours of inquiring at farms and small-holdings and tramping through many muddy yards.

My leg was causing me considerable discomfort when Holmes, who had turned down a narrow lane which appeared to lead nowhere, suddenly reined in the horse.

'I believe we have found it, Watson!' he said softly, his eyes glittering in the glow of the side lamps.

We had halted at a gate leading to a rutted track at the

far end of which we could dimly observe in the fading light the roof and chimneys of a house, partly obscured by the surrounding trees. A board nailed to the gate-post announced in peeling white letters the name 'Bedlow's Farm'.

'But why this one?' I inquired.

To me it looked no more likely than several other farms which we had passed on the road and which Holmes had dismissed out of hand.

'Observe the heavy chain and padlock on the gate, both of them new,' Holmes replied. 'Note also the fresh pieces of straw caught upon the hedge. I am convinced we have found the Pied Piper's lair. It is too late to make a reconnaissance tonight but we shall return tomorrow at first light.'

He was as good as his word. At six o'clock the following morning, Holmes, already dressed, shook me awake and at a quarter before seven, having breakfasted on bread and bacon, we set off once more in the trap, Holmes with his field-glasses on their strap about his neck, I with my service revolver in my pocket.

We approached Bedlow's Farm circumspectly on foot, first leaving the trap in a little copse about half a mile from our destination, well hidden from the lane. From there, we took a circuitous route across the fields which led us eventually to a sloping meadow behind the farm and its outbuildings which we had only glimpsed the night before.

From the vantage point of this rising land and hidden

behind a hedge, we had a clear view down the slope towards our objective.

The house itself was a mean building of brick and slate which appeared unoccupied although a wisp of smoke from one of its chimneys suggested someone was in residence.

Facing it across the yard was a long, low barn with a pair of closed doors painted black, beside which stood a large dog kennel.

I was able to discern these details through Holmes' field-glasses which he lent me once he himself had studied the place. But I had barely focused on the kennel and its occupant, a huge, brindled mastiff, when he plucked urgently at my sleeve and requested that I return the glasses to him.

Even at that distance, his keen eyesight had picked out some movement in the yard.

Whatever it was, he watched it in silence for several moments before he said softly, 'Two men have just entered the barn; our quarries, Watson, for they answer the descriptions we have been given of the Pied Piper and his confederate. While they are still inside the building, I suggest we withdraw while our presence is still undetected. I must also alert Inspector Unwin and his men without any delay.'

We returned by the same route by which we had come and, having retrieved the trap, set off immediately for Wellerby where Holmes dispatched a telegram to Inspector Unwin in London.

It was a long message which I read over his shoulder as he penned it. It read:

SHOOTING PARTY ARRANGED FOR LATER TODAY WITH PIPER STOP WILL MEET YOU AND YOUR FRIENDS OFF THE 4 27 TRAIN FROM CHARING CROSS AT WELLERBY STOP PLEASE BRING FISHING LINE STOP HOLMES

'A fishing line, Holmes?' I inquired. 'What on earth do you want that for?'

'You shall find out later tonight, Watson,' said he with an enigmatic smile.

II

Inspector Unwin seemed as puzzled as I by the request for the fishing line although he had complied with Holmes' request and, when we met him and his colleagues at Wellerby station, he produced it from his pocket.

'Although it beats me what you need it for, Mr Holmes,' he said.

He was a heavily built, round-faced, cheerful man, dressed appropriately for the occasion in tweeds as were his fellow officers, two of whom were carrying large leather cases which I later discovered contained rifles.

But Holmes was no more forthcoming about the purpose of the fishing line than he had been with me, apart from remarking, 'It will have its uses.'

While waiting for the arrival of Unwin and his party Holmes and I had taken luncheon at the Maltby Arms. Leaving me at the hotel to rest my leg which was causing me considerable discomfort, he then departed on some mysterious errand of his own from which he returned with the pockets of his ulster bulging with parcels, the contents of which he declined to reveal.

Having met Unwin and his colleagues off the train, we again retired to the Maltby Arms where, over dinner at a corner table and out of hearing of the other guests, Holmes gave them a brief account of our inquiries which had led us to Lower Bagnell and to the Pied Piper's secret hideaway at Bedlow's Farm. Then, tearing a page from his note book, he quickly made a sketch of the farmhouse and its outbuildings as well as any surrounding trees and bushes which would give us cover, circumstances which I myself had taken no heed of but which he, with his remarkable powers of memory, had noted exactly.

In low voices we discussed what stratagem should be employed until, by the time coffee was served, our plans were perfected and each man among us knew exactly what part he had to play in the coming ambuscade.

We set off at half-past nine, Holmes and I in the trap, Unwin and his men in the hotel's dog-cart which Holmes had taken the precaution of retaining earlier in the afternoon.

It was a chilly night with a waning moon which cast sufficient light for us to see by but which, or so I fervently hoped, would obscure our own movements from any hostile observers.

I must confess that my heart was beating high at the prospect of the adventure to come and, as I sat beside Holmes in the trap, both of us silent, I was reminded of the time in Afghanistan before the battle of Maiwand in

1880 when I had again experienced that same sensation of fearful but excited anticipation. In the fever of the moment, I even forgot the pain in my leg which had troubled me during the afternoon as the muscles grew tired and which the rest had not quite remedied.

We left the trap and the dog-cart in the same copse which Holmes and I had used but we took a different route from the one we had followed that morning. It brought us to a small neglected orchard, close to the rear of the farm, where the trees offered us plenty of cover and from where we could see ahead of us the house and its outbuildings. Although the barn was in darkness, one window on the ground floor of the house was bright with the yellow glow of an oil lamp.

Here, at a signal from Holmes, we halted and all watched mystified as he removed the several small packets from his pocket and laid their contents on the grass. They were a piece of prime steak, a penknife, a ball of thin twine and two small phials of liquid. Using a convenient flat stone as a cutting board, he proceeded to slice a long, thin portion from the steak which he sprinkled liberally with the contents of the phials. In the night air, I caught the unmistakable odours of aniseed and chloral hydrate. Then, rolling up the meat into a shape not unlike a beef olive, he tied it up with a piece of the twine before attaching it to one end of the fishing line.

'The lure,' he whispered, the faint moonlight gleaming in his eyes and making them glitter like stars.

Then, with the fishing line looped up in one hand, the

baited end of it swinging free, he set off alone, crouching low, towards the farmhouse while we waited under the trees.

The silence was so intense that even the smallest noise which broke it seemed magnified beyond normal. I could hear the night breeze stirring the branches above my head and the clear sound of running water although I knew that the nearest stream was two fields away. Even my own heartbeats seemed to thunder out like the regular tattoo upon a drum. Only Holmes was silent, nothing more than a dark shadow moving noiselessly across the grass, his stooped silhouette almost invisible against the tangled foliage and the looming bulk of Bedlow's Farm.

As he reached the low fence which separated the orchard from the yard, I saw him pause and slowly draw himself upright.

Whether it was this movement or some slight sound inaudible to us which disturbed the dog, I cannot say. But there came the sudden rattle of its chain which to my ears sounded as loud as a fusillade of shots while its deep growl seemed to echo across to us like the low rumble of an approaching storm.

I recall thinking with an inward groan that all was lost. At any moment, we would hear the farmhouse door burst open as Van Breughel and his accomplice came running out to challenge us. In the ensuing confrontation, we should be forced out into the open to meet them in a headlong charge in which, although outnumbered, they would have the advantage of knowing the terrain as well as access to all available cover offered by the house and its outbuildings.

It was similar to the situation I had experienced in Afghanistan where, as Assistant Surgeon, I was only too familiar with the appalling consequences of such an encounter.

But even as these thoughts clamoured in my mind, I was aware of a stillness about me, as if all movement, the motion of the breeze among the trees as well as the distant stream, had been suspended.

The figure of Holmes was likewise motionless, standing upright now, his right arm raised above his head. Then, as I watched, I saw the arm whirl suddenly into action. A dark missile flew silently from his hand to be followed shortly afterwards by the faint, dull sound of something soft hitting the ground. The chain clinked once more but gently this time as if the great mastiff had stirred only a pace or two from its kennel and then there came to us clearly on the night air an eager, slavering sound.

The lure had been taken.

We waited for several more minutes in this state of breathless inanimation until Holmes' tall silhouette once more dropped out of sight and we heard the rustle of the grass as he came creeping back towards us.

'A lucky cast,' he announced in an exultant whisper. 'The drugged meat fell almost at the creature's feet and it snapped it up at once. No dog can resist the smell of aniseed. You see now, Inspector, why I asked for the fishing line? All the other ingredients for my lure were available in the local town but not the means to deliver it.' He consulted his pocket-watch. 'We shall wait for another five minutes for the sleeping draught to have its full effect and then we shall make our move.'

'Holmes,' I said in a low voice, struck by a discrepancy in his account, 'how were you able to acquire chloral hydrate without a doctor's prescription?'

He gave a quiet chuckle.

'I have a confession to make, Watson. I took a sheet of your writing paper some time ago in case of need which I have been carrying in my pocketbook ever since. It was a simple matter of forging your signature, an easy enough task as your handwriting is so deplorable that a mere scribble sufficed.[8] But in a good cause, I knew you would not object.'

'Of course not, Holmes,' I replied. Under the circumstances, there was little else I could say.

While we had been speaking, the light in the downstairs window of the house had been extinguished and two others had appeared in the upper storey, gleaming like two yellow eyes in the darkness. It seemed the occupants of Bedlow's Farm were preparing to retire.

Holmes rose to his feet. It was time to go.

Using the trees as cover, we moved as silently as we could across the grass, keeping low so that we would not

---

[8] This remark by Sherlock Holmes tends to support the theory of my late uncle, Dr John F. Watson, which is printed in full in the Appendix and which suggests that Dr John H. Watson's handwriting could have caused the confusion over dating in certain of the published accounts. Aubrey B. Watson.

be visible against the sky-line, should either Van Breughel or his confederate happen to glance out of the upstairs windows. In this manner, we gained the low fence which separated the orchard from the farmyard. Here we paused to take stock of the situation at closer quarters.

The house lay over to our left, silent although the lamps still gleamed in its facade. Facing it was the barn with the kennel standing guard beside the closed doors, the huge mastiff stretched out on the cobbles before it in so deep a drugged sleep that not a muscle twitched in its massive frame as, climbing the fence, we stealthily approached.

It had been agreed that we should surround the building, taking advantage of whatever cover the yard and its outbuildings offered, using Holmes' plan as a guide. Now, with a wave of his hand, Inspector Unwin gestured us to our assigned positions. Two of his men stole round the side of the building to guard the rear while the rest of us slipped as silently as shadows into our places of concealment. Mine was behind a large rain-barrel, close to where Holmes was crouching under the protection of a log-pile.

As I took out my revolver, I glanced across at him. His figure was barely discernible in the darkness although I could just make out his lean form, tense and eager, every muscle strained for action like a tiger waiting to spring.

The signal came shortly afterwards.

There was a loud thud as Inspector Unwin lobbed a stone against the front door of the house, followed immediately afterwards by the sound of his voice, ringing out across the yard.

'Van Breughel!' he shouted. 'Can you hear me? Give yourself up. We are armed police officers and we have the place surrounded. If you and your accomplice come out with your hands up, no harm will come to you. You have my word on that.'

There came an answering crash as one of the upper windows was flung back and a man's head appeared in the opening, outlined against the glow of the room. From the glitter of the lamplight on the lenses of spectacles, I assumed it was Van Breughel.

'Surrender? Never!' he screamed out in a shrill voice which had in it all the overtones of madness as well as defiance. 'You will have to come for me, Mr English policeman, but, by God, not before I take you and some of your men with me!'

With that, raising a gun against his shoulder, he took aim and fired several wild shots into the darkness.

As I tightened my finger on the trigger of my own weapon, I saw the flashes from his and heard the whine as one of the bullets passed harmlessly, thank God, over the log-pile where Holmes was concealed to bury itself in the wall of the barn.

It was as much as I could do to restrain myself from returning the fire. Indeed, I had steadied my revolver against my arm and was looking down the barrel, the man clearly in my sights. As he stood there, silhouetted against the lighted window, I could have picked him off as easily as a sitting target. All my instincts urged me to pull the trigger. And yet I refrained. If my army experience had taught me anything it was not to act precipitately but to obey the orders of a superior officer, in this case Inspector Unwin, and he had given specific orders that no one was to open fire without his permission.

So I held back which was the wisest action I could have taken for what happened shortly afterwards decided the issue without the need for any of us to participate.

A second figure appeared at the window which, from its broad-shouldered outline, could only have been Van Breughel's accomplice, the same man who had driven the van and purchased the straw from Armitage's farm.

A violent quarrel then broke out between the pair, the subject of which we could only guess at from their angry gestures and by the occasional words or phrases which were audible above the general fury of the altercation.

Van Breughel's companion appeared to be urging him away from the window, dragging him by one arm while with the other he struggled to gain possession of the rifle.

I heard him shout, 'Give in! It's hopeless!'

Whether the weapon was fired by accident or with deliberate intent, there was no way of telling from our places of concealment.

All we saw and heard was another flash and report as the gun went off followed by a dreadful scream and the broad-shouldered man fell backwards out of sight.

Van Breughel appeared briefly at the window. I swear that he grinned down at us although Holmes later asserted that it was pure fancy on my part and that I could not, at that distance, have discerned any expression on the man's features. However, there was no mistaking the jaunty wave of his hand, a last gesture of defiance, as he tossed an empty cartridge box into the yard before he stepped back and there came the sound of a final shot.

There ensued several moments of absolute silence, made all the more intense by the noise and violence which had preceded it.

It was broken by Inspector Unwin who rose to his feet and called to us to come forward. It was only then as I relaxed my grip on my revolver that I realised my palm was sore where its butt had bitten deep into my flesh.

After we had burst down the front door, we found the two bodies in one of the bedrooms, Van Breughel's just below the window, his head shattered by the bullet which had penetrated the skull. His features were unrecognisable although the steel-rimmed spectacles lying broken beside him identified the corpse as his. His companion was stretched out on the floor a little distance away, a large gaping wound in his chest just above his heart.

I had no difficulty in pronouncing them both dead.

Inspector Unwin stood gazing down at them, his hands behind his back and an expression of distaste as well as disappointment on his broad, ruddy features.

'Well, gentlemen,' said he, addressing all of us, 'it is not the outcome I had looked for. I had hoped to take the pair of them into custody. However, there is no point in crying over it. The milk has been spilt and that's an end to it.'

'You will inform the local constabulary?' Holmes inquired. 'What account will you give them to explain away this affair?'

'I shall keep pretty much to the story we've already prepared with just a change of ending,' Unwin replied cheerfully. 'Me and my men have been on the trail of these villains for the past few weeks on account of an armed raid on a post office in Marylebone. We traced them to this hideout where we found them dead. What do you suggest, Mr Holmes,' he added with a twinkle. 'A quarrel over the proceeds of the robbery? A falling out among thieves? I think that would explain their deaths most satisfactorily. But before I send one of my men to the police station in Wellerby, there is unfinished business we must attend to in the barn.'

Taking the oil lamp from the table, he led the way down the stairs and across the yard to the outbuilding where he opened back the double doors and we followed him inside.

Even now, long after the event, I find it difficult to bring myself to recollect that scene, let alone describe it.

The barn was old with an earth floor and a raftered roof, hung with cobwebs which over the years had gathered in tattered, dusty wreaths.

But before my eyes had grown accustomed to the dim yellow light from the lamp to discern these details, I was horribly aware of two other sensations.

The first was the smell of the place which compounded of the musty odours of the earth and the old timber of which the barn was constructed, the sweeter scent of straw but, overpowering it all, the fearful stench of rotting food and of the excreta of rodents which caught the back of my throat.

Added to this was the noise, more dreadful even than the odours, which assailed us as we entered. It was a scratching, grunting, rustling sound, demonic in its pitch and its intensity, which assaulted us from every side and which was so deafening that we could hear nothing above it, not even the sound of our own footsteps.

As Unwin turned up the lamp and the light grew stronger, we then saw the full horror of the place which, until that moment, we had only smelt and heard.

Lining the walls of the barn were several dozen large steel cages with thick mesh sides, each containing half a dozen rats of a similar size and colouring to the one which I had already seen preserved in the glass jar in Holmes' bedroom.

But if the dead specimen had been hideous enough, the living creatures were infinitely more monstrous. Disturbed by the light and our presence, they scuttled up and down the cages, thrusting their evil snouts against the mesh and lifting back their muzzles to expose their sharp orange teeth, their scaly tails rustling eagerly in the straw and their little eyes gleaming ferociously in the lamplight.

Holmes, who had clapped a handkerchief about his nose and mouth, turned to address us.

'I doubt,' said he 'that there is a poison strong enough to exterminate them, even if we had some about us. But eliminated they must be, every last one of them. If only one or two escape into the wild to breed, God alone knows what the consequences would be. Are you ready to use your guns?'

I shall pass over the next half-hour without comment except to say that, after we had lifted the lids from the cages, the noise and stench from the giant rats was covered by the sound of rifle and revolver fire and the odour of cordite.

When it was all over, we made a bonfire in the yard of the bodies, covering them with straw and dousing them liberally with paraffin before setting them alight.

As we stood watching the flames leap, Holmes said quietly to me, 'Watson, may I borrow your revolver?'

I handed it to him and he slipped silently away, for what reason I could not guess until I heard a single shot and realised the purpose of his errand.

'The mastiff?' I asked when, a moment later, he returned as silently as he had departed.

'Like the other inhabitants of this dreadful place, it was too vicious ever to be tamed,' he said.

Holmes and I were not present when the bodies of Van Breughel and his confederate were removed from the house later that night, after Inspector Unwin and his men had searched the building and had consigned to the flames any papers pertaining to the Pied Piper's scientific experiments, with the exception of the contents of the large valise which he had insisted on keeping with him on his journey from London and which, because of the paucity of his tips to the porters who had carried it, had laid the trail for Holmes and Inspector Unwin to follow.

It was thought prudent that Holmes and I should withdraw from the scene before the official police from Wellerby arrived although we heard the final outcome a week later, after our return to London, when we dined with the Prime Minister and Mycroft at the Carlton.

It was rare indeed for Mycroft to leave his lodgings in Pall Mall or to dine anywhere except at the Diogenes Club where he spent most evenings.

On this occasion, he made an exception. The rules of the Diogenes forbade any conversation on the premises with the exception of the Strangers' Room and, as the Prime Minister had issued the invitation, Mycroft, very unwillingly, agreed to accompany us to the august setting of the Carlton.

I must confess though that, while impressed by my surroundings, I was disappointed at first acquaintance by the Prime Minister. In contrast to Mycroft's portly and dignified presence, he struck me as a small, insignificant man with a little, clipped moustache and pale, short-sighted eyes behind gold-rimmed pince-nez.

Of the two men it was Mycroft who was the more commanding figure and I thought of Holmes' comment that, because of his prodigious capacity for retaining and collating information, his brother was indispensable to every Government department and that it was on his advice that much of our national policy was decided. Indeed, there were occasions when Mycroft *was* the Government.

It was Mycroft who took charge of the conversation.

'I thought,' said he when the waiter had withdrawn, leaving us alone at our secluded table, 'knowing your preference, my dear Sherlock, and yours, too, Dr Watson, for a case to be satisfactorily concluded, that I should begin by informing you of the facts we have learnt of the man calling himself Van Breughel and his accomplice. By "we", I of course refer to Her Majesty's Government although the whole truth is known to no more than two or three persons who were privy to the affair from its outset.

'First Van Breughel. Discreet inquiries through the Dutch authorities in Sumatra have established that his real name was Wilhelm Van Heflin and that he was employed as a manager by an Amsterdam-based company which grew and exported coffee. He was born in Rotterdam of an English mother and a Dutch sea-captain. Because his father's calling took him away from home for long periods, Van Heflin was largely brought up in this country by his mother and consequently came to think of himself, despite his surname, as English. I give you these details because they are relevant to Van Heflin's subsequent career.

'It was during his childhood in England that he met and formed a close relationship with a cousin, Jonas Bedlow, his mother's brother's son who was later to become his accomplice.

'While Van Heflin was still a youth, his father retired from the sea and the mother took the boy back to Holland although the ties with England were still maintained and Van Heflin continued to consider himself a British citizen.

'It was only after he left school that he learnt the truth about his antecedents. It came as a bitter blow to him. As both his parents had died in the meantime, he returned to England, his intention being to apply for a post in the Civil Service. He was an intelligent youth and was confident that his application would succeed. It was only when the facts of his birth were looked into that it was discovered he was a Dutch not a British citizen and his application was refused.

'According to our sources in Sumatra, he was still complaining bitterly against what he considered his betrayal by the British Government thirty years later. There is no doubt in my mind that it was because of this rejection that he turned to plotting revenge against our Government and people. It is also, I believe, why he sought a post on the other side of the world in order to put as much distance as he could between himself and this country.

'However, Van Heflin's career in Sumatra was successful and he rose quickly from humble clerk to manager of one of the coffee plantations. It was then that he began to experiment with the rodents which are indigenous to Sumatra. Van Heflin's private papers, which were found in his valise, confirmed that he was engaged in certain tests which involved the keeping of records, such as dates, numbers and weights.

'In the mean time, while Van Heflin's career flourished,

that of his English cousin, Jonas Bedlow, had declined. On his father's death, he had inherited the family farm, never a very prosperous enterprise and one which suffered further under Jonas Bedlow's inept management. He was consequently short of money and was willing to agree to any proposal put forward by his cousin, Van Heflin, to establish his fortune.

'The valise also contained letters from Bedlow which, together with Van Heflin's private papers, make it quite clear that, having retired from his post in Sumatra, Van Heflin booked a single passage to England, bringing with him his "specimens", as the dreadful products of his experiments were always referred to. Bedlow was to meet him at the docks with a covered van, having first prepared the farm to receive its appalling new livestock.

'You are already familiar with the rest of the account, of how Van Heflin sent the jar containing the dead "specimen" to Downing Street, accompanied by the blackmail letter. But you may not be aware how Van Heflin proposed that the half a million pounds should be paid over to him by the British Government. That, too, was revealed in his private documents.

'It was as fiendishly clever as the rest of the scheme. It was to be entered into a secret bank account in Switzerland, identified only by a number. Once Van Heflin received assurances through the personal columns in *The Times* that the money had been transferred, he in turn would have kept his end of the bargain. The rats would have been killed, their bodies crated up and sent to Downing Street. Can you imagine the consternation this would have caused, my dear Sherlock? I believe you reported that there were more than ten dozen of the vile creatures.

'It was the intention of both Bedlow and Van Heflin that, once the farm was emptied of its revolting tenants, the place would be sold and the pair of them, using false papers, would travel to Switzerland, there to enjoy the proceeds of their evil plot. No doubt one might have unwittingly come across them from time to time in London, staying at the best hotels and dining at the most expensive restaurants, at the same time laughing quietly up their sleeves at their success in outwitting the British Government. The prospect does not bear thinking about.

'I know it is quite useless, my dear brother, offering you any official recognition for your services to the State. You would almost certainly refuse such a distinction. However, as Unwin and his fellow officers have been rewarded by promotion, we felt that we could not allow the occasion to pass without acknowledging the part both you and Dr Watson have played in laying these villains by the heels. Sir, would you care to perform the small ceremony we have prepared?'

The Prime Minister, who had listened in silence to Mycroft's speech, smiling affably and occasionally nodding his head to show concurrence with the sentiments expressed, now rose to his feet.

'Gentlemen,' he said, in the expressive voice which had on many occasions entranced the Members of Parliament and which had earned him the title of the Kean of the House of Commons, 'it gives me great pleasure to thank you most heartily on behalf of myself, Her Majesty's Government and the whole British nation and to present you with these small tokens of our esteem and gratitude, which a certain lady, who shall be nameless, thought might be appropriate and who took the liveliest interest in the design and choosing of them.'

With that he shook both Holmes and myself most warmly by the hand before passing over to us two packets containing the 'small tokens' which were nothing less that two magnificent gold pocket-watches, complete with chains on which were hanging tiny platinum figures in the shape of a Pied Piper to serve as seals.

I wear mine when the formality of the occasion demands such splendid personal adornment and, for any one who inquires into the significance of the seal, I have prepared an answer.

'It was given to me,' I reply with an air of intrigue, 'by a most charming and gracious lady whom I am afraid I am not at liberty to name.'

Appendix

An hypothesis regarding the internal evidence as it relates to the chronology within the published Holmes canon

Students of the late Sherlock Holmes' adventures will be familiar with the problems appertaining to the dating of certain events and deductive investigations which arise from Dr John H. Watson's published accounts.

This has peculiar pertinence to the precise date when Dr Watson married Miss Mary Morstan and to those adventures which took place soon after the wedding. I refer in particular to the inquiry of the Five Orange Pips and those other cases which Dr Watson states occurred in the same year, 1887, namely that of the Amateur Mendicant Society,[1] the Camberwell Poisoning affair,[2]

---

[1] This investigation was published in The Secret Files of Sherlock Holmes under the title of 'The Case of the Amateur Mendicants'. Aubrey B. Watson.

[2] These investigations are published in this second collection, The Secret Chronicles of Sherlock Holmes, under the titles of, respectively, 'The Case of the Camberwell Poisoning' and The Case of the Paradol Chamber'. Aubrey B. Watson.

and the case of the Paradol Chamber[3] as well as the loss of the British barque *Sophy Anderson*[4] and the adventures of the Grice Patersons in the island of Uffa.[5]

It is quite clear that, at the time of the case involving the Five Orange Pips which took place in 'the latter days of September' of 1887, Dr Watson was already married for he accounts for his presence at his former lodgings by the following statement: 'My wife was on a visit to her aunt's,[6] and for a few days I was a dweller once more in my old quarters in Baker Street.'

However, in 'The Sign of Four', during the course of which adventure Dr Watson first met and fell in love with Miss Morstan, Miss Morstan herself, on consulting Sherlock Holmes on the fate of her father, Captain Morstan, gives the date of his disappearance from the Langham Hotel in London as occurring on 'the 3rd of December, 1878 – nearly ten years ago.'

Furthermore, she adds that 'about six years ago – to be exact upon the 4th of May, 1882', an anonymous advertisement appeared in *The Times*, requesting her

---

[3] See previous footnote.

[4] These cases have not so far found their way into print. Aubrey B. Watson.

[5] See previous footnote.

[6] In some editions, the word 'aunt's' is given as 'mother's'. However as Miss Mary Morstan states quite categorically in 'The Sign of Four' that her mother is dead, one must assume that this latter reading is either a slip of the pen on Dr John H. Watson's part or a printing error left uncorrected by either a publisher's editor or by Dr John H. Watson himself. Dr John F. Watson.

address. Subsequent to her publishing it, she received through the post the first of six valuable pearls which were to be sent to her over the following years.

Later in the same account, Dr Watson states that it was on the evening of the same day that Miss Morstan consulted Mr Holmes, 'a September evening', that he and Holmes accompanied Miss Morstan when she went to meet her unknown correspondent outside the Lyceum Theatre.

It hardly requires a mathematical genius to deduce that the adventure of the Sign of Four must have taken place in September 1888 or, at the very earliest, September 1887. Miss Morstan would not have described the events which occurred prior to these dates as being 'nearly ten years ago' or 'about six years ago' if they had happened more than twelve months before the dating she gave to Sherlock Holmes.

However, as Dr Watson positively states, a fact which has already been noted, that the adventure of the Five Orange Pips occurred in 'the latter days of September' 1887, by which time he was already married, then even the least discerning reader will be aware that there is some confusion not only over the dating of Dr Watson's marriage but as to exactly when these cases already referred to actually took place.

Further complications arise on a careful perusal of The Adventure of the Stockbroker's Clerk' which, although undated, happened 'three months' after Dr Watson had purchased the practice in the Paddington district from old Mr Farquhar, a transaction which Dr Watson himself describes as having taken place 'shortly after my marriage'.

Moreover, the case occurred in June of that year which, as Sherlock Holmes remarks, was 'so wet' that Dr Watson caught a summer cold.

On the evidence, the case involving the Stockbroker's Clerk should therefore also be assigned to the year 1887 as it followed so closely after the marriage and the purchase of the Paddington practice.

Counting back approximately three months from June of that year, the actual wedding ceremony must have taken place in April, or at the latest, May of 1887.

This is quite evidently impossible.

It would have been a whirlwind romance indeed which allowed Dr Watson not only to meet Miss Morstan in September 1887 and to purchase the Paddington practice but also to have married her four or five months before he first became acquainted with her!

How, then, has such confusion arisen?

To quote Sherlock Holmes' own words in 'The Red-Headed League': 'It is quite a three-pipe problem.'

Having made a study of the great consulting detective's methods, I have applied the same principles which he would have brought to bear on the problem and have come to the following conclusion – that the dating in 'The Five Orange Pips' must be incorrect and that this adventure, as well as the others referred to in the same account, together with the case of the Stockbroker's Clerk, should be assigned to the year 1889.

The mistake could have easily been made.

Medical practitioners are notorious for the illegibility of their handwriting and as Dr Watson wrote the accounts of the adventures he shared with Sherlock Holmes from handwritten notes, sometimes at a much later date as is clearly the case in 'The Five Orange Pips', it is perfectly feasible that a carelessly formed figure '9' could have subsequently been read by him as a '7', thus giving rise to the error of dating, a mistake which quite understandably he failed to notice.

He was, after all, an exceedingly busy man, being fully occupied with carrying out his duties as a general practitioner as well as assisting Sherlock Holmes in the many investigations they undertook together.

Alternatively, the mistake could have been made either by a secretary who may have been engaged to produce a typescript from Dr Watson's handwritten manuscript and who misread the date 1889 for 1887 or, if that were not the case, by a typesetter at the printer's who made a similar error, a mistake which Dr Watson himself passed over when he came to read the proofs; that is, if he indeed checked them himself and did not leave this chore to his publisher's reader.

This revised dating scheme would place Dr Watson's first meeting with Miss Morstan, during the investigation of the Sign of Four, in September 1888 with the purchase of the Paddington practice and his marriage shortly before this event occurring in the spring of 1889, to which same year such cases as the Five Orange Pips and those already referred to, including that of the Stockbroker's Clerk, would also be assigned; a more satisfactory chronology than that apparent from Dr Watson's own – and, in my opinion, incorrectly dated – records.

A spring wedding would also accord with Dr Watson's statement that it was in July 'immediately succeeding' his marriage that he was associated with Mr Sherlock Holmes in three memorable investigations, two of which he later recounted under the titles of 'The Adventure of the Naval Treaty' and 'The Adventure of the Second Stain'. The third, 'The Adventure of the Tired Captain', has not so far been published.

If my dating scheme is correct, these three cases may be assigned to July 1889.

The same explanation regarding Dr Watson's handwriting may be applied to the problem of dating another later adventure, that of Wisteria Lodge, which Dr Watson states occurred in 1892.

This, too, is clearly an error. As fellow students of the canon will be well aware, after Sherlock Holmes' apparent death at the hands of his arch-enemy, Moriarty, at the Reichenbach Falls in May 1891, he was absent from England for three years, not returning until the spring of 1894. It is therefore quite out of the question that he investigated this particular case in 1892.

I suggest that Dr Watson's handwriting was again responsible for the mistake and that the case should be assigned to 1897, the last figure being so hastily written that it was later misread as a '2'.

This would place the adventure of Wisteria Lodge in the same year as those of Abbey Grange and the Devil's Foot which took place respectively in the winter of 1897 and March of that year, the same month in which the Wisteria Lodge case would have taken place according to my theory.

This change of dating conforms with Dr Watson's comment in 'The Adventure of the Devil's Foot' that 'due to hard work of the most exacting kind', Sherlock Holmes' health began to deteriorate and he was advised by Dr Moore Agar of Harley Street to seek a 'complete change of scene and air'.

If, as I suggest, the investigation at Wisteria Lodge occurred in March 1897, not 1892, then Sherlock Holmes would have indeed undertaken a particularly complex inquiry of a 'most exacting kind', to use Dr Watson's own words, and one which Sherlock Holmes himself referred to as 'a chaotic case'.

It was, moreover, conducted under peculiarly difficult conditions. The weather was most inclement and could well have contributed to the breakdown in Sherlock Holmes' health. Dr Watson describes them setting off for Wisteria Lodge on 'a cold and melancholy walk' of two miles across a 'wild common' on a 'cold, dark March evening with a sharp wind and a fine rain beating upon our faces'.

It is little wonder then that, shortly afterwards, Sherlock Holmes should have been forced to consult Dr Agar and, on his advice, to rent a cottage near Poldhu

Bay in Cornwall in order to recuperate. It was, however, hardly a restful retreat for it was here that Sherlock Holmes and Dr Watson became involved in the adventure of the Devil's Foot.

Although I am personally convinced of the correctness of my theory regarding the dating within the canon of these aforementioned cases, I should not wish, in all modesty, to force my ideas on other Sherlockian specialists and I therefore remain open to any alternative suggestions which fellow students of the great consulting detective's life and times, and those of his chronicler, Dr John H. Watson, may care to put forward in rebuttal of my own hypothesis.

John F. Watson, D. Phil. (Oxon),
All Saints' College,
Oxford.
24th June 1930.

The Secret Journals
of Sherlock Holmes

A further seven tales have been rescued from the battered tin dispatch-box which came into the possession of the famous Dr Watson's namesake. Deliberately unpublished to protect the names of those they concern, now, finally released to the public a multitude of previously unseen cases are revealed.

An American millionaire receives threatening letters from a sinister Black Hand . . . A mysterious box terrifies a shop keeper . . . Holmes and Watson feel the influence of an old enemy from beyond the grave . . . And a tragedy occurs which Sherlock Holmes will never be able to forgive himself for failing to prevent. And in addition, the brilliantly conceived proposition: An Hypothesis regarding the identity of the second Mrs Watson.

To discover more great books and to
place an order visit our website at
www.allisonandbusby.com

Don't forget to sign up to our free newsletter at
www.allisonandbusby.com/newsletter
for latest releases, events and exclusive offers

Allison & Busby Books
@AllisonandBusby

You can also call us on
020 7580 1080
for orders, queries
and reading recommendations